The School for Dangerous Girls

The School for Dangerous Girls

ELIOT SCHREFER

Point

This book was originally published in hardcover by Scholastic Press in 2009.

ISBN–13: 978-0-545-15563-2

ISBN–10: 0-545-15563-0

12 11 10 9 8 7 6 5 4 3 2 1   9 10 11 12 13 14/0

Printed in the U.S.A.   40

This edition first printing, April 2009

The text type was set in Rotis Serif

Book design by Becky Terhune

For Angélica

Chapter One

All of the girls fell silent.

The woman took a few seconds to look around the room, making eye contact with each of us. When she finally spoke, her voice was cold, with a slight accent that said she had lived years in places beyond our reach.

"Welcome to Hidden Oak," she said. "My name is Dr. Spicer, and, together with Dr. Zsilinska, I'm in charge of the psychiatric wing of the school. During this first month you'll be undergoing some of the most strenuous tasks this school will require of you. The Hidden Oak family works because we're very careful about keeping you surrounded by the most appropriate influences. Some disorders can be aggravated by exposure to like minds, and some can be aided. Therefore we will need to make frequent evaluations of you and your social groupings. Please don't resist this process; it is for your own good."

I was on my bed, pressed against the wall. The pounding and yelling outside my door got more and more frantic. Any moment, they'd bust in, and then they'd send me away. No time to say good-bye to Trevor, the boyfriend they hated so much. No time even to change clothes. I'd be stuck wearing a shirt that smelled like the bottom of my drawer. And that's what switched me from being scared to being mad. I started yelling back.

I knew why they were sending me away, and in a small way I even agreed. But I was still going to make it as hard as possible for them. After my parents had arrived to "deal with the incident," I'd shut myself into my room and hadn't come out or talked to them or eaten any food except for the couple of candy bars under my bed.

And now I was waiting for the moment my dad finally busted open the lock, when my mom would come in and grip my elbow in that death clutch of hers, screaming at me to look at her. And, sure enough, the door crashed open, and I saw in her expression how her grief had mixed with her usual disappointment in me to combine into something new and foreign and powerful. As she threw me toward my dresser, her nails left red trails over my arm.

She blamed me. And now, I was going to be punished.

"I will share a few of Hidden Oak's initial rules with you before I go any further. There is a uniform code here, and to help enforce the dress policy, we will be locking your belongings in storage until you leave. You may not access your luggage for any other reason. Feminine products and any permissible medications will be dispensed through the school pharmacy. Any book you may have been reading you can check out from the library once the term starts."

She smiled like she'd made a joke.

None of us laughed.

"You may not make phone calls or access the Internet while you are here. Your cell phones are already locked away. We ask you to register your e-mail address and password with us; we will check your messages for you, print out anything appropriate, and leave it in your mailbox. If you are uncomfortable with us having access to your e-mail, simply don't give us the password. But this means you will not receive any messages whatsoever. Your parents have been instructed to contact the school directly in the event of an emergency.

"You must understand: Your parents have signed you into our custody for at least eighteen months. In the eyes of the state, we are now your legal guardians. Your enrollment is considered involuntary, and cannot be revoked except at our discretion. In the past you may have turned to acting out as an escape route. Misbehaving now can only result in *decreasing* your freedom. Is that clear?"

None of us said anything. Dr. Spicer stared at the girl at her side, a tall girl with a scowl and a hip, boyish haircut. The girl stared back, and for a second it was a contest, like they were pushing something invisible between them. I could see it hover and then slide to the girl's side. She looked away and said, "It's clear."

Then Dr. Spicer stared down each of us in turn, and extracted the same answer. She ended with me.

"It's clear," I said.

"We've done the best we could for you," Mom said, not for the first time. She'd been cooking breakfast, and hadn't thought to put down the spatula. It was caked with egg and green chilies, and the idea of her having spent half an hour making a breakfast I'd refused to come out and eat just about broke me inside.

"I don't want to go," I said, keeping my voice low and pressing my palm against the raised lines on my arm. They'd started to dot with blood. "I know I can't stay in Texas, and I won't go back to Roanoke with you guys. But isn't there someone else I can stay with?"

My mother's eyes began to brim with tears — and not the sad kind.

"After what's happened here," she said, "I can't possibly ask anyone I care for to take you in."

They were through with me.

They were ready to toss me away.

Dr. Spicer held my gaze for a moment. I shivered.

"I'm glad we all understand," she said. "I'll continue. Our campus used to be home to Heath, one of the largest and most prestigious boys' schools in the United States. In the early 1990s, due to an event I've chosen not to discuss, the school closed. Years later, our current headmistress obtained a charter to found a unique therapeutic boarding program that would provide a safe learning environment for girls on the brink. You.

"Girls who attend Hidden Oak have similar basic traits, though these traits can manifest themselves in very different ways. What you all have in common is that you have failed to respond to more traditional therapies.

"You are all lonely. You are all self-hating. For whatever reason, you have decided that you have no control over your future. Perhaps you never received affirmation at school. Perhaps you feel that your guardians never gave you enough attention, or perhaps they gave you inappropriate attention. You are unable to imagine a happier future, so you rely instead on immediate gratification. Your despair is so entrenched that you can handle it only on a moment-to-moment basis, turning to drugs, promiscuity, self-mutilation, and criminal behavior."

"I didn't kill him," I said.
"Just pack your bags," Mom told me.

"Most of you have been informed that you're chemically depressed. For a minority of you, this might actually be the case. The rest of you have been misdiagnosed. What you are is negatively minded, which is *not* the same as chemical depression. You are dishonest with your most basic self. Once we refocus your mind, these depressive symptoms should subside.

"We will not accept self-pathologizing as an excuse for bad behavior. If you get an F on an essay because it isn't finished, do not claim you have attention deficit disorder. You got an F because you didn't work long enough or hard enough. Due to chronic overuse, we will not be prescribing any attention-focusing medications. None."

This probably wasn't the best time to let my mind wander. But I couldn't help but look at my fellow inmates. Truth be told, I wasn't impressed. I wanted deviant girls to have spiked bracelets, scars, angry expressions. Well, there were a few angry expressions, for sure. But otherwise we could have been any group of girls waiting for the first day of school.

The only girl I'd really met was my future roommate. Her name was Carmen, which is the kind of name a girl should have if she's rose-between-her-teeth gorgeous. But this girl was a Martha, or a Bertha, or some other character from an assigned book you wouldn't bother to read.

I wondered which of the other girls would become my friends. If any. I hoped there would at least be one. But there was no guarantee. Other girls were always nasty to me. At the far side of the room, there was a pair of really big skanks who could have been sisters, and next to them was an Asian girl (Filipina, maybe?) with that unfamiliar set to her face that said she was actually foreign, not Asian American. I watched two girls pass a note and felt a pang of jealousy, because bonds were already being formed. The only person near enough for me to pass a note to was Carmen. But she didn't seem the type.

I switched my attention back to the doctor. Because now she was getting to the good stuff.

"Most of you also have a history of significant alcohol or drug abuse. You may have already wound up in a hospital, or in jail. You may have resorted to theft to finance your habits. You may have attempted suicide during an altered state. Most of you have disordered eating. Many of you have a history of sexual or physical abuse. In your previous school situations, you have, consciously or not, used these histories to impress others, to prove how different and deeper you are than the average person. You have taken a perverse pride in being so far off course. This is an inappropriate source of self-esteem. Don't expect to get out of bathroom duty because you had a flashback to cutting your arms. You will have frequent individual therapy sessions, which are the sole venues for expressing such feelings. This rule, like the others, is not intended to be harsh or unfeeling; it is for your benefit.

"There will be no exclusive relationships here. You are not here for sex or love. You are here to get better."

They didn't let me say good-bye to Trevor. They acted like he'd never existed.

But he'd existed for me. At that moment, he was all that existed for me.

They wouldn't even drop me off at the bus station in person, and had a taxi take me. As I waited before the smudgy glass doors, I realized how alone I'd suddenly become. How alone I'd always been.

Dr. Spicer's hair kneeled on her scalp in rigid steel curls. I tried not to stare at them.

7

She cleared her throat and stared us down. Her meaning was clear:

Pay attention. Because I can destroy you.

"I'll end with the most important rule at Hidden Oak: You may never discuss your past with your schoolmates. Every girl here has dark stories that she would love to share late at night when the lights are down, but you may not, under any circumstances. You have been enrolled here as a last-ditch effort, because your problem behaviors have ingrained themselves. This is your one chance at rebirth. Fail at Hidden Oak and you can only expect failure until the end of your life. Is that clear?"

She shifted her focus around the room until each girl nodded.

"You think your life has been spent battling insurmountable forces that keep you from being happy. We won't dispute the fact that harsh things may have happened to you. But outside of those few uncontrollable events, the significant majority of your crises have been created through *your own* destructive and dangerous thought patterns.

"You are your own worst enemy. And together we will defeat that enemy."

She didn't ask us if we had any questions. She didn't tell us we had anything to look forward to.

She barely even pretended that we were worth saving.

I looked at my new classmates, these "destructive and dangerous" girls. You could see it on our faces: We didn't want her to know she'd hit the mark. There was something rigid about our group scoffing, like it was a reflex more than a real response. I would have expected some of us to have argued back. How could we survive with no phones, no clothes, no e-mail, and no talking about our pasts?

But despite our seeming disbelief, no one had said anything the whole time, other than, "It's clear."

Chapter Two

I've been called many things in my life.

As a little girl, slapping my doll against the bus seat: *hyper.*

By my grandparents, when I stuck my hand in the pitcher of milk at a wedding to make sure it was cold: a *trouble-maker.*

In elementary school, I was *headstrong.*

In middle school: a *puta.*

Freshman year, I was called (by an English teacher, obviously) a *malcontent.*

All of these were true at the time. And I didn't mind them much, since they were the opposite of boring.

But once I arrived at Hidden Oak, I became more. I was a *deviant,* a *criminal,* an *arsonist,* a *murderer.* Throughout it all, one word always stayed attached to me. I stopped thinking about what it meant; it was *me,* as undeniable as my name.

Dangerous.

*　　　*　　　*

I wasn't feeling particularly dangerous when I arrived. If anything, I felt like a shrunken version of myself. I didn't know what to expect or who I was going to be.

I was, I believe, the only girl in the history of the school to arrive by bus. I had so much freedom during those two days of travel from Texas to Colorado, so many opportunities to lose myself in the world. In Austin, Oklahoma City, or Denver, I could have wandered off instead of hovering near the snack machine and waiting for my transfer. But honestly, I didn't even consider avoiding whatever hell the school had waiting for me − I was way more scared by the idea of being totally alone in the world.

My parents had taken my cell phone away, so that I wouldn't call Trevor. I didn't have enough money to buy a new one, so at each rest stop I found a pay phone and called him collect. I didn't know if I was doing it right, though, because the calls never went through. I would say my name and wait to be connected, but each time the robowoman told me that the call couldn't be completed.

I don't know. If I were Trevor I think I'd have gone online to find out the numbers for pay phones at stops along my trip and called them over and over, letting them ring and ring until I heard the other end pick up. He knew the exact times I'd be alone in these sketchy cities. I'd written them on his forearm.

Once I'd stopped inking my schedule on him, I'd sat up to get away from the marker fumes, only to see this look of suffering in his eyes. I'd figured he was sad that I was going away. But during the final leg of the bus trip, as I stared out the window with my forehead pressed against the glass, I got the horrible feeling that he'd only been suffering because I'd basically tattooed myself onto his arm.

All I wanted right then was to talk to him and have him tell me I was wrong.

At the end of the trip, I discovered that Hidden Oak was buried deep in the Colorado forests, with no bus station nearby. When the driver let me off at the side of the road, I couldn't see anywhere to go; it was like he had chosen a random spot on the highway. Then I saw, partially hidden by a hill, a dirt road leading up a mountain. Nailed to a nearby trunk was a sign: HIDDEN OAK SCHOOL FOR GIRLS: 4.3 MILES.

I was a ways up the dirt road and taking a rest (my suitcase wasn't that big, but it wouldn't roll over the rocks) when I heard a car drive up behind me — one of those bulky black sedans that people with drivers have. It passed me slowly and then stopped. The driver's side window rolled down and a hot older guy asked if I wanted a ride. Then I heard a woman's sharp voice inside the car, and the guy ducked his head back in. As the car abruptly pulled away, a girl in the backseat turned to stare at me.

If it weren't for my suitcase, the haul up to the school wouldn't have been too hard. But since I had to stop every few feet to rest my arms, by the time I arrived I was pissy as hell.

I knew I was in bitch mode. I always *know*, but that

doesn't mean I can do anything to stop it. I wasn't really seeing the school buildings, even — only that this place was pretty damn big and castle-like. I just wanted to find someone in charge so I could tell them precisely how wrong it was that no one had warned me I'd have to climb half a mountain to get there.

As soon as I made it through the main door, I hurled my suitcase inside so it made a dramatic thump.

The posh man from the car was in there, with his brittle wife. Their daughter, a frumpy girl who looked like the heroine of a movie where the whole point is that she eventually gets made over, shot me the quietest of looks, like she would apologize for her parents the moment they went away.

Of course, she was destined to be my roommate. God is cruel that way.

I said "excuse me" as I pushed in front of the whole family, because I knew how to be polite.

I was in a stone hallway that opened onto some kind of courtyard at the end. Next to us was a door with cloudy glass and chicken wire, labeled ADMINISTRATION.

The mother was about to say something nasty, and I was wondering why the handsome dad with the kind face hadn't left her for someone younger and nicer (and prettier), when the door opened.

It was a Hostile Hag. I knew the type. Usually they were vice principals. Or career waitresses who tell you they're not refilling your coffee anymore, just so you'll have to leave.

"We're here to register my daughter," the mother said at the same time as I said, "I need to speak to your leader." The mother was louder, which was just as well because "leader" sounded dumb, like what an alien would say.

The HH looked at me first. She was shorter than me, but her attitude projected twice as big. "Who are you?" she asked.

"Angela Cardenas."

"Cardenas? You were supposed to arrive hours ago. You've missed your entrance interview, and the assembly is about to start."

"Well, maybe if someone had met me at the bus, I wouldn't have had to lug my suitcase through wolf country for like sixty hours. So let's not get into 'supposed to.'"

She stared at me, and I could see this ice age settling in.

"Sorry," I said in my sweetest voice (which is really sweet), "I didn't mean to be rude. All I'm trying to say is that I'd really appreciate talking to someone in charge."

What would I tell them? I didn't belong at some reform school, for one thing. And if I had to be here, I wanted to be sure I wrangled as many privileges as I could, right from the start. Like being in a minimum security wing, if the school had anything like that.

"Where are your parents?" the HH asked, glancing down the hall.

"I came on my own."

"Excuse me," the brittle woman said, "are you registering her now? Because we were here first."

14

"The headmistress will be right with you," the HH said to her. She took me by the arm, giving me that bicep pinch only little children are supposed to get. "And you need to come with me."

It was time for me to meet my fellow inmates.

Chapter Three

After the assembly, the Hostile Hag dragged me straight back toward the office.

I figured we were going to get my suitcase. But instead, she hurled me into a little room and left. Some mechanism clicked inside the door. I didn't really understand what that meant for a few seconds. The bars of the dead bolt shone in the gap between the door and the wall.

Now the escape urge kicked in, and I wanted to be out of this place, to bust out and get back to Trevor.

But it was too late.

I felt so mad that I was hot. I unbuttoned the top button of my shirt and leaned against the door, both because it was cool and because I wanted to eavesdrop. When I couldn't hear anything, I balled my hands, struck the wall once twice three times, and sank to the floor.

It had to be at least twenty minutes before I heard the

door unlock. I staggered to my feet and straightened my shirt.

Into the room walked this skinny woman with purple-beige circles under her eyes, like she was exhausted but had slapped some makeup over to cover. She had this limp gray hair that she probably thought looked blond, and a cone of extra yellow hair on top that was totally fake.

She was wearing what I would come to recognize as the uniform of the Hidden Oak faculty: pastel sweater over white cotton pants. She looked like a cross between a tennis instructor and a nurse.

"Angela Cardenas?" she said. "I'm Dr. Zsilinska. Please have a seat." A beaded string around her glasses made noise as she spoke. So it was more like "Please [clack] have a seat [clack]."

The room was the size of a medical examination chamber. Two plastic chairs were against opposite walls; no matter where I placed myself, we would basically be touching legs. I sat and pulled my knees to my chest.

She was clutching a manila folder. I recognized the form stapled to the front, filled out in the purple ink from the pen my mom kept clasped to her checkbook.

"It's for your own good," she'd said. Which was just a less guilty-sounding way of saying "We want you out of here."

"Welcome to [clack] Hidden Oak," Dr. Zsilinska said. She'd clearly been doing this new student intake thing for years; her smile had been around too long for anything real to remain in it, like curiosity or fear.

"Thanks."

"I understand you took the bus here. If we had known you weren't arriving by car, we would have had someone pick you up from the Denver station. We assumed your parents would be escorting you in person. Tell me — did you have any trouble on your journey?"

I shook my head.

"You must be very independent. That's not a short journey for a fifteen-year-old to make on her own. Do you wish your parents had made the effort to bring you?"

I snorted. I had been to plenty of shrinks, and it was way too early in the session to ask a big question like that. Amateur.

"At Hidden Oak, one of our most important rules is that you answer all questions adults pose to you. You don't have to answer in the way you think you're supposed to, but you do need to say something."

"Why should I do anything you tell me? Obviously, I don't want to be here."

"I don't think it's that obvious, Angela. Many of our girls are delighted to finally come to a place like this."

"I'm delighted for them."

Dr. Zsilinska looked at me for a long moment, as if to tell me I was revealing more than I thought. Then she made a production of opening my folder. "Before I introduce you to the campus, I'd like to pose a few preliminary questions about your history. To confirm that you and Hidden Oak will be a perfect fit."

"Okay." This I would enjoy. I was curious about what in my history she would focus on. Because then I could figure out what a "Hidden Oak girl" was, exactly. Once I knew that, my options would open up. If I wanted to stay, I'd play it all up. If I wanted to get kicked out, I'd show myself to be the opposite of what they expected.

"When did you first move in with your grandfather?"

Oh. We were already getting into *that*.

"Last summer," I said. "A year ago."

"What led your parents to send you to live with him for the past year?"

"You're assuming I was sent to him. I chose to go."

"You're right, I did assume. Why, then, did you choose to go?"

"I grew up in a boring town in Virginia. I spent middle school finding out that I didn't like any of my friends. I was ready for change. I was bored." Of course, I didn't add that I'd learned to fill that boredom by making out with older guys and tormenting the girls who rejected me.

"You were bored?"

"Yep, that's pretty much it."

"And that was why you asked to go live with your grand-father in Texas."

"My grandmother had died a few months before, and my parents were worried that if my grandfather fell in the shower or left the burner on or something, there would be no one there to call for ambulances, stuff like that. So I said I'd stay with him and go to high school in Houston."

19

"And your parents trusted you to take care of your grandfather?"

I couldn't stop my eyes from narrowing. "Of course they did. I'm no monster."

"It wouldn't take a monster not to be up to the responsibility. That must have been a lot of pressure on you, caring for him."

I knew where this was going. If she wasn't going to say it, I would. "You're wondering if I had something to do with what happened?"

"Not specifically, but if that sounds logical to you, let's tease it out. *If* taking care of your grandfather put pressure on you, *then* . . ."

"Yes?"

"Then what? Finish the sentence."

No. I spent enough time there in my head. I wasn't about to talk about it with her without a fight. "Then nothing. I wasn't under pressure."

"Did you find Houston any less boring than Roanoke?"

"Of course. Houston's got culture. Like museums and bars."

"Did you visit 'museums and bars'?"

"Are you really asking about my museum habits?"

"Please answer the question, Angela. I have a higher tolerance for pertness than the rest of the staff here, but you don't want to test it."

"Yes. I visited museums and bars."

"You're well under the age for visiting bars."

"I think it's my highlights. They make me look older."

"Whom did you spend time with in the bars?"

"The chess team?"

Dr. Zsilinska closed my chart and took off her glasses, making the biggest clacking sound yet. "Angela, I'm afraid that if we can't make it through your entrance interview without you throwing up these walls [clack], it will be hard for me to find you a place at Hidden Oak."

Kicked out before I even began – perfect. But since going back to my grandfather wasn't an option, I'd get sent back to Roanoke and my parents. I had to tell Dr. Zsilinska something revealing, or at least something that sounded like truth, and soon. I took a deep breath and tried to choke back my snarkiness. I've spent my life trying to choke back my snarkiness, with occasional success.

"I was spending time with older guys, Doctor. At the bars. They made me feel like I didn't have to make my own decisions anymore." The last part was crap, but I knew it was expected. I had almost said they made me feel like I was with a substitute for my father, but that would have been too much.

"That's a very mature conceptualization," Dr. Zsilinska said, totally suspicious but with this note of optimism, like all she wanted in the world was for me to be open enough for her to affect me. "Perhaps you've heard another therapist suggest as much?"

"Yeah, maybe," I said. I pulled my knees tighter to me, and felt that familiar wave of bad feeling that meant I was concerned about too many things at once. I realized I wanted to ask Dr. Zsilinska where my luggage was, I wanted to complain about having to walk to the school, and I was also trying to figure out the best way to answer her questions. I needed to get some of these thoughts out of the way to start feeling good again.

"Is my suitcase safe?" I asked. "It's got all my personal stuff in it."

"Your suitcase is fine. You'll have access to its contents whenever you eventually leave us."

"You mean I really can't have it until then?" The idea that I wouldn't have anything of my own panicked me. "What is this school *about*, Doctor?" I wanted to say her name but couldn't remember it – I'm terrible about names; all I'm thinking about when I meet someone is doing the handshake right, and I'm too distracted to think about memorizing anything on top of that.

"We'll get to the rules and practices of Hidden Oak in a moment, Angela. First we have to get through with you."

But I was saved by a knock on the door. The HH poked her head in.

"Carmen Pope's parents want to talk to you before they catch their flight," she said before closing the door again.

"I intended us to have more time this morning," the doctor told me. "But you were also supposed to arrive hours ago. Don't worry, we'll continue soon. And when we do, you'll tell me everything that happened on June tenth."

Yeah, right – we'd see about that. But at least, I guessed, that meant I'd passed the test.

I'd proven myself a big enough screwup to belong here.

Chapter Four

I was told to wait in the administrative office for a prefect to show me to my room. So I sat in a staredown with the HH until this blonde with legs to the ceiling opened the door.

"So sorry I'm late," she said.

"Maureen." The HH nodded in my direction. "You've got a live one today."

Maureen looked at me for the first time. "Oh! Hey, what's your name?"

She wasn't someone I'd ever have wanted to be friends with, but she did seem like someone who had some major social pull. If I wanted to make my time at Hidden Oak easier, I knew I'd have to impress her.

"I'm Angela," I said. Then I added, unfortunately, "*Don't call me Angie.*" Whenever I decided to impress, my brain turned to the bitch channel instead.

"Okay, I won't," Maureen said, in a voice that said she'd be fine never calling me anything, ever again. I had to fix this.

"Ready?" I said, smiling really sweetly.

Maureen stared at me, her niceness clearly becoming more a duty than a feeling.

"Are we waiting for someone?" I asked.

"No. Oh gosh, no one's explained it to you yet. You have to wear a blindfold while I walk you to the freshman house."

"For real?"

"I guess you didn't get your Hidden Oak equipment yet. You can use mine for now." Maureen pulled a black ribbon out of her back pocket and wrapped it over my eyes. It scratched my eyelids. She took my hand and led me down the hallway.

What the hell kind of school has a blindfold as standard issue? I thought. If Maureen hadn't been so fresh-faced and pretty, if she weren't obviously some local star, I wouldn't have let her lead me anywhere blindfolded. Sure, I'd be the first to say I had major trust issues. But there's no underestimating peer pressure, right?

It seemed to me that blindfolding students right off wasn't really what a school like this should be doing. Wasn't being blindfolded by strangers how Zsilinska would say I'd lived my life until coming here?

I realized I was smiling while blind, which had to look crazy, so I made my face drop into my usual mask.

The main school building was pretty quiet, so I was able

to fixate on the sound of my footsteps on the uneven tile floor. *Vup tup, vup tup, vup tup.* We turned a corner and I felt a breeze. "Are we in a courtyard?" I asked.

"Good call," Maureen said. "The main building is built around a fountain. You can't hear the water because it's not on until the rest of the girls arrive. It's only you freshmen for the first month."

"What are you in for?" I said, jokingly.

"I can't tell you," Maureen said. "And you can't ask me or anyone else that, ever again."

"You're not serious."

She released me and took a moment before she held my hand again. Her skin felt clammy now. "This school is giving you a chance to start over. Maybe the only chance you'll get in your whole life. Don't mess it up."

"Okay, whatever." Goody-goody.

Then we were on grass. I felt my sneakers dampen with dew. Maureen's fingers worked on the blindfold knot. I wished I'd had a chance to take a shower after my bus ride, that my hair wasn't greasy beneath her hands. I could smell that gross human oil smell as she removed the ribbon.

"Pretty, huh?" Maureen said.

"Yeah." And it really was. Mountains formed a ring in the background, thick trees flocking their base. We were at the center of their bowl, in a campus that looked like something from a Roman history textbook. Only the buildings weren't Roman, I guess. But they sure were ruined. This had been a huge school at one point, based on how far the ruins extended. Most of them had been reduced to walls in grass, the tops covered in uneven bricks. The patches of rubble had been there so long and were so tangled in weeds that they looked like they were designed to be that way, like shabby brick art. Only a few buildings were intact, painted white and standing out in the tall grass. The large one we came out of — the main one, I guessed — was the size of a big church. We were heading toward a smaller one a ways off, which looked more like an old mansion.

"Hidden Oak is very important to us," Maureen said. I hated the way she said *us* so softly and exclusively, the way a nun would say it. Like Hidden Oak had given her some way to live better than the rest of the world. I didn't believe a word of it. No matter what this school had done for her, no matter if there was some fountain of youth next to the soda machines and a spring bubbling out hot happiness in the boiler room, it was still a lie. I wondered what she got sent here for. Probably got pregnant by the tennis team captain and ripped the head off a teddy bear.

We were halfway to the rickety mansion by now. Some crud fell from a gutter as we approached. "This will be your home for the next month," Maureen said. "Your intro session can be hard, or fun. It all depends on your mind-set. You won't have any real classes yet, so you should try to think of it as a sort of weird vacation."

"How did you get to be a prefect?" I asked.

"By not getting into trouble," she sniffed. "And I suggest you do the same. Hidden Oak respects girls who respect Hidden Oak."

I doubted I was prefect material.

The mansion might have looked painted white from a distance, but when I got closer I saw that it was just that the wooden sides had been so weather-beaten that all the color had faded away. Planks curled away from the walls like unclipped fingernails.

We walked up the creaking porch steps and entered a main hall. It looked like a horror movie set – dingy walls, a dirty rug, a black iron chandelier creaking over a wide stair-case. And it didn't get better as we walked farther. I guess I'd always figured a boarding school – even a boarding school for "dangerous girls" – would have leather-bound books everywhere and walnut-paneled walls. But instead it was like we were in some dead person's house. A shadow of dirt and dust had settled over everything.

We started at one end of the landing and peeked in bed-rooms, each cell-like and furnished only with two stripped beds, until we came to one that had two girls in it. The frumpy girl who had arrived the same time as me was mak-ing her bed with navy blue sheets. The hip girl with the boy haircut watched.

"Hey," Maureen said to her. "This isn't your room. Why aren't you down at dinner?"

"I'll go in a sec," she said, watching my new room-mate try to fit the last corner of her sheet under the straining mattress. "Guess I must have got lost. I don't think this one's ever made a bed before in her life. Missing your maid, hon?"

"Is this my room?" I asked.

"First come, first serve," the hipster girl said as if she was spitting out a seed. "You were the last one here. Congrats."

"Hi," I said to the shy girl as she stood up from the mattress. "My name's Angela." I figured if I was going to live with her, I might as well be friendly.

"Let me do the introductions," Maureen snapped. She turned to me. "Her name's Carmen. That's all you get to know. Come on, all three of you. We're going downstairs."

"Aye-aye," the cool girl said. I could swear she had an accent — French, maybe?

"No more words," Maureen said. "And that'll be the last time any of you are visiting each other's rooms." At least for the moment, the hip girl shut up.

Maureen took the steps daintily, like pageant stairs. "Every morning you'll find a schedule posted on the bulletin board downstairs telling you the day's plan. It's pretty full — meals are basically your only free times. If you're tempted to go outside, don't even think about it. They'll tell you you're allowed as far as the woods, but if they even suspect you've gone farther, you're sunk. So just don't bother going outside at all. There's nothing much out there, anyway, except for deer crap and wolves."

We passed into the dark first floor. I listened for the rowdiness of a dining room, but I couldn't hear anything in the whole building except for the creaking of wood. "I know you're all going to be bitchy at first. We all were. But if you do that here, you're just building a history — and trust me, you don't want to have a history at Hidden Oak."

She opened the door to a quiet room that I assumed from the hush was a library. "Go ahead, guys. Take any open seat. See you in a month."

The hip girl peeked in. "And so it begins!"

Carmen and I joined her. The room was full of long wooden tables that had drawers and looked like they weren't supposed to be for eating. The chairs had been spaced out so that everyone was facing away from one another. All girls from the orientation meeting were eating in perfect silence, except for the occasional fork hitting a plastic plate. A few of them looked up at us balefully. "Grub's up," the hip girl whispered.

The only remaining seats were at the front, near where a sharp-faced old lady sat with a magazine folded on her lap, like for swatting bugs. We slotted ourselves in.

In front of me was a worn orange tray of shredding plastic, which contained spaghetti swimming in equal parts red sauce and water, a banana with a huge blue-brown bruise, and a glass of what was probably supposed to be milk but looked like frothy tap water.

"Could I borrow a napkin?" Carmen whispered, craning to reach me. She had none, and I had two. I held one out to her.

"No talking!" the old lady barked. "No contact whatsoever the first night."

I froze, the napkin held out inches from Carmen.

"What?" the hip girl said. "Since when is giving a napkin an act of terrorism?"

The lady hurled her folded magazine to the floor. Her

steel barrette glinted in the fluorescent lights as she walked to hip girl's tray, grabbed the overripe banana, and placed it on the girl's palm. The girl was too surprised to do anything when the old lady took her other hand and squished it on top, so that the banana made a slurpy-farty noise and oozed all over the girl's fingers. "Does anyone have a napkin?" the old lady called.

None of us said anything, of course. This test was impossible to win. But since the old lady was focused on punishing the hip girl, I took advantage of the moment to slip a napkin to Carmen.

I would have expected to see banana bits appear in the old lady's hair as the hip girl retaliated, but she just sat there, her cheeks pink with anger and her hands shaking under the banana goo as she tried to wipe it off with her napkin.

She didn't bother eating. It's not like she missed anything, anyway. With the weird, heavy vibe in the room, I couldn't eat anything, and neither did most anyone else. We regarded our food in silence, staring at our trays as our stomachs clenched tight.

This was the start of our new lives.

Chapter Five

Once Carmen and I had filed back into our room, the door locked with some magnet that we'd been told would only release if there was a fire.

We'd been drifting through our day, trying to pretend it was any other school, but at the sound of that lock it was me and Carmen, sealed into a little room with a toilet that constantly made running sounds.

After spending dinner staring at a bunch of unfriendly girls, all I wanted was to be alone, so I shut myself in the bathroom. The door wouldn't lock, so I sat on the toilet seat and braced my feet against the door. It was a classic smoker's pose, and triggered a physical memory of sitting on the bike racks after school in Virginia. I desperately wanted a cigarette. Anything smokeable.

The walls were covered in some type of old linoleum and looked like floors. The sink had psychedelic blue streaks where its copper taps had been dripping for years. The shower's gray tiles were either grouted in black or covered in mildew. I realized I was breathing really quickly, and my toes were twitching. I sighed, and when I did, I held my hands against my face, like I was trying to keep my mind inside.

"Can I get in there for a sec?" Carmen called.

"Yeah, just a minute!" I chirped, my voice unwavering even as my mouth got in a crying shape. It was my mother's biggest influence on me, this getting oversweet when I'm most sad.

I tried not to think of my mother. She didn't deserve to have me thinking about her right now. I had to be rid of her the same way she was rid of me.

I realized the only time I'd actually be by myself in this place would be when I was asleep. All I'd have to do first would be to wash my face and take a shower. I stood at the mirror, my hands on the sink rim for support. *All I have to do is wash my face and take a shower.*

But of course my toiletries were in my luggage, locked away somewhere. The only beauty products in the bathroom were a thin bar of soap, wrapped in wax paper like at a hotel, and two pumps in the shower, one filled with red fluid, the other with blue.

That's what did it, the idea of washing my hair in Red #5. I curled myself up on the toilet seat — I could make myself so small sometimes — and pressed my face against my knees. I didn't think I was making that much noise, but then I noticed how quiet it became each time I took a breath.

So quiet, in fact, that I could hear other breaths against the door. I creaked it open to see Carmen, face red and puffy.

"What the hell are you doing?" I asked. The last thing I needed was a roommate who liked to listen when I peed.

She darted to her feet. The speed of it made a long line of clear snot fall from her nose.

"I'm sorry," she blubbered. "I heard you crying, and it made me cry, too."

I tore off a few squares of toilet paper and handed them to her. "It's okay," I said.

Carmen blew her nose. She was wearing a John Lennon T-shirt that was way too big; no doubt she was convinced she was obese. "I have to take my contact lenses out," she said, "but I don't have my case or anything."

"Oh," I said. "Maybe we should tell someone. That seems like something you should be allowed to have."

She shook her head. "Nope. Not allowed to wear contacts. Dr. Spicer said they only indulge our vanity."

Carmen stood at the sink, washed her hands, and plucked a contact lens out. It quivered on her finger. "I've worn them since I was in sixth grade." She stared at it, and even though I told myself it was a stupid contact lens, I joined her. We stared at its swirling world, its soapy film and floating bits of eye grit. One or the other of us sniffled every few seconds. Then Carmen held her finger upside down over the toilet bowl. "Good-bye, Mr. Contact Lens."

It was the line of someone who still owned stuffed animals, but I said it, too. "Good-bye, Mr. Contact Lens."

Once both lenses had slid into the water, Carmen told me she was now officially blind, so I guided her to her bed and passed her glasses to her. With her red nose and spectacles, she looked like the smart mouse from a cartoon. We lay back on our beds and stared at the ceiling.

"What made you start crying?" she asked me.

"Do I have to give something specific?"

She laughed. "Nope."

"All right. The big reason is I don't know how to wash my hair without products."

She laughed again, but she stopped when I didn't join in.

"Really?" she asked.

"I don't know how I'm going to deal. I can take anything else."

I heard her turn on her side to look at me. "You *do* have real pretty hair."

I fanned it over my pillow. My hair took massive upkeep — there was my natural brown, then black lowlights and blond highlights and a pair of vivid red streaks, and a couple of mermaid-like braids that I kept tight and clean. I knew I would be taking flak for it — stressed girls would zone in on the first sign of pride.

"You ever notice that people always compliment girls' hair when they're ugly?" I asked.

"I don't think that's true," Carmen said.

"I'm not saying that's what just happened or anything. It's weird. Like the hair looks better in comparison, or maybe ugly girls have to work harder on their hair, or maybe there's just nothing else to say to them."

34

Carmen didn't speak.

"I don't know what I'm talking about. Ignore me."

"Seriously, you're really pretty."

There were plenty of ways girls could say something like that and not have it mean anything big. Like while we were brushing each other's hair, or after having teased each other, or while looking at photos. But Carmen's voice was full of so many different things — flattery, yes, but also envy and self-doubt and maybe even attraction.

"Thank you," I said, but it came out stiff, and the air turned awkward. Even though we'd made this small connection, we were still strangers. Sharing a room and, I sensed, sharing a future.

We didn't say another word. Carmen started snoring but it was a sweet wheezing, like a sick child. It actually helped me fall asleep.

Hours later — I couldn't tell if it was for real or in my dream — I heard a scream.

Chapter Six

We were supposed to be awake and down to breakfast by seven, which I figured would be near impossible. But I sprang awake at five. After a moment's disorientation, I sat up in bed and stared around the dark room. *I'm not alone in this*, I thought. There were probably a good fifteen other girls awake all around me, staring at the walls.

Carmen hadn't changed out of her John Lennon T-shirt — I think she might not even have taken off her bra — and was sprawled out on her bed, arms pointed to the floor, as if I had knocked her out. A small barred window showed a ruined wall outside, which itself had a blank square where there'd once been a window. Through that square I saw a patch of the dense trees of the surrounding forest. We really were isolated here. That wouldn't have been so bad if the school were more fun — my mind wandered to all the preppy boys who had once run around this campus in their ties and crisp shirts, throats exposed to the breeze as they sat against this very ruined wall. . . .

After running through a couple of fantasies, I stopped looking out the window and returned my focus to my room. Whenever I was anxious, I counted to settle my mind. There were forty-one wooden planks across the floor; fifty-one and there could have been three groups of seventeen. There were three lamps. Carmen's comforter — aha — it was twelve squares along its length, eleven wide. That made thirty-three quartets of squares, or six groups of twenty-two.

Feeling weirdly comforted that at least numbers worked the same way here, I decided to come up with a plan:

1. Make some friends who wouldn't screw me over.
2. Get word to Trevor, somehow. Possible: He hitches a ride up. We escape.
3. Find out how to get in touch with Pilar.

Pilar Felix was the whole reason my parents thought to send me to Hidden Oak in the first place. She was a distant cousin, maybe not truly related at all. My family was always like that — sprawling and impossible to figure out. Pilar's parents usually sat near mine at family gatherings, our mothers gossiping until early morning. Pilar was never actually there, because apparently she had tons of piercings and her parents were embarrassed to have anyone see her. Tía Lucia had about given up on her. Between Pilar's escapades (she ran away — a lot) and my own troubles, I know my mother and Lucia had lots to talk about. At least I *came* to the reunions, even if I spent most of my time in the parking lot with the off-duty waiters.

Two years ago my mom told me Tía Lucia had decided to enroll Pilar in some school called Hidden Oak, a boarding school for *chicas peligrosas*, and if I wasn't careful, she would do the same to me. I never heard anything more about it, mainly because I chose that moment to put my headphones on. Next time the school's name came up was after the incident with my grandfather, when my parents suddenly realized they didn't want me back with them in Roanoke.

I figured Pilar had already been at Hidden Oak for over a year, so I'd have to wait until the weird freshman orientation was over to find her.

But first, I would have to figure out how to wash my face with a bar of cracked yellow soap and not break out.

I knew the first breakfast was going to be important. It was when we'd finally talk to one another, find out who was truly crazy and who was the kind of crazy that was cool. My social future depended on playing this morning right.

Since I was up so early, I figured I might as well be one of the first girls down to the dining room. Worst thing, I figured, would be to arrive after the social groups had been set, once the fun table had no chairs left. Bonus: If I left the room early, I wouldn't be stuck with the liability of Carmen.

I showered, rinsing some of the blue stuff through my hair, dried it with the dryer attached to the wall (it blew really hot – small miracles), dressed in the same clothes from yesterday (guess we'd be receiving our uniforms sometime after breakfast), and headed down a few minutes early.

The dining room looked the same, except the chairs weren't facing away from one another anymore, and some wet-looking boxes of cereal were lined up at the back, next to a stack of plastic bowls. I took a bowl, dumped some cereal and milk in, and sat down. There wasn't any coffee. When I asked the lady scrubbing the cereal table for some, she shook her head in this mean way, and I called her a bitch softly enough that I couldn't get in trouble for it.

For the longest time it was only the two of us. I didn't want to be done with my cereal by the time everyone else arrived, so I toyed with it, swirled the flakes until they fell apart into milkbroth.

It turned seven, seven-ten, and then, finally, the rest of the girls arrived in a clump. Of course – the first one of them had been nervous to enter the dining room alone, so the rest bunched up behind her. They had already gotten acquainted back in the hallway, and were chattering as they came in. They avoided my table entirely. I didn't take that personally; why would they throw another competitor into the mix? But it still meant I was alone, with all of them chilling behind me. I debated getting up to join them, but then Carmen lifted her tray and moved next to me.

"Hey," she said. "Mind if I sit with you?"

"'Sup?" I said, waving at the chair.

We didn't say much to each other, just ate our cereal and waited for something interesting enough to comment on.

The table full of girls fell into an awkward silence, and someone whispered something and laughed. Suddenly I could feel the heat of their attention at my back.

"They're talking about us," Carmen whispered.

"I know. Ignore them."

One of the girls made kissing sounds. How completely mature.

I turned around. "Who did that?" I said.

The girls all stared at the table. One of them snickered, and a couple others started chuckling. "Seriously," I said, "what the hell?"

A weirdo girl on the end, who was clearly barely clinging to the group, looked right at me and made a big air kiss. She had this wasted look, like someone had scooped half of a normal girl out. At the end of her air kiss, her body fell into an odd posture, like she was reaching for something.

Since life had done nothing but prove to me that the best defense is a good offense, I looked right at her and said, "Was it you, spaz?"

The girl carefully placed her arms at a more normal angle. "Naughty spic-spic," she said. The other girls looked at one another in shock and glee, glad to share the drama.

"What the *hell*," I said, getting up.

She stared at me levelly.

"Girls, girls!" called the hip girl from yesterday. As she busted through the swinging doors, I saw her hair had strayed from the previously cute lines of her boy style, and the area below her eyes was blue and puffy. "Save it for the TV special."

She sailed toward the rest of us like we'd been friends for years. "Hey, Jew-Anne," one of the girls said. *Jew-Anne? Really?* "How'd the night in solitary go?"

"Just fine, ladies," Jew-Anne said, floating past me and Carmen and clambering onto our table, sitting Indian-style in front of us. The hairnetted cleaning lady looked at her with distaste and a good amount of fear. I wondered, for a moment, why they didn't have someone else there to discipline us, especially after last night's dinner. It's almost as though they wanted us to bully one another.

"How'd you get out of jail?" the girl who'd been slamming me asked, obviously milking her connection to this foreign creature for as long as she could.

"You know, a good screaming fit. Oh, that and I slept with a guard," she said perkily, cupping her chin. "*Now . . .* what *are* we fighting about?"

"Don't worry about it," I muttered.

Jew-Anne looked at the other table. "Anyone want to fill me in?"

"Bitch hunt," said the carved-out girl.

"Ah," Jew-Anne said. "Who here's a bitch?"

No one raised her hand, so I did for the hell of it. Jew-Anne read me like a line of fine print and nodded. "I'm sitting with you."

And she did, sliding off the tabletop and into a chair, making a whoosh sound, like it was the bottom of a waterslide.

"Is your name really Jew-Anne?" Carmen asked, scandalized.

"Yup. J-U-I-N. My mum's French. It means June."

"Oh, I thought . . ."

"Jew-Anne? I mean, I'm a Jew, too, but that's a coincidence. I'm all sorts of things. But we can start with Juin Carpenter."

"So are you American?"

"I told you my name's French, pumpkin."

"I know, but you're speaking English and all."

"Mom's French, Dad's American. Grew up in Paris, so I have *dis funk-y accent.* Your names?"

"Carmen Pope."

"Angela Cardenas."

"Cardenas and Carpenter. We'll be seated next to each other all the time."

This undisguisable look of envy passed over Carmen's face. "Have you been here before?" she asked. "You seem to know what's going on."

When Juin responded, she only looked at me. Poor Carmen.

"Yeah, this is my second go-around. Orientation didn't quite work out last year."

"Why not?" Carmen whispered.

Juin smiled. "I slept with a guard," she said, then added, "He was totally worth it."

I rolled my eyes. There weren't even any male guards around to sleep with. Juin caught my look. "Dr. Spicer. Secretly and totally a guy. Know that and you'll get through anything."

"Uh-huh," Carmen said, believing every word.

"Of course she isn't," I said, to prevent Carmen from embarrassing herself.

"You've seen Spicer naked, Cardenas?" Juin asked.

I didn't answer for a moment, because I was distracted by the network of lines on Juin's underarms, some sunken and white, others fresh and red.

"You like the battle scars?" Juin asked. "Juin the Pain Pirate, that's me. Word of advice, ladies — barter yourselves a knife early on."

After breakfast we lined up to get our uniforms, which were this hideous striped-overalls-and-polo-shirt combination. Each of us had to choose a different color, I guess to make sure we couldn't ever fight over whose clothes were whose. Since my name's early in the alphabet, I had a pretty big selection left. I chose yellow, of course, which has been my favorite color for as long as I can remember. (I like it because it's the most fluorescent you can get without actually being fluorescent.) I looked hideous, like a cartoon misfire, but so did everyone else. And at least I wasn't Mariana West, who got stuck with throat-infection green.

Then it was off to the yards for an "endurance challenge." We lined up alongside the back wall of the mansion, two arm's lengths apart. Once we had lined up, the otherwise normal-looking PE lady busted out with this booming voice and informed one of the fat girls that she wasn't going to survive the morning. Only then did she give us her name, Dr. Hundrick.

You have to be kidding, I thought. *Even the gym teacher's a doctor?*

She made the fat girl, who I think was named Connie — but that could be just because that's a fat name — run to the edge of the forest and back before a minute had passed. Of course Connie failed, coming in at twice that time. So Dr. Hundrick made her do it over again, telling her she'd pass if she beat her previous time. Connie failed that, too, because she was already exhausted. Then Dr. Hundrick made her run again to beat her third time. Connie finally made it, and puked as she went back to her spot. Dr. Hundrick didn't do anything about it, just gestured that the next girl should step around the puddle.

Dr. Hundrick picked another girl to run the challenge, then another. She was clearly starting with the least fit girls, and I was glad that I only got called near the end. Little did Dr. Hundrick know I only looked fit because I didn't ever eat much.

Of course someone was going to refuse. Her name was Arden, and she had permanent makeup tattooed on her face. When Dr. Hundrick said she had to compete, the girl told her off. So Dr. Hundrick sent her to the administration, and told us that we probably wouldn't be seeing Arden for a week or two. We rolled our eyes — but she ended up being right. In fact, we never saw Arden again.

Juin was next. I figured she was the fittest of all of us — she had this rangy body, with muscles you could see fighting against one another — but she took off at this limping pace. She missed the minute mark by far, but because of that barely had to break a sweat beating her first time. When she was back against the wall, she gave one of her trademark ass slaps and lay out in the sun. I figured Dr. Hundrick would call Juin out for not trying, but she just made a mark in her ledger.

I ran the challenge fine, beating the minute mark, and Dr. Hundrick smiled approvingly. I guess I was one of the only girls who didn't act like a smart-ass with her. Which didn't mean that I wasn't going to start acting up eventually, of course. I knew it was best to evaluate the scene first.

Afterward it was showers, then lunch and another orientation meeting and setting up shrink schedules, followed by a stupid bonding game that actually had its intended effect because we made fun of it so hard. After that: a substance abuse seminar and calisthenics and a group meeting where they literally made us say what we were thankful for in life.

Once dinner was over there were twenty minutes free before bed checks, so we had our only unmonitored time of the day. But "free" was a relative term — there were only certain places we were allowed to go. In fact, the whole day I'd noticed that we were always led through the same few hallways. The paranoid part of me wondered what they were hiding. And the free-spirited part of me just wanted more space to explore. I guess that's one of those things you don't realize you have until it's gone — the simple ability to walk outside without permission, to drive where you want or call who you want. I pictured Trevor at some restaurant — not even somewhere glamorous, just a Taco Bell. And I was jealous. I missed him — and I missed that freedom.

Half the girls used their "free time" to go straight to bed, and the rest went downstairs to the basement common room. I went to my bathroom and sat on the toilet seat to be alone for five minutes, then went downstairs to join them.

Juin was holding court. The others might have pretended to have been talking among themselves, but whenever Juin said something, you knew everyone paid attention. As I walked in she was telling them precisely why she thought the school was a complete lie. She had chosen hot pink for her color, and she looked like the sole wildflower in a field of greens, blues, and browns.

"Take that big first speech by Dr. Spicer," Juin said. "We're all self-destructive? And we all have abuse problems, and self-loathing?" She pronounced the T and the H in *loathing* as individual letters, reminding me of her foreignness. "Bull. Oh, I don't doubt that some of you crackers hate your body because your daddy massaged it, and Mummy never looked you in the eye after, but a little self-hatred keeps a person interesting."

"And those cuts, Juin?" asked one of the girls, who had looked away while Juin was saying the daddy and mummy parts.

"I love my cuts," Juin said. "They're *vitalizing*."

"Anyone seen Arden?" Carmen asked.

"Don't cry about Arden, pumpkin," Juin said. "She's on to better things. We're the ones who need crying for, because our lives are about to get really messed up."

"Why?" I asked.

"Don't think they're trying to help us. That's a front. Why do you think they left us alone at breakfast? Don't think that no one was watching. They're trying to *evaluate* us."

"Yeah," I said. "Obviously."

"It's to weed us out. They're going to push us harder and harder, until the weak ones start peeling away."

"What for?"

Juin shrugged. "I don't know. I didn't get that far last year."

"I can't wait for the regular school year to start," said the caved-in girl who made fun of me at breakfast. Her name was Riley, and she stood in the dark corner of the common room, her eyes glittering. "I want to get the hell out of this holding pen."

"Maybe they want to see which of us turn out to be totally psycho before they let us loose on the others," Carmen proposed.

"All I know is there's nothing gooey about this hellhole," Juin said. "Keep on your guard, ladies."

The faces of the girls who had been busy making themselves popular at breakfast clamped down. Juin may have become our impromptu queen, but she was peaking too soon. I could feel the animosity building. The girls were thinking, *Who the hell does she think she is?* There would eventually be a revolution, and Juin would be out. Juin must have felt it, too, because she clapped her hands, said, "Whatever. Take my advice or leave it. Every girl for herself," and went upstairs.

Every girl for herself — that didn't sound too hard.

It's what I'd always been best at.

Chapter Seven

The next morning I sprang awake early and took a shower, being careful not to let the slide of the curtain rings wake Carmen. Afterward I wrapped myself in my yellow towel and sat on the end of my bed, toying with the ends of my hair. I must have stayed like that for a while, because I heard Carmen roll over and groggily say, "Are you okay?"

"Yeah, I'm fine," I said, shifting away so she couldn't see my face.

I heard her fumble for her glasses. "You don't sound okay."

"Don't worry about it," I said in that way that asks to be asked again.

"I didn't sleep well at all," Carmen said, sighing. "I guess I really miss home."

"Why? What got you sent here?"

"I can't tell you, remember?"

"Carmen, we're all alone. You can tell me."

"Shh! No, I really can't!"

"You've *got* to be kidding." But then I saw that Carmen was pointing at a spot above our doorway where there was one of those triangle mirrors, like what you see in the corners of convenience stores. "No way," I breathed.

"Yup. You don't really think they'd lock us away in a room and let us do whatever we wanted without anyone watching?"

"That's so hard-core!" I said.

"Tell me about it."

"There could be any pervert watching on the other end. It's — what do you call it? — unconstitutional."

"What are you going to do, call the Supreme Court?" Carmen asked. I didn't like this new *I'm an expert about the real world* tone she was taking on.

"We *can* get ourselves out of here," I whispered. "I got here on my own; we can get back out on our own."

"Angela, shut up. They're *listening to us.*"

I stared down at my legs, and was temporarily distracted to see a map of dry skin. I hadn't moisturized for days.

"I don't care," I finally said. "They can listen away."

"Look," Carmen told me, "I'm sure they're not doing anything our parents haven't agreed to. The jerks."

"I think you can say 'assholes.'"

Silence. Then Carmen said, "I'm glad you're my friend."

"Me too," I said. And I was. Carmen might not have been the coolest, but she was a good listener. She wouldn't turn on me.

"I wish I could know what got you here," she said.

"Me too," I said again. I was suddenly really curious. What could mild little Carmen have done? I dragged my bed over to the door. "We can't get kicked out if they don't see us talk."

"Oh my god," Carmen said, giggling nervously but doing nothing to stop me.

By placing both my bare feet on the whining bed rail, I was barely able to reach the mirror. I stretched my fingertips around the rubbery edge and pulled. The plate twisted and snapped back into position.

"Which one of us is taller?" I asked.

Carmen paused before answering. "I guess me. By a little bit."

So we switched places, me on Carmen's bed and her on mine, a foot on each bedpost, reaching so far that when she grabbed the mirror she fell at the same time, landing on her ass in the corner and sending the bed skating into the wall. She sat there, stunned, clutching the mirror to her chest like a shield.

Which was when someone knocked on the door.

I gestured for Carmen to stay put as I slid my bed back against the wall. "Yes?" I called. Then I walked to the door and, after I heard the lock release, cracked it open to see the Hostile Hag. "Can I help you, ma'am?"

"Oh. *You're* Cardenas?"

"Yes, ma'am, I am."

"You were supposed to be meeting with Dr. Zsilinska five minutes ago."

"Whoops! Well, I'll throw some clothes on, then."

"Hurry."

I closed the door, pulled on my yellow granny panties and uniform, and made a *whew* gesture to Carmen, who was still sitting in shock.

On the way to the administration building, I asked the HH for her name, figuring it was best to get on good terms.

"If you don't learn my name, I won't feel obliged to remember yours, and that's best for both of us," she replied.

It was a weird thing to say, for sure, and I thought I detected a lot of dissatisfaction beneath. Not with me, but with the school or maybe the whole world. I was good at picking up on negativity; it had found me allies in all sorts of situations.

"Can I ask how long you've worked here?" I asked.

She snorted. "Long enough."

"Like years?"

"Save the questions for the counselors. I've learned not to get all chatty."

"Have the girls here been mean to you in the past?"

"I'm not your age, thank the good lord. I'm not worried about which of you likes me and which doesn't."

"I wish I wasn't, either," I said, surprising myself.

I let us walk in silence for a while so she wouldn't think I was pumping her for information. "Any advice?" I finally asked.

"It's going to get all kinds of nasty," she said. "Don't be too quick to make friends with the badder girls. That's the best way to get sent to the headmistress. The worst thing a girl here can be is conspicuous —"

"Wait. Headmistress? Who's that? Why haven't we heard about her yet?"

She shook her head, pointed to a door marked COUNSELING, and waited for me to knock.

I'd been so close to finding something out ... but the secret had sealed back over.

Chapter Eight

"Good morning, Dr. Zsilinska," I said as I walked in. We were in a larger room than before. This time there were boring-looking books on a shelf, big gray cushions on the chairs, and a frosted glass container full of those strawberry-wrapper candies that turn sharp in your mouth and cut your tongue.

"You're ten minutes late, Angela," she said. "It's very important that you're on time to our sessions. Please have a seat."

I did. "I'm sorry that I —"

"I'll also ask you never to apologize. An apology is a defense; you've used them in the past to prevent further questioning."

I blinked. "No, I haven't."

"Oh? Isn't saying 'I'm sorry I'm late' really saying 'Please don't keep reminding me I was late, please don't hold it against me'? Isn't saying 'I'm sorry I caused that incident with my grandfather' the same thing as saying 'Please don't ask any more questions; let's be done with it'?"

"That's pretty cynical." And her mention of my grandfather was a cheap attempt at getting me to talk about June tenth. I wasn't about to go there with her, no matter how much she tried to trick me into it.

"If you'll forgive my saying so, you've arrived at the point where you don't merit anything but a cynical view."

"Well, jeez, that's an awesome start to therapy," I said, slapping the arms of my chair in mock glee.

"How *have* you felt about your experience here so far?" Dr. Zsilinska asked.

"I don't know. Super?"

Dr. Zsilinska chuckled, which caused that annoying reverb of her eyeglasses beads. "[clack] Honestly, Angela."

"I don't know. What do you want me to say?"

"I know it's difficult, but do your best to keep my expectations out of it. Let me start you off. Most girls would say they're angry at being so restricted, anxious about what's to come, and insecure about their standing with their peers. Would that describe you?"

"Um, that describes the last ten years."

"I'd also predict that, in your case, you feel you're more capable of handling tough situations than most of the other girls. Is that accurate?"

I thought about it. "Yeah. I'm stronger than them."

"And yet, if I may say so, you don't have the external image of someone proud of her strength. The slight stature, the elaborate hair, the preoccupation with appearance, the dainty countenance. Do you think your peers have noticed this disconnect?"

"Don't know. You'll have to ask them. And I don't think it's such a 'disconnect.' Say, when do I get to meet this headmistress?"

She looked up sharply. "Headmistress? Don't trouble yourself with her. She occupies herself with the school's public affairs and is frequently away meeting with trustees. And don't try to distract us from the task at hand: I'm not off base to observe that you are preoccupied with looks, am I?"

"My mom values pretty above anything else. I guess it rubbed off."

"Your appearance is also something you can control, isn't it? When you've so often felt your life was outside of your grasp?"

I rolled my eyes. "Yes, my appearance is something I can control. That's a *remarkable* insight."

"It must weigh on you, then, that you have no say over your wardrobe here."

"The shower soaps suck. There's not even conditioner. I figure with the amount my parents are paying you guys, you'd provide conditioner."

"We don't withhold conditioner to cut costs, Angela."

"I want to ask you a question about Hidden Oak."

"Of course. I'll answer what I can."

"What are you *really* trying to do here?"

"The mission of Hidden Oak is to aid you in what we determine to be the best manner."

"To make me get better?"

"Ideally, yes."

"But most of us aren't shipped here because our parents are so keen on us getting helped. Most of us are shipped here because our parents wanted to get us out of their hair."

"I'd say that's unfair. Who has the cynical world-view now?"

"We can't go home for breaks, summer is only a month off, and even then we have to go to camps you're affiliated with. We can't even bother our parents with phone calls, unless they call us. Plenty of other reform schools allow parents to be part of our lives, but Hidden Oak keeps us, well, hidden. We've all been given up on, haven't we? Why don't you let us do what we want? No one's really going to be checking up on you guys."

"Of course there's a kernel of truth to what you say, but you're being unnecessarily negative. Your isolation is part of the therapeutic process. It's critical that you're unable to revert to the behavior patterns you had back at home."

"I have plenty of experience with liars, Dr. Zsilinska, and I can't help but think that you're hiding the truth."

She looked up sharply. "[clack] I've been as open as I can in answering your questions, Angela. Don't abuse the privilege."

"Does Hidden Oak make a lot of money?"

"That question is inappropriate to our goals."

"Do *you* make a lot of money?"

"You're a smart girl, Angela. Surely you realize how consistently you've directed the flow of our conversation away from yourself and back to the school, and to me. Surely you realize, as well, what that indicates about your willingness to self-evaluate. I'll remind you that your time with me is your last chance to put your life back on course."

"I want to get in touch with one of my family friends who goes here. Can you help me do that?"

"You know one of the older girls? Who?"

"Pilar Felix."

I caught her speechless for a moment. She tapped a pen on her lips to cover. "First-years won't be able to interact with older students for two weeks yet. Right now, I'd like to direct our conversation to your feelings."

"You know what? I'm not up to much more self-examination today, Doc."

Dr. Zsilinska swiveled her computer monitor so I could see it. On it were dozens of streaming black-and-white videos. She moved the cursor to one box and clicked to rewind it. I watched myself get down from the bed and boost Carmen up. Her fat white legs gleamed on the screen.

"Perhaps you could explain what brought this vandalism on."

"You should've told us we were being recorded," I muttered. "We have privacy rights and stuff."

"By signing you into our custody, your parents severely curtailed your legal rights," Dr. Zsilinska told me. "What's important is that you felt you could dismantle school property. Even more striking is the brazenness of it. You had to know that trying to rip down a camera would most definitely be caught on that very camera, no?"

"I don't know. I was mad. I felt violated."

"But at the time you had no thought of the future consequences?"

"Guess not."

"I sense that you've lived your life this way, looking for moment-to-moment satisfaction with no thought to the future."

"I'm tired of you making me sound so sick."

"Forgive me for not sugarcoating it, Angela, but you *are* sick. If you don't work hard to correct yourself, once you turn eighteen, your parents will no longer feel any responsibility to get you help, and you'll be able to indulge in drugs and promiscuity and other destructive behaviors until they kill you. So, yes, I'd *hate* to make you feel *sick* right now, but this soul-searching, however uncomfortable, is your one shot at getting your mind in order."

"So you're saying what, that my life is ruined because I don't think about the future enough?"

"I'm saying you don't value yourself enough to accept present discomfort and ambiguity, even if it means a better future. If I gave you twenty dollars on the condition that you give me a hundred dollars tomorrow, you'd do it, because the present Angela doesn't give one lick about tomorrow's Angela. If your abusive boyfriend invited you out for a romantic evening, the present Angela would go, even though that means he'd still be around later to beat the future Angela. It's not that you don't look out for yourself — you'll always do what's best for right now. But you're afraid that we'll all find out that you're a fraud, that you're worthless and unworthy of love or respect. And since you're convinced that people's accepting you is only temporary, you figure you might as well sell the future Angela short, since she's doomed, anyway."

"Trevor never, ever beat me," I said. Normally doctors' analyses left me irritated or bemused. But what Zsilinska was saying made me furious instead. "Who the hell told you that?"

Dr. Zsilinska smiled. "It was just an example," she said. "But is there something that you want to tell me about Trevor? I know, for starters, that he was your boyfriend back home."

I had no idea what my parents might have told the school about what happened. I'd kill to get my hands on my file.

"He's a great guy and he would never hurt me," I said. "He loves me."

All Dr. Zsilinska said was "I see."

I was reminded why therapy sucks.

But I was also intrigued — not by what Dr. Zsilinska was saying, but by what I saw on the security screen when she showed it to me. All the girls were in bed. Except for Juin.

Juin wasn't in her room at all.

Chapter Nine

By the time that first week was over, we had gotten past whining about our exhaustion and into not caring whether we were awake or asleep. Which was actually a lot more pleasant.

Not caring about things seemed to be a good life philosophy at Hidden Oak, because our social lives sucked. Thank god I at least had Carmen, who turned out to be one of those quiet girls who can't shut up once she gets going. We spent all our days together.

The rest of the girls blocked me with a huge *who does she think she is* vibe. I'd totally predicted it: I was too outspoken, too visibly different (most of the girls had this summer-cottage-rich-girl look going on, and I wasn't the freckled blond type). No one froze my bra or anything, it was just whispers and the usual nastiness of unhappy girls. Riley, especially, always shut down conversations as soon as I joined them. Sometimes it'd just be rotating a shoulder to block me from view. Or she'd stretch around me to whisper in another girl's ear. Or she'd bring up a joke someone had made the day before, when I wasn't there. She was already on the fringe of the group, and made her position more secure by keeping me out.

I only ever really found out about what mischief the other girls were up to when they got in trouble. There was that weird chemical smell we woke up to one morning, and suddenly Mariana West disappeared for two days. The Filipina, whose name was Teresa something, banded up with Veronica Menghe to cut through a sink pipe using dining hall knives, just for the hell of it. They weren't caught, so the very next night they were up to more trouble, loosening the bolts of Riley's sink so that when she next used it, it fell and cut her shin. She wound up having to get a bunch of stitches. Teresa and Veronica disappeared for a while, too. Kiara Baines had somehow snuck a switchblade in, and she would pull it out before the doctors arrived at group sessions and just lay it on her lap, so we could all watch and wonder. Until Spicer arrived early one day, and Kiara, too, was sent to solitary.

Juin came over to eat with us once in a while, but it was no act of social charity, because she'd become an outsider, too. The queen of us all, and an outsider at the same time. I heard someone say she was actually twenty. Someone else said she had AIDS. Another girl claimed she was a faculty narc, and that was why she knew so much about the school.

One day these "group interviews" appeared on the

schedule. Along with four other girls, I was assigned to meet in a second-floor room that had always been off-limits before. Craving something new, we were in a good mood.

The door swung open when we tried it. At the center was a long oval table, set with a lace tablecloth and heavy silverware. Someone had laid a big spread of food on it. It was the same grub we were used to from the dining hall — greasy rolls with cold cuts, grapes half gone to wine — but in such abundance that it suddenly looked really good. Dr. Spicer sat away from the table, in a corner of the room, next to a wide window that looked out at the grounds. It was a rainy day, but it wasn't a depressing rain; it was the kind of rain that created interesting water currents on the window and made you happy to be inside.

"Sit down, girls," said Dr. Spicer.

The night before I had gotten into a shouting match with Teresa, which ended with me holding a fistful of her hair. Today I had made a decision to avoid conflict at all costs, so I let the others choose their seats first. Unfortunately, avoiding conflict meant getting stuck next to Riley, who was as likely to steer her fork toward my eyeballs as her melon cubes.

"Go ahead, eat," Dr. Spicer said.

We stared at the food.

"Are you going to watch?" I asked.

"For now, yes."

The good humor drained out of us. "Isn't that a little weird?" I asked.

"Go ahead, please."

It was like eating at my grandparents' house. You'd ask someone to pass you the salt even though you could have reached it yourself, just to fill the silence. Finally, after a couple of minutes of mechanical chewing and staring at the walls, Riley said, loud and out of nowhere, "This is messed up."

The girls all laughed, and I couldn't help joining in, because it was so true.

Dr. Spicer didn't say anything, just scribbled into her notebook. Despite her *I've got the master plan* image, she often seemed dulled, like she had been ruining girls' lives for one year too many. I caught her doodling once — nothing exciting, just rows of circles in the margin. Since she didn't scold Riley, we all freed up. Rebecca asked if anyone else had a funky smell coming from her toilet, and wondered if it was related to that weird chemical smell from before, and her roommate Sammie said she thought it was coming from the shower drain, and so on.

I was pouring myself some more of that mystery red dining hall juice when Dr. Spicer loudly called out: "Hold."

We all froze. I slowly lowered the pitcher, fitting it over the red circle it had already left on the tablecloth.

"In about five seconds I'm going to ask each of you to vote one of the other girls out to run laps. Five, four, three, two, one. Rebecca, you go first."

Rebecca, who had an awesome snake tattoo along one forearm, said, "I have to name someone?"

"Yes, or elect to go outside yourself."

I glanced out the window. The rain had strengthened during the lunch. The tops of the trees were waving.

Why did we play into her game? After days of doing nothing but follow directions, it had gotten harder to remember not to. It was more comfortable to obey.

Rebecca stared at the far wall and tugged on the end of her ponytail. "I choose Riley," she said finally.

Smart choice. Riley didn't have enough connections to get revenge. We all said Riley. On Riley's turn, she refused to say anyone's name.

"Riley, please change into your gym clothes. Dr. Hundrick is waiting for you on the patio. If she doesn't see you in five minutes, you can expect five hours of basement solitary. You're dismissed."

"You're not serious," Riley said. She wasn't going to cry, but I watched a vein in her skinny throat go throb, throb, throb. "I hate you all so damn much," was what she finally said as she got up and stiffly walked out of the room.

"Continue your lunch, girls," Dr. Spicer said.

No one really ate after that. There was some soup in a tureen, which Laurel suddenly offered to ladle out for everyone, all polite-like. The same Laurel who two days earlier had left a syrupy globe of spit on my door.

I predicted how it was going to go. We'd keep getting cut, until one of us was left, Rebecca or maybe Laurel. Sure enough, a few minutes later Dr. Spicer stopped us.

"Angela, your choice."

"Laurel." I probably answered a little too quickly.

Rebecca said the same. I was waiting for Laurel to say "Angela," but she named Sammie instead.

Dr. Spicer told both Laurel and Sammie to run laps.

Then it was just the rain hitting old windowpanes, Dr. Spicer at the wall, and Rebecca and me, seated at opposite ends of the long table, like a frigid old couple.

"When you enter the main school next week, you'll find that we operate a small commissary, where you can purchase treats and toiletries using credits you receive as rewards for good behavior. I have a hundred credits to offer today, not an inconsiderable sum." She gave a small pad and pencil to me, and one to Rebecca. "The rules are these: When I direct you to, you'll write either *self* or *share* on the pad. Then I'll read your responses. If you both write *share*, you'll receive thirty credits each. If one of you writes *share* and the other writes *self*, then the one who wrote 'self' will receive fifty credits and the other nothing. If you both write *self*, neither of you will receive anything. We'll go for three rounds."

I asked Dr. Spicer to repeat the directions, and strategized while she was talking. We'd be best off if we shared each time. But if I counted on Rebecca thinking the same thing, I could write *self* and get more. Looking back now, I obviously should have chosen *share* each time, if only to keep Rebecca as a friend. But the idea of conditioner and Clearasil . . .

As we got ready to write our first answers, I saw the three castoffs running in the rain, hair plastered to their heads. It felt blissful to be inside.

Rebecca and I didn't look at each other. We wrote and

passed the notebooks to Dr. Spicer. She read the pads and nodded. "Neither of you receives anything."

I grinned. Selfish bitches, both of us.

The next round, Dr. Spicer read the pads and declared: "Angela, fifty credits."

Rebecca didn't even look at me. She stared into her fingernails.

Next round, Dr. Spicer shook her head. "Nothing for either of you."

"You're such a jerk," Rebecca said, finally looking at me. She was smiling a little. She always kept perspective, Rebecca.

"You can go," Dr. Spicer said. "You know, if you had both shared each time, you'd each have ninety credits."

"Got the message, Doc," I said, thinking about Pantene.

The sick thing is: I thought I'd won something.

But of course, by playing the game, I'd lost from the start.

I just didn't know what I'd lost yet.

Chapter Ten

After writing so many e-mails to Trevor and having so many phone calls with him — all of them in my head — one afternoon we were finally allowed to write messages to send outside. I was sure everything I wrote was going to be read — and there was always the possibility that it was all a lie from the faculty, that the messages would never make it any farther than Dr. Zsilinska's office. But of course I tried. After trying to locate a Web browser on the computer I'd been led to (no luck), I opened the word processor and let out the words I'd long been holding in.

Trev,

I don't know if this is going to be the same when you get it, because the doctors here read it and say they'll e-mail whatever's acceptable on to you. Guess it's so I won't get any bad influences. That doesn't include you, of course. lol.

If you write me back, the nuns (the girls have started calling them the nuns, it seems to fit) will read your message and then print it out for me. There haven't been any printouts in my mailbox, and when I asked why, they said it was because no one wrote me. So write, asshole.

I'm surprised that not even my mom and dad have written. They may not be my biggest fans, but they must know it would make them look good to write their daughter. How about that? Just when I thought they couldn't hurt my feelings anymore, it happens.

So what's up? I bet you're getting this on Lawrence's cool new phone, while you guys are up to no good at the mall, waiting for his shift to end. He's probably standing there next to you, asking what's going on with the crazy chica. Tell him the girls here are all having sex with each other, or whatever. That'll get him going. Honestly, where are you sleeping these days? I think a lot about you.

One last thing: You know how you said it was probably good I was going away to Hidden Oak, because it would give us time to figure our own stuff out? I said yeah but I didn't mean it.

Miss you,

Angels

Normally if Trevor and I had no money but needed something to do, we'd head to the mall by my grandfather's house. But after June tenth that all changed, because my grandfather was dead and my mom and dad flew in and wouldn't leave me alone. From then on, whenever I was out of the house for too long my mom would drive to the mall to find me, because apparently she'd decided she was going to start caring about where I spent my time. I'd get my friend Gaby to man the phone and cover for me, and Trevor and I'd go farther away, to the other mall by the Y. Half of this mall's stores had closed, and all that was left were this coat outlet

69

and an arcade with a broken air-hockey game and machines with greasy joysticks.

One night Trevor and I'd planted ourselves in the food court, even though it was past closing time. The security goons drove by in their golf cart, told us we had to go, and drove us to the exit. But after Trevor hopped out, they sped off before I could get out, too, and they drove me once around the parking lot, laughing and teasing me when I scowled and looked pissed because I was scared they were going to take me back inside and rape me. They didn't do anything, just got their jollies freaking me out and dropped me back off with Trevor. He was laughing about it, too, and as soon as the guards left I pushed him right in the middle of his black sweatshirt, where the safety pins were.

When he got mad I pretended I'd only been playing at being pissed, which lasted until we were sitting at the curb waiting for his friend to pick us up and he asked why the hell I was being so quiet, and when I said those guards freaked me out, he said I should try to make myself into the kind of person who didn't freak out about what other people did.

What I'd wanted him to say, of course, was that other people sucked but we'd always be there for each other. All I needed was our little united front; even that would have been enough for me. But instead he told me that everyone in the world would let me way down if I let them. He didn't say he was any different. When we'd first started seeing each other he'd kept saying stuff like "I'll never leave you," and I realized, right then, that I hadn't heard him use the *never*, not for weeks.

"What's going to happen to us?" I said, leaning on his shoulder and waiting for him to hold me.

"Good question," he said, concentrating on a pebble he was fiddling between his fingers. It was like he was saying he was one of my worries, so it wasn't appropriate for him to say.

"What does that mean?" I asked.

"Look, your grandfather's dead. We both may know what really happened, but who knows what everyone else's thinking. And if they're going to look for someone to go after, I'm the guy."

"I wouldn't let them do that."

"How the hell am I supposed to know that, when I can barely ever see you? I spend whole days sitting around wondering if you're ratting me out. We're sneaking around a shitty mall, and half the time I'm looking over my shoulder for a cop car, or your dad with a shotgun. It makes all of this no fun, you know?"

I didn't know what to say. I didn't know that *fun* was the point of *us*. But I choked down what I was really feeling and tried to be entertaining. I pulled his hoodie over his head, then ran around the parking lot until he caught me. We fell behind the bushes. It didn't feel natural to be messing around right then, but we got high on the weirdness of it all.

I had no way of knowing that was the last time I'd see him.

When I finally got back to my grandfather's house I pushed past my mom and dad into the bedroom and cried and threw things a little, until my mom used a coat hanger to get the door open and started yelling.

It was the usual stuff, with the added touch that I was more disrespectful than ever to act up when my abuelito's funeral was that very weekend. Her speeches always followed the same pattern:

1. She'd moan about whatever my latest betrayal was, then
2. She'd choose a couple of her favorites of my past misbehaviors:
   a. biting my little cousin hard enough to leave a mark (I was *four*)
   b. exposing myself to the elementary school principal
   c. getting drunk at eleven (it was a *dare*)
   d. that bag of pot in my locker in seventh grade
   e. telling my mom I was sexually active only because we had to go to the doctor for that STD
   f. going back to the doctor because I kept losing all that weight
   g. failing physical science and Spanish ("Spanish!")
   h. the summer of piercings (three discovered and removed, two still hidden)
   i. crashing the family car (June)

   j. crashing the family car (August)

   k. expulsion (Roanoke Middle)

   l. expulsion (Holy Cross)

3. Next would be a general commentary section about how I was spoiled and selfish and didn't appreciate the amount of effort my parents put into raising me, then

4. I'd say if I was spoiled, it was because she and Dad had spoiled me, which would cause her to

5. Choose one of the following as proof that she was a good parent:

   a. throwing me the "sweet eleven party" (yes, yes, who gets a "sweet eleven" party — lucky me)

   b. driving me to dance and charm school classes (yeah, my eternal gratitude for the *charm classes*, Ma)

   c. getting me far more Christmas gifts than any of my cousins ever get, though I'd have to note that our cousins didn't have any money

6. I'd go on to point out that only when enough guilt about being such a crappy parent built up would she make some dramatically generous gesture, when *all I wanted was a mom who would actually listen when I had something to say*, who hadn't left me to be raised by a nanny, who cared about me beyond how I made her look, and *get out of my room*, followed by

7. A variation of the same Mom closing line: "I've tried to make us happy together, but you've opposed me at every turn."

Slam.

This time was extra bad, because I knew the bad spot I was in with Trevor. I didn't have anyone else to turn to.

That's when I gave up.

I stopped eating. I stopped talking.

I started fighting.

And I ended up here.

Chapter Eleven

The whole time, they watched us. We had no idea how much they watched us. When we were together. When we were alone. When they were in the room. Or when they were following us through the surveillance cameras. We thought that sometimes we didn't have to be on guard. We were wrong. They saw it all. And they were taking notes.

We should have thought more about what their master plan was. But we were too busy battling one another to pay them much notice.

With all the "unmonitored" time they gave us, we had the luxury to strengthen our friendships and hassle our enemies.

They knew that would happen.

They made that happen.

And we had no idea.

They were the real enemy.

* * *

Of course my group told the others what the "interview" was going to be, and they all hatched these elaborate strategies before they even went inside. But they ended up meeting with Zsilinska, not Spicer, and she made them role-play and catch one another and do more lame bonding exercises. Then the next day they were surprised by having to play the weird game instead. Poor Carmen got cut first and had to run laps for half an hour.

"What's this teaching us?" Juin asked as the three of us sat at dinner that night. "When you think about it, all their supposed 'good intentions' are full of holes."

Carmen nodded along but said, "I guess they're teaching us to share more?"

"What are we, eight years old?" Juin spat out.

"We're selfish, selfish girls," I said, with a sex-kitten frown.

"No, I get it. I know what Spicer would say if we asked her: 'Egoism is untenable, Juin.'"

I had no idea what *untenable* meant, but I believed Juin fully.

"And I guess we would have learned that lesson. If we were all dopes. But we see through to the next layer, so all we really learn is that we're powerless, that we're going to keep on being manipulated by those we're meant to trust, that it's okay to treat fellow human beings like lab rats if you have more authority. Any of you guys google Hidden Oak before you came here?"

Carmen and I shook our heads. I had other things — Trevor, my grandfather's death, my parents — on my mind.

"Well, I didn't, either," Juin continued quietly, "until after I got booted during last year's orientation. And let me tell you, the first few pages of hits are all propaganda, bogus articles praising the school's bold techniques and other crap. But look deeper, and you find these blog entries from these girls who've been kicked out. They're totally ruined, practically bleeding on the screen, you know what I mean? And you better believe there've been attempts to close the school. None have worked, because no court's going to believe what a bunch of hysterical teens say."

Juin had worked herself up and looked all righteous and pissed, so I wasn't about to say anything to poke a hole in her argument. But she wasn't pointing out the most obvious conclusion — that Hidden Oak had never been shut down because it *worked*, at least for most girls. Instead I asked her where she was the night I saw her empty room on Dr. Zsilinska's surveillance video.

She didn't say anything, just puffed her lips and laid a long finger against them. Then she continued like my question had been edited out of the broadcast. "And you don't even want to know why the old Heath school got closed. It's this total ghost story."

"What happened?" asked Carmen.

Juin stood at the porch rail and stared at the skyline. "You're not ready to hear yet."

"Drama queen," I said.

"I'm going for a walk," Juin declared. Of course we weren't allowed to do any such thing, but she left her dinner plate and traipsed outside, wandering into the fields, fingering the tops of the tall grasses like it was all her plantation or something.

I wondered why none of the adults in the dining room said anything. Once she returned (there was nowhere to escape *to* – that was the hardest thing about Hidden Oak), I had my answer.

They'd let her go so they could punish her when she got back.

She spent the next five hours in a moldy room in the basement.

Solitary confinement. It would seem almost pleasant compared to what waited for us.

Juin missed the next stage of all the weird tests and interviews. I went in with my usual group. We were in the same room as before, but two of the chairs had been set against a wall. Dr. Spicer gestured for me and Rebecca to sit in those. Then she sat there and looked to us to do something. Riley, Laurel, and Sammie stared sullenly.

"What's up, Doc?" I said.

"You and Rebecca are in charge," she said. "You won last week. That comes with responsibility to decide which person is going to get the one hundred credits at the end of this round."

"I'm not sure I want to decide that, Dr. Spicer," Rebecca said. Like me, she had probably seen the look of otherworldly anger Riley had shot her way. Getting to play queens meant that we could be assassinated.

"What are your criteria going to be?" Dr. Spicer asked.

Clearly, there wasn't going to be any getting out of this.

"What do we do?" Rebecca whispered to me.

"Something ridiculous. Pick a number one to twenty."

"Okay."

"All right," I said. "Rebecca has picked a number from one through twenty. You guys each have one? Good. Now, let's hear."

"Ten," Sammie said.

"Eleven," Riley said.

"Nine," Laurel said.

"You guys suck," Sammie said.

"The number was fourteen," Rebecca said.

I held up my finger. I couldn't have Riley win, not after she'd called me a spic, not after she talked about me behind my back and done her feeble best to sabotage my attempts at making friends. "Executive order," I said. "The number is now ten."

"Sweet," Sammie said.

Dr. Spicer said, "Riley, Laurel, to the fields."

That night at dinner Carmen and I sat alone as usual, busy ignoring our salads and moaning about how tired we

79

were. I had Trevor on my mind and was fighting the urge to dump my feelings about him on Carmen, cameras be damned.

"You notice," she said, "that we're slowly getting divided?"

"Eh?" I asked, waving a speared tomato at her. "What do you mean?"

"In the beginning we were all mixed. I'd be in group therapy with you one time, Connie the next. But now it's the same people over and over. Like I'm never, ever with Juin. I'm always with the good girls. Or the better girls, I guess I should say."

"I don't think I've been placed with any one group," I said.

"You totally have. You're with the bad girls."

"No, I don't think so." And I really didn't. There were worse girls out there than me and Rebecca and Laurel. That chemical smell that had filled the house before had been from one of the more whacked girls burning her uniform in her sink — and because we were shut into our airless rooms, we all spent the next day hacking and coughing from the polyester vapors. Then there were Arden and Delores, both eventually kicked out, one for attitude and the other for abusing prescriptions. There was Bee, who traded the few permitted medications (if those lucky doped-up girls held their pills under their tongues and spat them into Bee's cup once the faculty was gone, she'd arrange for someone to throw them extra commissary credits next time a game came around). Shanice supposedly hurled a punch during a session after Dr. Zsilinska called her narcissistic. Teresa was in basement solitary way more often than she was out of it. Compared to all of them, I was with angels. My girls dreamed of escape, starved, or hurt themselves. Normal stuff.

"But why keep the bad with the bad, and the good with the good?" Carmen asked. "It seems like they should be doing the opposite, you know? Like mix us all together so we'll help one another get better."

"That's real sweet, Carmen."

"Seriously. I don't get it."

It made perfect sense to me. The bad girls were with the bad girls for the same reason cities have slums. The government wants to keep the undesirable people together, so they don't dirty everything else. I was going to tell Carmen as much, but then I heard this huge racket in the hot-food line.

Riley was on the floor, running circles on her side. Juin was standing over her, dangling a cardboard cup of steaming water. She let droplets periodically fall out, and each time a splash hit, Riley screamed and thrashed and sped up. The two girls' trays had spilled, and Riley's hair was clotted in turkey casserole, her bangs twisting into one creamy yellow mass.

The other girls in line formed a half ring around them, rooting Juin on.

A dining hall lady tried to grab Juin's arm, but Juin batted her away and kept dribbling hot water. By this point Riley was yelling hot nonsense, saying only half of one word before seizing on another. The dining hall lady tried to grab

Juin's hand again, which made her pour the remaining water on Riley, whose fists balled up under the scalding stream. I definitely thought it was wrong that Juin was spilling boiling water on someone, but I have to say I was also sad to see the cup empty.

The HH arrived with reinforcements, and Juin obviously knew better than to try to take on everyone at the same time. She was led away like a white-collar crook. As she left she pointed directly at me and mouthed something I couldn't make out.

That night, as Carmen and I were getting ready for bed and waiting to hear the ten P.M. magnetic locks snap on, I heard the door squeak open and turned in time to see a hand appear and slip half a dining-hall plastic spoon between the two plates of the lock. Then the hand disappeared. Ten o'clock came, and the lock ticked but didn't click into place.

"Hey, Carmen," I said coolly, pointing at the plastic spoon, "what the hell do you think that's about?"

"Huh," she said, combing her fingers through her hair.

We didn't remove it, of course. *We* hadn't placed it there, after all, so they could hardly punish us, and the possibility of an adventure not planned by doctors was too exciting to pass up. We got into our beds and stared at the door, our eyes gleaming in the dark.

Something, finally, was happening.

Chapter Twelve

We waited.

And waited.

Finally, I fell asleep. And then, all of a sudden, the overhead light clicked on. I opened my eyes and stared at it unthinkingly, focusing on the sunspot a bug corpse made in the plastic globe. Carmen was sitting up, shielding her eyes as she fumbled for her glasses.

"Time for class, girls," Juin called.

"It's the middle of the night — there can't be class," Carmen mumbled. She never quite got when people were being funny.

"Let's go," I said.

It would have broken some magic to ask Juin where we were heading, so we slipped on shoes and complimented her method for getting past the locks as we crept down the creaky main staircase and passed out the front door, which had been similarly blocked by a dining-hall spoon. She carefully replaced it as we eased the door shut.

Seen in the moonlight, the Hidden Oak grounds were an ancient graveyard. The gates, the plastic flags set into the ground by landscapers, the ruined buildings, all looked like crypts and gravestones. The gravel paths had disappeared — instead there was only a dark expanse, layered with ruins that blocked squares and diamonds out of the silver-black silhouettes of the trees.

Juin didn't have a flashlight, so we picked our way along like children lost in the woods. She seemed to know where she was going, darting between the crumbly stone walls with practiced steps. We didn't say anything; questioning would have made us undeserving of the adventure.

We slowed as we passed by the main building, which had a few scattered lights on.

"How are we going to break in?" I whispered.

"No way," Juin said. "We'll have plenty of time in there soon enough."

We sped up and passed out of view of the school. We approached the line of the woods without any apparent direction, but as we neared, I saw a trail cutting between the trees.

I shivered. I hadn't put socks on, and I could feel cold dew through my canvas shoes. Being out here in the dead of night made me feel really uneasy. I had to be careful not to let it show.

"Where are we going?" Carmen asked.

"Shut up," Juin said, holding up a hand and pausing us at the base of a fallen tree. "Listen."

We stopped.

"Do you hear it?" Juin asked.

We shook our heads.

"That's too bad," she said, like she was disappointed in us. "Come on."

Juin started down the trail. Carmen looked perplexed, but I gave her a *she's just playing with us* look.

The trail must have followed a stream, because there was a patchy line of trees on the side, and then empty space. We followed the sound of the water for a while, until we had to stop before another fallen tree. We traced it off the trail, until it started tilting up at an angle. At the end was a small building that had somehow gotten wedged beneath the branches.

"Ruined tree house," Juin said. "The boys at the old prep school must have built it. The tree fell, of course. But the walls are steady."

One long leg and then the other, she passed through a tilted window. Carmen and I stole glances at each other and then followed with considerably more difficulty. Especially Carmen, who landed on the floor with a thump.

We were sitting on the former wall of the tree house, which was now a floor of broken wooden shards. The air was moist and smelled like soil. A pair of small creatures skittered away into the darkness before I could identify them.

"How did you *know* about this place?" Carmen asked.

"Between getting placed in solitary all those nights and sneaking out here for others, I don't think I've slept in my actual room even once," Juin replied. She pulled a pillow and sleeping bag from a corner. "I just make sure I'm back before daylight. No one does bed checks during the night. And the cameras don't see anything in the dark. Believe me, I'd have heard about it from Spicer if they did. They trust the room locks to keep us in. Morons."

We assembled on the floor. It was a relief to be unwatched; I felt like I used to whenever my parents went out of town, those first few minutes when I could stretch out and fill all the space around me. I looked over at Carmen, who didn't seem nearly as blissful. "We shouldn't be here," she said.

Juin rolled her eyes.

"No, really," Carmen said. "I'm going."

"Are you serious? You just got here," I said.

"I know. But I changed my mind."

"Come on."

"Let her go," Juin said. "See you later, pumpkin."

Carmen tried to scramble out the window, but got caught with one leg out and one in. She worked her way back inside.

"I don't know what you think you're doing," I said to her. "I mean, breaking out is major enough. Once you've gone this far, you might as well stay around."

"You looked like a fat monkey somebody trained to climb out windows, anyway," Juin observed.

Carmen stood looking out at the black forest. We could hear the swaying of the trees as a breeze passed through. "Someone else is out there," she whispered.

Suddenly the night felt huge, the fallen tree house feeble protection.

Juin came to stand next to us at the window.

A treetop swayed, and I heard the crunch of gravel, then a kerplunk and a girl's voice cursing away.

"Oh! Riley's here," Juin said.

"Riley!" Carmen gasped.

And it was. Her face appeared right in front of us. I fell back, startled.

"Come on in," Juin said, lifting a hand out to help Riley through the window.

"Stupid stream," Riley said, sitting on the floor and shaking out a soggy boot.

"What the hell is going on?" I asked.

"I invited her to join us," Juin said.

Riley looked up from where she was sitting on the floor, daring me to object. She had a bright red-yellow blister on her cheek where she'd been scalded by Juin. Carmen crossed her arms and stared coldly at her.

"No, seriously," I said. "What the hell? Last I saw, you guys were mortal enemies."

"No, *you* and Riley were mortal enemies," Juin said. "I was defending you. But we're past that now, aren't we, Riley?"

Riley nodded, avoiding my eyes.

"Riley has this tic thing that makes her unable to control herself sometimes," Juin continued, "so she comes across as hostile. And getting teased about that her whole life has made her prickly. But she's promised not to be prickly with the coven. Haven't you, Riley?"

Riley nodded. I was in shock at the changed dynamic between them.

"Why don't you say you're sorry to Angela?" Juin said.

Riley muttered something that very well might have been an "I'm sorry."

Meanwhile, Carmen was stuck on something else Juin had said. "What do you mean, *coven*?" she asked.

Juin laughed. "Coven. A circle of witches — look it up. But we're a coven of *bitches*, don't you see? And I've decided it's time we convened."

"Why us?" I asked. Maybe I should have been scared, like Carmen, but I was suddenly excited.

"Let's say I'm curious about some people," Juin replied. "And you and Riley are the ones I'm most curious about." She placed a finger on my breastbone. "And we'll be starting with you."

Chapter Thirteen

Like a bird fleecing for a nest, Juin had stolen random bits from the mansion to make the tree house feel ours. She unknotted a sack she'd rigged from one of her pink polo shirts and dumped out forks and knives, three socks (one with the heel cut off), a hard roll, cigarette papers, a key ring without keys, an old bus ticket, and two pens. Then she put everything back into the sack and whizzed it around her head so the contents shuffled.

"Pick your signature thing," Juin told me.

I reached in, and the first thing I touched was . . . the hard roll.

I could've cheated and moved on to something else. But I felt Juin would know. This was, in its own bizarre-o way, a test.

I took out the roll and held it up. "This bitch is high in carbs," I proclaimed.

Juin chuckled. Carmen looked liked she was still ready to flee, and Riley looked resentful, like she'd wanted the stupid roll for herself.

"Now," Juin said, "tell us why you're here."

I took a breath and prepared to speak.

Carmen stopped chewing her lip and opened her mouth to stop me.

"Don't start. I don't care," I said. "We're way off in the woods. There's no cameras out *here.*"

"It's going to be fine," Juin said, her eyes gleaming white as she rolled them in the moonlight. "Really."

I glanced at Riley. She stared at me intently, waiting for me to start.

I knew I had to tell them about June tenth.

But I couldn't make myself jump right in. So I started with easier stuff. "I was skipping most of my classes. I didn't have too many friends in Houston, just a couple of guys. My age. We'd check in each morning and then head straight back out. The high school was in a suburb, so there wasn't much around. I spent most of my time at the bookstore, browsing CDs and that kind of stuff. Well, I was in the *libros en español* section, and this guy was there, too. Trevor."

"Describe him for us," Juin said, closing her eyes.

"Um, brown hair, brown eyes. Skater type, but he didn't really skateboard, he just looked like it. He wanted to be an actor."

"How old was he?"

"Probably twenty-three? He said he was nineteen when we met."

"Sexy?"

"Yeah. Really, really sexy."

"And you fell for him?"

"Not right away, but yeah."

"How did your grandfather feel about Trevor?"

I knew where Juin was slowly edging me. "He didn't know for a while, until he came home one day and saw me and Trevor in the living room watching TV. It actually went okay, so I got more comfortable. Trevor came over more often. My grandfather must have told my parents eventually, and they must've flipped, because suddenly my grandfather's tone switched. One day he just got all nasty, said I'd been misleading him. He had that grumpy side, and didn't understand that my parents would have disapproved of any guy I was seeing. Especially one who was older, wore ripped jeans, dyed his hair, didn't have a job — want more? Basically, my parents are really conventional. They want the McMansion with flimsy walls, they want me looking pretty and doing the shy-girl-with-breeding act. It's that whole Mexican-American newly rich insecurity thing. If there'd been debutante balls in Roanoke, I would have had to go."

I stopped. Carmen was riveted and Riley was trying to look bored.

Juin opened her eyes and said, "Go on."

"Well, none of this stopped me from seeing Trevor. He'd still come over to my grandfather's house. We'd just make sure that he wasn't home first. It was fun."

"I bet it was fun. And then?" Juin asked.

"What?" I said.

91

"Nobody is sent to Hidden Oak because she was just sneaking around with her boyfriend."

Did I trust her? Did I have a choice? All I knew was that now that I'd come this close to revealing myself, there was no way I was going to stop.

"How do I start?" I said. "Trevor didn't really have a job or even a home. He slept at his dad's some nights, but hated it. Other nights he'd sneak into my bedroom, or he'd sleep in the trees behind the mall parking lot, where they store those security golf carts. He was really poor, and my grandfather had money. So I gave him some of it."

"Where did you find the money?" Carmen asked.

"My grandfather's checkbook."

"You wrote him *checks*?" Riley snorted. "Didn't you know you were going to get caught?"

"Of course."

"But that didn't stop you?" Riley asked.

"Guess not."

I was about to start arguing with Riley, but Juin put a stop to that.

"It wasn't just the checks," she said. "What happened?"

I took a deep breath.

"Trevor and I weren't in a great place. We'd been fighting. I guess it was because I kept getting all needy, calling him even when I knew I'd already been calling too much. He had always been worried I was too young for him, anyway, so when I got emotional, it made him sort of shut off. And when I felt this glassiness from him, it made me more needy, made me keep asking him if he loved me and all that. I totally wasn't playing by the cool rules.

"He'd already told me he wouldn't be coming to my grandfather's that night. But he got drunk, and called me at like one in the morning, saying he was in the neighborhood and was going to stop by, anyway. I thought about saying he couldn't come over, because I knew rejecting him would fire him up and give me some power back, but I couldn't. I really wanted to see him. We have this system where he'll walk down the neighbors' yard, hop their fence into my grandfather's, and then rap on my window. So I sat in my window seat, waiting to hear him knock and for my life to restart.

"When he showed up, he had that weird look he gets when he's high — his skin was paler and his lips were redder. It makes him look a little sick but also hot, like he's living this extreme life. I let him in and couldn't resist kissing him and peeling off his shirt, so we hooked up for a while. By now it was probably two-thirty in the morning, and we were both getting really tired. So we got into the bed —"

"We need details," Juin said. "I want to picture this. What kind of bed?"

"A full, I guess. You know, for two people but not really. Shaped like a sleigh."

"Sheets?"

"White with little red flowers. Trevor used to make fun of them."

"Was he a good kisser?" Carmen asked, her chin cupped in her hands.

"Very. I didn't enjoy anything as much as kissing him. Well, I wish he didn't smoke, because his breath kind of stunk a lot of times, but otherwise, yeah, a great kisser."

"Continue," Juin said.

"So we fell asleep, and I woke up because my grandfather busted in. He didn't sleep that well after my grandmother died, and I guess he'd been up checking his account online and found out about the checks."

"How much?" Riley asked.

"All together? Five thousand."

"Damn," Juin said.

"Was that a lot for your grandfather?" Carmen asked.

"Yes," I said, suddenly — and for the first time — really ashamed. "Half his savings. Trevor was going back to school. He needed the money to pay for his first semester."

"No excuses in the coven, just facts," Juin declared.

"You come up with that right now?"

She nodded. "Continue."

"So, um, my grandfather came in, and he was so mad. Then he saw Trevor and got even more mad, so mad that he turned a scary kind of quiet. He shook Trevor awake. You never know what mood Trevor's going to be in, especially not if he's high and woken up. Trevor didn't move at first. His eyes shot open and stayed fixed on my grandfather. There they were, totally still but passing each other this weird energy, and I knew, right then, that this wasn't going to be some simple fight.

"My grandfather asked where his money was, and Trevor said he didn't know. Then my grandfather said that was a

94

lie, and Trevor stood up and, you know, they started talking to each other louder and louder, until Trevor was pushing my grandfather out of the bedroom. I should have been telling him to stop, but I didn't. I sat there. How wrong is that?"

Carmen stared back with her eyes empty of judgment or pity, her look that made you want to tell her everything. I concentrated on her.

"I got out of bed and went into the living room. It was dead quiet."

"You were wearing . . . ?" Juin prompted.

"What? Panties and a lame old T-shirt for some Disney band. I saw my grandfather on the floor, half under the glass dining-room table. He was totally awake, and he was trying to get up, trying to get his elbows under him. That's when this cloud passed over him, somewhere between his brain and his face, and he stayed on one elbow, looking at us like suddenly we were far away."

"Heart attack?" Juin asked.

"Yeah. Well, a stroke. He died a few hours later."

"Did the police come?" Carmen asked softly.

"Nope. He had a history of smaller strokes. This was just the one that did him in."

"So he was probably going to pass away soon, anyway," Carmen said, taking my arm in her lap.

I nodded. I didn't know if that was true. He was pretty old, but he also seemed pretty healthy.

"Nah," Juin said. "He was basically killed. But it wasn't you, pumpkin. You can't think that."

"My parents thought it might as well have been me that did it. When they found out about the checks, they almost turned me in. The only thing that stopped them was my promising never to see Trevor again."

"And what happened to him?" Carmen asked.

I shrugged and wondered why I didn't feel like crying anymore. It seemed, suddenly, that Trevor was beside the point.

Juin nodded, and motioned that we should all lie back. We did, and spent the next few hours like that, dozing on one another's ankles and talking about whatever came to mind.

I figured we'd have some drawn-out conversation about what Riley had against me, and why Juin had poured that boiling water on her, but we never did. Riley had just been being a bitch, and I guess we all got that. We'd all moved on. So instead we talked about bands and boys, and wondered who had once built the tree house, before it'd fallen. When we got up, Carmen said, drowsily, "Let's do this every Saturday."

And so we did . . . for as long as we could.

Chapter Fourteen

Morning bed checks were very predictable, coming some-time between 6:20 and 6:30 A.M., depending on whether the woman on duty started on our end of the hallway or the other. We weren't allowed to have watches, but Juin told us the sun was supposed to rise at 5:45 or so in late summer, so as soon as it started to get light we stole across the wet grass to the mansion. I concentrated on its roof as we crossed the grass, its white beams lit pink in the dawn.

On the return from our second meeting of the coven, an issue arose: the front door.

Juin had left a spoon across the lock to keep it from bolt-ing, but it must have fallen while we were off in the tree house. When we got back to the building, we found it rest-ing neatly on the ground, as if someone had just taken a break from eating dirt. When Riley tried to force open the door, Juin snapped at her to stop, since she was making too much noise.

"How are we going to get in?" Carmen whispered.

"Give me a second," Juin spat.

Carmen looked pleadingly from Juin, the general, to me and Riley, the lieutenants. I shrugged and sat on the stoop. That day I honestly didn't care whether we got away with it or if we got caught. If I got kicked out, I told myself, I'd be totally on my own. I could go to a warm state, like Arizona or something, and find someone who'd give me money or a room. I found myself wanting a cigarette, something to fill my fingers and my thoughts. But of course there were no cigarettes allowed at Hidden Oak.

"Come *on*," Carmen said. "Five more minutes and we're, like, busted."

Huh. Interesting. I couldn't make myself care.

"Okay, I've figured something out," Juin said. "I gave myself a break in the bathroom before I picked you guys up, and I left the window open to let the smoke air out. Unless someone decided to be an early-morning goody-goody, it should still be open."

"You've got cigs?" I asked indignantly.

"The bathroom's on the second floor," Carmen said mournfully. Actually, it was even worse than that. The bathroom windows were little circles way up high on the roof. You'd have to climb to the very top to get in.

"Follow my lead," Juin commanded.

She put a leg against each side of the doorframe, then shinnied until she reached the top. As the rest of us held our breaths, she pulled herself over and scrambled up the weathered shingles. It didn't look easy, even for Juin, and I knew it would be a true struggle for Carmen.

Without saying a word, Riley followed her. She was able to work the odd angles of her body agilely, like some super-evolved alien creature.

"You go next," Carmen said.

I said no and threaded my fingers for her to stand on. Once she'd placed her wet sneaker into my hands, I lifted. She tottered about in the air, finally crashing against the top of the door frame. Between my heaving, Riley's tugging, and Carmen's own frenzied struggles, we got her up. I followed, and the four of us lay against the roof. No sooner had I caught my breath than Juin crept up to the second-floor hallway window. "Damn," she said. "They've already started room checks."

"What?" Carmen shrieked. She was at the edge of the roof, halfway into the gutter. "Starting at which end?"

Juin shook her head sharply and started back down toward us.

"What are you doing?" Carmen asked.

"For the team," Juin said, and pitched Carmen over the side.

Carmen fell wordlessly, and thumped a second later when she hit the ground. I stood at the edge and stared down at her, lying on her side like Riley had been the week before when Juin had been scalding her. Carmen gasped against the grass, her breath knocked out.

"What are you doing?" I said, grabbing Juin's arm.

Juin shrugged me off. "It's four in solitary or one. Come *on!*"

She gestured me and Riley toward the bathroom window. I wanted to go down and help Carmen — she was my closest friend here, and it was definitely wrong for Juin to have pushed her off the roof. But now that Carmen was on the ground, Juin was right — there was no point in leaping down to be with her. It wouldn't help anyone for more than one of us to be caught. At that moment, I hated Juin — not just for doing what she'd done, but for being right about it.

Juin and Riley and I slipped through the tiny window (Carmen might not have fit through it, anyway, I told myself) and dashed to our rooms. I made one final glance out the window and saw Carmen get to her feet just as the room checker emerged to investigate the noise.

I closed my door soundlessly behind me and leaned against it. In the space of a few seconds, I had gone from feeling empty to feeling totally distraught. It was my first time ever being alone in the room, and I felt loneliness and guilt press on the center of my chest, the invisible third and fourth roommates that, I realized now, Carmen had always been silently working to keep at bay.

Chapter Fifteen

At breakfast that morning we were surprised to find Dr. Spicer seated at the head table. Conscious of Spicer's stare, I chose a spot at the opposite end of the dining hall from Juin, making a big show of avoiding her. I'm not sure if it was just to minimize the appearance of collaborating, or because seeing Juin reminded me of how bad I felt about Carmen.

Halfway through breakfast Spicer got up and reminded us about the severity of Hidden Oak's no-sneaking-out rule, and then left. That was it. No mention of Carmen, no reference to any specific infraction. It was as if Carmen had never existed. When Sammie asked me where she was, I didn't know how to reply.

"What was that about?" I asked Juin, lingering so I could walk with her as we filed out.

"I don't think we'll be seeing Carmen for a while," she

said. She looked preoccupied, but at the edges of her mouth she was smiling.

After breakfast we had to meet with Zsilinska for meetings scheduled five minutes apart and called *Ladders.*

"How are you, Angela?" she asked me as I sat down.

"Great, thanks."

"I want to ask you a question, and I want you to answer me as honestly as possible. Do you think you can do that?"

"Yes, Dr. Zsilinksa."

"You've always sounded ambivalent about your relationship with Trevor. Why did you never break it off with him?"

I hadn't really talked to Dr. Zsilinska about Trevor, not like I had with the coven. Then I realized: Dr. Z had read my e-mail to him. Of course.

She pushed her glasses up her nose, setting her beads to clacking, and I stole a glimpse of her clipboard while she did. All of our names were printed along one side on a sheet of paper, a blank box after each.

"Um, I told him we were through plenty of times."

"But you never meant it. Why did you never mean it?"

"I really did mean it. Every time."

"Please answer my question, rather than redefine the conditions."

Apparently I hadn't ever really meant it. I decided to play along. "I guess sometimes I said I wanted to break up because I knew it would make him affectionate again."

"Why did you want him to be affectionate?"

"Because it felt good."

"Why did it feel good?"

"Because I felt special."

"Why did you feel special?"

"Because it felt good." I smirked.

"You've entered a loop. Give me another answer."

"What do you *want* me to say?"

"Something else. Why did you feel special?"

"Because it meant he was looking out for me."

"Why would his being affectionate mean he was looking out for you?"

"Because he wouldn't waste time on someone he didn't care about."

"Why wouldn't he?"

"Because it wouldn't make sense."

"Thank you, Angela. I'll see you for our regular session tomorrow. Don't forget there's a general meeting this afternoon."

"He cared about me, okay?"

She didn't look up again. I glanced at her notebook as I left. Beside my name she'd written *Overly Trusting.*

Even by the afternoon assembly, Carmen hadn't returned. I was starting to get really worried. Not just about her well-being, but about what they might find out from her — I could imagine interrogations breaking her down so she'd give up our names and lead them to the

103

tree house. The coven would be over before it had really started.

At the assembly, Dr. Spicer started by calling out a bunch of girls' names, fully a third of us. Laurel's name came up, and Connie's, and Carmen's, even though she was still missing. The girls who were there all stood up, and Dr. Spicer told them to go upstairs, get their belongings, and meet her outside.

Again, I was surprised at how cowed we were. A bunch of us left, and the rest just eased over to fill their spaces. I did a quick appraisal of who remained. Overall we were the worse-behaving group. But it didn't work out perfectly — there were definitely some real misfits who got sent away, and some brown-nosers staying.

Once the hubbub was over, there we were, a newly lean huddle, peering at Dr. Spicer beneath the fluorescent bulbs of the big basement room. Rebecca raised her hand and asked, "Where did they go?"

"Not all students are fit to stay in the mansion until the end of orientation," Dr. Spicer said.

"But where did they *go*?" I asked.

"There's no more need for questions," Dr. Spicer announced.

That night at dinner, I slid my splintering orange plastic tray next to Rebecca's. "What's the word?" I asked.

She shrugged. "Everyone's wondering where the others went. It's all anyone's talking about."

"So what are the theories?"

"Hmm? Oh, general thought is that they've been kicked out."

"Bull. Why would a school kick a third of its students out? And if they did, why wouldn't they have already kicked out someone like Juin or Teresa?" The day before, Teresa had been discovered hoarding medications, plenty enough for a suicide or a poisoning. She'd since disappeared back into solitary.

"What's your theory, then?"

"I dunno. Did anyone see where they went, exactly?"

Rebecca shook her head.

"Then my theory's that we should go investigate the main building tonight," I said.

Rebecca raised an eyebrow.

"There's a way to get out," I said. "Juin discovered it. She'll come with us."

"Count me in," Rebecca said. Then she stared into her tray as she bit into her sandwich, Rebeccaspeak for *conversation over.*

That night, Rebecca, Juin, Riley, and I sneaked out of our rooms and met on the porch. It was one of those humid nights where it might not be raining, but still whenever you move you get wet. Fog crept over the grass.

I couldn't help thinking that it was as if I'd replaced Carmen with Rebecca, and I felt guilty. I missed her a lot, and really wanted to know where she was and how she was doing. I convinced myself that having another pair of eyes along would only help that.

"So it's decided," Juin said. "We'll go to the main building."

The moonlight was diffused by the clouds, so we couldn't see the building well, only a black chunk clipped out of the dim gray sky. We quietly stole away, our feet making hushed murmurs in the grass.

As we approached the main building, I saw a window glowing on the lower floor. I moved us toward it, but when we were still a hundred feet away, a dog started barking.

Juin cursed as we plunged into the thick grass.

The barks went on and on. We had fallen in a circular formation, and I was half in dirt and half in grass, Rebecca's knees in my face. I was the only one who could still see the building.

"What's going on?" Rebecca asked.

I didn't answer. I could see the dog in the window, small and white, its ears sharp quivering triangles. Its owner — a man, the first I had seen in weeks — stood behind it, staring out the window. He was old and shiny-headed, and wore a loose shirt and high-waisted pants that made me imagine he wore tweed suits during the day. But it wasn't that man or the dog that got my attention.

The light from the living room cast a softer glow on the next room, and only by concentrating could I make out much inside it. What I saw was a young guy wearing only pajama bottoms, standing at the foot of his bed. He had his hand raised, so at first I thought he was on the phone. But he didn't move, which made me think he was just standing in his bedroom in the dark, thinking. He crossed to the window, and I saw his narrow waist and tight stomach. I couldn't make out a single color or a hint of his expression, but I was transfixed. Bonding with Carmen aside, it was the best few seconds of my stay at Hidden Oak.

"Come on, what's going on?" Rebecca asked.

"There's a dog," I said.

"*Really,*" Juin said sarcastically. "What're you being so tight about?" I could hear her rustle in the grass, and then gasp, "There's a man!"

I felt a surge of disappointment; I had wanted to keep him to myself.

"Let me see," Riley said. "Ah, old and balding. Just my type."

Juin laughed, and I felt a surge of relief. They hadn't seen my guy yet.

"Listen, ladies," I said. "If there's a dog that's going to bark, we shouldn't go any closer to the main building. It's not worth it."

"So what do we do?" Rebecca asked.

"I think it's time for another meeting of the coven," Juin said.

If I felt strange before about venturing out without Carmen, it now felt like a much bigger betrayal. But still I followed Juin — that was her hold on me. It wasn't until we were in the tree house that I could muster up any kind of protest. While Juin was pulling out her bag of objects, I said, "Shouldn't we, you know, hold off on the speeches for Carmen?"

Rebecca didn't really know what was going on, and Riley didn't seem to care. So everyone looked to Juin for a reply.

"If you want, you can take notes and read them to her over tea," she said mockingly. "Otherwise, it's survival of the fittest here. Or haven't you noticed? If you want to be a bitch, you have to be a bitch. And she lost out."

"Survival of the bitchiest?" I replied. "I guess that means it's your turn to go, since you're the bitchiest of us all."

Juin stared at me hard.

Without another word, she reached into the bag and pulled out the first thing she touched.

The empty key ring.

Then, before we'd even had a chance to get comfortable, she launched into her story. There was no stopping her. I'd been the one to dare her to speak, and now she was the one to dare us all to listen.

"I was a creepy kid," she began. "I'll admit it. Mom and Dad could never seem to decide whether to live in France or the States, and I guess you could say all the moving around turned me into my own best friend. I took pleasure in myself a bit too much. I'm not talking about anything sexy, just that I would lock myself in my room and stare at the mirror. Or I'd burn magazines over the sink. Creepy stuff for a five-year-old, but not 'dangerous.' Yet.

"Dad couldn't decide where to live, and he couldn't decide who to live with. Whenever he'd cheat and leave, Mom would get withdrawn and I'd be eating cereal three meals a day.

Then Dad would come back with tears and promises and a toy for me, and we'd have three weeks of extravagance, until he would start coming home late from work again and Mom would boot him out. Repeat recipe.

"During one of those periods when Dad was away, I let my hamster die. It was summer vacation, I was alone in my room, and I had nothing else to do. You're looking at me weird, and I can't explain it. It *was* weird. I simply didn't give him any food. I'd check on him every once in a while, peering in the cage to see what was happening. I think I was waiting for him to ask for help. And of course he didn't. He curled up in his empty dish, a little circle of brown fur.

"I threw the hamster out, and if my parents ever noticed he was gone, they didn't say anything. But I knew I had done it, and I knew that I had really felt *something* when he'd died. I started looking forward to each time my dad left us, because the grief it made me feel was now mixed with having destroyed something; the feeling wasn't dull anymore, but sort of laced with live wires."

I looked at the network of old scars on Juin's arms. She was obviously ready to do whatever it took to make herself feel.

"When I got to be thirteen, Dad stopped coming by at all. I started lying big-time to my mom about where I was going and who I was going out with. She was too spineless to deal with me, and her weakness made me even more irritated, so we started avoiding each other altogether. I had this affair with a family friend named Etienne. We ran away from home and wandered all over France for a year, then we broke up and I was living on my own until I ran out of cash and rummaged up enough money to get to my aunt's place in Paris.

"She made me re-enroll in school, which I actually became fine with, after giving her hell for the first few weeks. But halfway through the semester, my mom came to visit. She treated it as though I'd just happened to be in when she came by. We sat in the front room and tried to be a mother and daughter again — we were so completely lonely — but she started moaning about how she'd been done wrong, and it sounded pathetic. I got furious and irritated like I always did, and I guess I looked like I was going to hit her, because she left.

"But she forgot her handbag. It contained a checkbook —"

"Jeez," Riley said. "You guys and your checkbook issues."

"Yeah, and it was handy for a while until she closed the account," Juin continued quickly, "but the important thing was that her handbag also contained her engagement calendar. There was all sorts of stuff written in that I wouldn't have predicted for my mother. Like men's names. She only ever talked about my dad to me, but apparently she was going out with other guys, sometimes three or four guys in one day. And that was why she was in Paris, because she had a date scheduled for the next day.

"So, yeah, school was getting boring so I didn't have much to do during the days, and I took off to follow my mom to the guy's workplace to see who he really was. What mattered most was that he was handsome — really handsome.

110

I watched them come out arm in arm, and wanted to be her. He always went to the same bar after work, and one day when my mother wasn't around, I followed him in. At first I just wanted to mess with my mom, but then I found I was really enjoying myself. And he liked me – obviously he liked messed-up girls, if he had gone for my mom – so we hit it off. I was seeing him for a month before I told him whose daughter I was.

"I really thought he would enjoy being with a mother and daughter like that. But he freaked. He told my mom, who tracked me down and slapped me around a bunch – nothing new there. Then she called my father and bitched at him, like it was his fault or something, and next thing I knew – ta-da – I'm flying back to America and being strait-jacketed off to Hidden Oak."

She was grinning widely, like she'd just told us a riveting story about some girl in a movie. Like her own doom was the best thing in her life.

"But that was just the first time you got sent here, right?" Riley asked.

"Yeah. I didn't get to stay long because they choose one girl to make an example of early on. It was Arden this year, and last year it was me. Once I got back to France, I wasn't about to stay with my mom, so I ran away the first chance I had. I vanished for a while, but you know what? The big wide world kind of sucks. Getting into it is fun for a break, but I started wanting a smaller playing field, you know what I mean? So when the next school year came around, I went home. A few strings were pulled, and Hidden Oak was convinced to take me back. And for whatever reason, the docs've decided to keep me around this time."

Juin clearly had broader horizons than any of us had ever known. I felt wary of the callous way Juin told her story, but I was mostly impressed that she was always in such control of her life, sailed through hard stuff so coolly. I wanted her to show me how to do that.

Should I have been suspicious that Juin's story was just so . . . Juin? Probably. But I would soon have far more serious concerns.

Chapter Sixteen

Carmen never returned. One morning, when I came back from breakfast, I saw that all her stuff had disappeared. Had they kicked her out? Or had she been sent to join the other girls that we never saw anymore? I tried to get answers, but no one — not Dr. Zsilinska, not the Hostile Hag — was speaking. It was like Carmen had never existed.

I should've been happy to have a room to myself. No more need to block the bathroom door. No more wheezy snores. No more stepping over someone else's clothes.

But instead, I was lonely.

And isolated.

Right where Hidden Oak wanted me.

At the next few afternoon assemblies, Dr. Spicer kept announcing more names of girls who had to leave, whittling our group down even further. Eventually only me, Juin, Riley, Teresa, and a couple other girls were left.

We were rapidly approaching the month mark, when Maureen had implied we'd be joining the main school. I'd been making marks on my bedpost, like a prisoner, and was up to twenty-seven.

There were sure to be fireworks at today's afternoon assembly, I knew, because Juin strode into it with this set expression, like she was getting into the cockpit of a fighter jet. I took a seat near the back and watched – when Juin had something to prove, it was bound to be quite a scene.

I had an idea why she was so pissed today, and it was partially my doing. The cease-fire between me and Riley had broken at breakfast. I took a corn muffin she'd wanted – I swear it was as petty as that – and Riley started saying, really loudly, that she was going to beat me just like Trevor had beaten my grandfather. I couldn't believe she was speaking my secret out loud – and while I stood there in shock, the stupid muffin that had been the source of it all dropped to the floor, and Juin went ballistic on my behalf. She slapped Riley down – literally – and when Riley tried to get back up, pushed her right back to the floor. Even after breakfast was over, Juin remained furious that Riley had broken our coven's rules, ranting about it in the bathroom. Riley tried to talk to her, but she really wasn't having any of it. Then Riley came up to me and – unexpectedly – said she was sorry. But that did nothing to lift Juin's bad mood. She got this look in her eyes that I knew by now – she was looking for a new target for her bad feelings.

Dr. Spicer walked in like she always did, smooth and business-like, like she was the president of a clothing company. She stared intently at us. There were only six of us left.

"Good afternoon, girls," she said.

"Good afternoon," we muttered. All except Juin, who stared back glitteringly.

"As you know, you have individual counseling this afternoon. But before I send you along, I have one more name of someone I'll be asking to leave."

Juin leaned back on one arm and shook out her hair. She watched Dr. Spicer with half-open lids, like she was waking from a nap.

"Yes, Juin?" Dr. Spicer asked reluctantly.

"I was wondering, Doc," she said, "what would happen if that girl decided she wouldn't leave unless she knew where she was going."

Dr. Spicer was not amused. "Sit up," she said.

Juin stayed slouched. "I mean, you're teaching us to be responsible and safe, right? And it doesn't seem too prudent for us to go along with anyone who tells us to go off somewhere, when we don't even know where that somewhere is."

"I am not 'anyone.' I am your guardian while you are residing in the psychiatric mansion, and you are under my exclusive control." Dr. Spicer winced for a fraction of a moment, after she said "exclusive control." I saw it, and apparently Juin did, too.

"That's what this is really about, isn't it?" she said, her

115

voice rising. "Not therapy, not rehabilitation, but control. Precisely, your reveling in it, and our having none of it."

"That's enough. You're treading a thin line."

"Hmm?" Juin said. "I don't quite get the image."

"Do you want to spend your last days here in solitary?"

"I wouldn't mind it. I've got some deep thoughts to sort out."

Dr. Spicer stood. "I'd like the girl whose name I call out to go upstairs and get her belongings immediately."

Juin sat up, suddenly rigid. "I don't think you heard me, Dr. Spicer. We're not ready to have another one of us picked off."

Dr. Spicer smiled icily. "It's not you, don't worry."

"Oh? Well, you gave something away here, Doctor. Your sarcasm says that it's a good thing to be 'picked off.' So there *is* a destination after this purgatory. Heaven for those who've done good, hmm?"

I looked at the remaining group: We'd been whittled down to a group of hardened bitches, most of us actual felons. I liked everyone there.

"If you cause any more disruptions, you'll be placed in solitary immediately."

Juin was tightrope-walking on some internal borderline — I could see it. She opened her mouth, then bit her lip and hurled herself into a sitting position so hard that I heard her head knock against the wall. She didn't look embarrassed; she just set her face harder against the pain.

The next words out of Dr. Spicer's mouth shocked me even more.

"Angela, I'd like you to go upstairs and get your things."

I blinked. "Me, Dr. Spicer?"

She nodded. I sat there, staring at my hands.

"She's not going," Juin said.

"It's not your choice," Dr. Spicer countered.

"Where the hell do you think you're taking her?" Juin yelled.

"Angela, please go upstairs now."

I crossed my arms, clutching myself helplessly. I wasn't sure who I wanted to cross less, Dr. Spicer or Juin. I felt far more loyalty to Juin . . . but Dr. Spicer had way more power.

Juin came over and hugged me from behind. It should have felt reassuring, but she was holding me like a hostage.

"Do you want a whole week in solitary, Juin?" Dr. Spicer asked. "Because you're about to get it."

"As if being on my own and away from you a-holes is some major penalty."

"In your case especially, I think solitude is one of our harsher punishments. But don't worry — by next week you'll find far more variety in our ways to deal with you."

"I don't think I want to go," I said. It had been a while since I'd spoken; my voice felt raw.

"I'm sorry?" Dr. Spicer asked.

"I'm not going," I said, strengthened by Juin's presence behind me.

"Solitary confinement for both of you, then."

It took Dr. Spicer and three attendants to get us downstairs.

Chapter Seventeen

"This is a pit," I said, as if anyone could hear. I had been dragged down the iron stairs by the main entrance, through a double-locked doorway, and along a steam tunnel. To put my rage somewhere, I counted my footsteps: 122. We climbed a few stairs, and I guessed from the change in the paint color that we were in some other building's basement. A pair of colossal boilers choked the room, and as we weaved between them, sharp flakes of rust peeled onto my shirt. The attendant opened a door behind one of the boilers and pushed me inside, locking the door after me.

It wasn't being alone that got to me — it was not knowing where I was. I was in some distant building's basement, locked who knows how far below ground. No one knew where I was, except for my captors. If my captors forgot about me, I'd die here.

I imagined my mother seeing me now. Is this the kind of imprisonment she'd wanted for me all along?

A few weeks ago I would have imagined Trevor sneaking in, picking the lock, and coming to save me. But I just couldn't picture it anymore. I was alone with my aloneness.

The walls were stained concrete, like a garage floor, and there wasn't a chair or anything — just a stained mattress, a metal sink, and an exposed toilet. I saw all of this dimly; the only illumination was from the small, double-paned window in the door. I stood against it and stared out, my only view a caged lightbulb and half a boiler.

Juin might have claimed that solitary gave her time to think, but I knew it was going to be pure misery for me. Whenever I found myself alone as a kid, I'd always buried my attention in a book or a video game. When I got older, I started compulsively calling friends or boyfriends all night until I was tired enough to go to sleep. Even on weekends, when I'd sleep in, I knew that the first twenty minutes of dozing would be bliss and then I'd start feeling depressed. Thinking without a purpose left me exhausted. And now I was stuck in a room with nothing to do but think. No magazines, no distractions. Just me, a caged lightbulb, and a toilet.

I walked over to it and stared in. I felt like doing anything to get myself distracted. Making myself puke, slamming my wrists against the handle. Instead I sat down next to it and toyed with my hair, reaching over and flushing the tank once in a while, just to hear the roar.

I was probably in there a couple of hours and had begun singing tuneless songs to myself when I heard the door unlock. I immediately stopped singing, wanting to make whoever was opening the door realize how unhappy I was. Hard as I tried to look stony, I knew I looked like a hungry puppy. I wanted out. I wanted company.

The top lock rattled, then the lower, and the door creaked open. I was surprised to see a man standing there, a man I recognized from the night I'd sneaked off with Juin, Riley, and Rebecca. Not the young one, but the old one with the white dog. He wasn't dressed fussily, just wore a pair of loose trousers and an untucked shirt.

"Angela Cardenas?" he asked, sighing.

I stood and nodded.

"Come with me, please." He winced apologetically at my surroundings and passed me a garbage bag. "Here are your new uniforms. Come on, I'm going to show you to your rooms in the main school," he said. "You first-years arrive piecemeal, so we introduce you gradually, sort of like fish to a tank."

I grunted and followed him upstairs. When we got to the landing, he paused and motioned that I should go first. I started, and heard him breathing heavily as he climbed behind me. "Fish to a tank," he said, chuckling. "Am I the most stereotypical biology teacher, or what?"

"You're not a doctor?" I said.

"What?" he asked.

I mumble when I'm uncomfortable. "You're not a doctor?"

"Nah. I got my master's, but that's it. Hold on a sec."

We were halfway up the second flight of stairs. We'd passed a couple sets of doors, but I had no idea where they led.

"Do you know where you are?" he asked me.

I shook my head.

"Oh, sorry. I'm not usually the one to introduce new students, but I have B period free and the secretary's home sick today. You've made it through the first-year selection process, and I'm pleased to inform you that you're with the main group of girls, the less restricted group. You're known as the gold thread. Your peers will talk about nothing but gold and purple thread while you're here; you'd think we were a sewing factory."

He was waiting for me to laugh, so I did. It sounded close to a hiccup.

The man went on.

"You'll be sharing a suite with one other first-year and an older girl, whom you can rely on to show you around and answer your questions. Of course you can ask a teacher, too, like me. I'm Mr. Derrian."

I turned and offered my hand. He looked at it strangely for a second — he wasn't expecting this gesture — then shook it.

"Look," he continued, "as long as you behave, you'll find life in the school much easier than it was during orientation. Select your friends carefully, and you'll stay out of trouble. And if you stay out of trouble, you'll find this isn't much different from any other boarding school."

"What . . . happens to the girls who cause trouble?" I asked, thinking of Juin and Riley and the others left in the mansion.

He sighed. "I'm afraid that it's vitally important that you don't ask about any of the purple thread girls. You won't run into any of them during your stay here."

I nodded, finding it hard to process the full impact of his words.

"Look, Angela," he said, looking into my eyes. "I want you to remember my name. Derrian. Most of the teachers here were brought in after Hidden Oak was formed, and they're – well, you'll see. But a few of us are the old guard, who stayed on from back when this was a boys' school. You'll find us significantly more sympathetic. Okay?"

I nodded.

"Your room is directly out these doors, first one on the left. Two-oh-one. There's no key, and you'll have to take whatever bed is left available. Your schedule is posted on the inside of the door, and we'll expect you in your first class in forty-five minutes. If you feel lost, ask any of the girls. Again, I'd suggest you be as careful as possible about whom you fraternize with."

I nodded again. He patted my shoulder, then started down the stairs. I waited until I heard a door close behind him. Then I started to shake. I knew this was progress, going from being locked into my room to being in a room where there wasn't any lock at all. But it was all overwhelming.

I had no idea who I'd find when I stepped out into the hallway, who I'd be able to trust.

Chapter Eighteen

The hallway was empty. I heard the distant clink of plates, the sounds of breakfast. I pushed open the door to 201.

It was a pretty awesome room, way nicer than the one I'd had back in the orientation mansion. The wall at the far end was taken up by a window that looked out over fields and ruins. Beneath the window was a twin bed with an exposed mattress; along the opposite wall was a set of bunk beds, made up with different colored sheets. I thought I recognized Carmen's navy blue on the top bunk, and my heart leaped.

I approached the free bed suspiciously. It was by itself, and had a view; why would this be the one left over? I sat on it and looked out the window at the ground below. A dingy sparrow sprayed itself in a pile of dirt. I could live my life sitting on this bed, if it allowed me to look outside, to remind myself that there was always something more out there.

Maybe they were saving the best bed for me because they knew I'd feel out of place and wanted to make me feel better. I ripped open my bag and discovered that they'd given me new uniforms – the more typical plaid skirt/ white shirt combo everyone associated with private-school girls. It was like they were saying *Welcome to the gold thread – you're normal now.* I found a clean set of yellow sheets at the bottom and stretched them over the water-stained mattress.

My stomach growled, but there wasn't much time for breakfast. The caged clock above the door showed I only had fifteen minutes until I'd have to report to my first class. Clipped to the door, as Mr. Derrian had promised, was my schedule:

Angela CARDENAS, first-year
Classification:	Gold Thread	
Security Elevation:	4(A)	
Faculty Advisor:	Harold Derrian	
Psychiatric Advisor:	Roberta Zsilinska	
Breeding Group:	M	
Class A	Spanish 3	ALSANZ, Elizabeth
B	Geometry	SHEPARD, John
C	UNASSIGNED	Report to study hall
D	English I	BINGHAMTON, Martha
E	Biology I	DERRIAN, Harold
F	World History	CHURCHILL, Mathieu
G	Arts	Various
H	Team Sports	HUNDRICK, Adrienne

Breeding group? I thought. *What the hell?*

A complicated calendar with a list of classrooms was posted next to my schedule, and after studying it for a minute I discovered that a) we'd be having classes *seven days a week*, and b) my first class would be Biology with Mr. Derrian, the same professor who got me out of solitary. His room was directly below. Before heading out, I looked around the room for a bathroom, but there wasn't one. (I did discover, however, a sly little camera hidden above the closet.) I dashed down the hall to check myself out in the mirror. My face looked greasy, but at least my hair was wild and kind of interesting. I changed into a fresh uniform and headed downstairs.

The halls were narrow and full of girls, and I felt conspicuous walking among them, though no one paid me any notice. I looked for familiar faces, but I didn't recognize anyone yet. The school was a two-story square that encaged a courtyard, and it would be pretty easy to figure out my way around. I soon made it to the biology classroom, and waited by the door for Mr. Derrian to arrive.

Girls filed by in boisterous groups, some talking loudly and foully, others quiet and sullen. I smiled at the first few who came in, but after I didn't get any reactions back, I stopped.

Eventually two girls arrived that I recognized: Connie and her equally huge friend Melissa. I nodded at them, and Connie shook her head in return: "Oh god, we've got Cardenas. I thought for sure she'd go purple."

Connie left Melissa and sat by herself at one of the slate lab tables. I followed her. "Okay if I sit here?" I said.

"Fat chance," she said, which I thought funny of her to say, considering. "Derrian assigns us lab partners."

"Yeah," said a voice behind me. "And that's my seat."

I cleared out of the way of Connie's lab partner, a bullish girl with bracelets tattooed on her wrists and a hole through her nose where there must have once been a monster piercing.

A bell rang, and still there was no Mr. Derrian. The girls started murmuring, and I could feel more and more attention being directed at me.

"What's your name?" asked one girl.

"That's *Angela*," Connie said before I could answer.

"What's up?" I said.

"You're real pretty," said Connie's lab partner, whose smile showed some silver teeth.

I didn't smile; she'd said it like I wasn't really pretty, but just thought I was. "And you're just *gorgeous*," I said back.

Whatever she was going to say was lost, because Mr. Derrian walked into the room, brushing right past me, and ordered everyone to take out a sheet of paper. I realized that I didn't have any stuff, while the other girls had notebooks and pencils.

"Stages of mitosis, with a two-sentence description of each," he said. "You have fifteen minutes."

Half the girls got to work, and the rest doodled, stared at the ceiling, or put their heads down. I raised my hand and waited for Mr. Derrian to notice. He squinted at me.

"Oh, hello, Angela, of course. Nice to see you again so soon. Come up to the front, please."

I went to his desk. He didn't get up, but peered at me carefully. "We're a week in," he said, "but you seem bright, so I imagine you'll catch up. Here's a textbook. Why don't you read about mitosis? Section two-four, I believe. You'll find supplies against the side. You're allowed one notebook and one pencil for each class."

"Where am I going to sit?" I asked.

"There should be an open seat. Next to . . . Carmen Pope."

"Oh!" I looked around. I hadn't seen it before, but there was a table behind the eye-wash station. And Carmen was sitting at it, doing her best to stay hidden.

"Hey, you," I said as I sat down.

She didn't look up. "Hey."

"I'm glad you didn't get kicked out," I tried.

"I'm taking a quiz."

I opened my textbook.

Even once she was done with the quiz, Carmen didn't speak to me. She just opened her textbook and read until Mr. Derrian started teaching again. When the bell rang for the end of class, she stormed out as fast as everyone else. I let her go – I could understand why she was mad at me, although I hoped we could get through it soon. I hung back, and was the last to leave. I looked back long enough to see Mr. Derrian give me a smile of encouragement and a long wink.

After Biology was World History, then English. I knew it was my first day, so I couldn't trust my feelings to stay the same, but I really felt like this time I would concentrate on my courses, that I'd stay interested. We were reading a novel in English class, and I left the room clutching a slim paperback with brittle brown pages. I would read this book cover to cover, I decided, and it would help me through. I dipped into the cafeteria long enough to grab a sandwich, and spent lunch period tucked into a bathroom stall, reading the first chapter. It was really good, all about this woman realizing she doesn't love her husband, and I felt like no matter how bad things got at the school, I could always read about people who were even more pissed off.

After lunch was a Spanish class for non-native speakers, which I obviously got placed into by mistake. But I played that I wasn't fluent so that I'd have an easy A. The teacher, Mrs. Alsanz, was this Midwestern woman with fluffy pink patches on the shoulders of her sweaters, and I bet she wouldn't have been able to spot a native speaker in Mexico itself.

After my afternoon classes I figured we were free to head up to our rooms, but when I reached the stairs I noticed that the other girls were all herding downstairs into the school's basement. I slowed and followed them.

There were a bunch of rooms leading off the hallway, and even though the doors were unmarked and unnumbered, the girls all robotically filed in. I wandered aimlessly down. After a second bell rang, it was just me standing in the hallway. I wasn't about to pick a random door and open it, so I sat down against a wall and put the paperback on my lap. I stared around for a while, taking in the security camera blinking at me, and was about to open the novel from

English class when I heard a voice at the opposite end of the hall.

"Excuse me, miss, what do you think you're doing?"

An extraordinarily short, round woman with coiffed icy-blond hair and a fur-lined jacket was standing at the opposite end, arms crossed. I guessed she was a faculty member, but it seemed weird that a teacher would be wearing six-inch pink alligator stilettos. "It's my first day," I said. "And no one's told me what's going on."

"Unlikely," she said.

I stared back at her, wondering how to answer.

"What's the real story?" she asked.

"That's it. I just came over from the mansion."

"They're not sending anyone else over. We've closed the gold thread."

"I don't know what to tell you, except I'm supposed to be here. Look." I pulled my crumpled schedule out of a pocket and thrust it at her. A little forcefully, probably. I didn't like being mistrusted.

She scrutinized it with a sort of suspicious admiration, like a well-executed forgery. "I'm going to have to talk to Dr. Spicer," she said. "You're not supposed to be here. I don't want the other girls tainted."

"Excuse me?"

She shook her head and headed down the hallway. Once she reached the far end, she turned and glared back at me. She snapped her fingers. "Come."

I followed her, gripping my stuff tightly. I raised my

middle finger at her somewhere in the pages of my history book.

She led me to the administration offices I remembered from my first day, and locked me in the examination room. I hugged my knees to my chest and stared through the small square of glass. Dr. Spicer arrived, and I heard her get into a heated argument with the woman. Then they both turned away.

A while went by, until I was pretty sure I'd been forgotten. I knocked on the door and called out. No answer.

Finally the door was unlocked again, by the dog-sized woman with the fur-lined jacket. She spoke mechanically. "My name's Mrs. Vienna. I'm the academic dean, and you can come to me with any classroom issues. Somehow you've wormed your way into the gold thread, and it's not my place to deny you an education. But if you cause me any trouble, you'll be in the purple thread immediately. And you don't want that."

"What exactly is the purple thread?" I asked.

"That will be the only time I'll tolerate you asking that question. You won't see any of the purple thread girls, and have no need to bother yourself with them. Now, I assume you've gotten yourself around for your first day, so there's little I need to go over. You've missed breeding group today because of all these shenanigans, but starting tomorrow you'll be expected in the basement from three to seven every day. I've found you a place in the second doorway."

That's right, breeding group, the weird thing on my schedule. I was tempted to ask what it was, but was sure by this point that she wouldn't answer any questions.

"I should hardly need to tell you that I don't appreciate being told what to do," she said. "And though you seem intent on faking your way through, it should soon be as abundantly clear to you as it is to me that you don't belong here. Give me the slightest excuse to kick you out, and I will. Is that clear?"

I nodded, my tongue pressed tight against the roof of my mouth.

"Run along. Dr. Zsilinska has agreed to see you early today. She's not officially on duty at the moment, so be sure to thank her."

Today I actually welcomed Dr. Zsilinska's clacking beads. It was good to have at least one thing stay the same between yesterday and today.

"What's going on?" I asked. "Are the rest of the girls still back in the mansion? What's all this thread business?"

Dr. Zsilinska looked up, surprised. "[clack] I'm sure you've been told not to ask about the threads."

"You can't do this, though. I've made friends, and then you take them away without giving me a reason. I'm expected to work on getting better, but I can't if you keep pulling the rug out on me. Like what's this breeding group? Are you mating us with spaniels or something?"

"You'll find out tomorrow," Dr. Zsilinska said.

"If it's some weird orgy, I'm going to flip."

The doctor surprised me by laughing. "It's not a weird orgy. I promise. Now, let's talk about your transition to the main school. Do you have any observations about your first day?"

I figured I'd better throw her a bone. "I think I'm going to like my classes this time," I said.

Dr. Zsilinska nodded. "That's a common reaction. It's amazing how that first month in the mansion gets you ready to actually learn something."

What did she want, a pat on the back? "I'm glad to see that not all the teachers are women," I said.

She looked up sharply. "[clack] [clack] Why's that?"

"Settle down, settle down. It seemed creepy, that's all, like some women's prison. It's more normal to have guys around."

"You've met Harrison, I assume?"

I shook my head. "Nope. Who's Harrison?"

Dr. Zsilinska made a note. "Which men have you met, may I ask?"

"Some of my teachers. That Derrian guy, and Churchill and Shepard."

"And how did you feel about them?"

"I felt like they were teachers."

"No other reactions?"

"I'm not sure what you expect me to say."

"It doesn't matter what I want you to say."

"Right." I rolled my eyes.

"You'll remember, Angela, that we've discussed how you've historically derived too much of your self-esteem from your relations with men. There's a reason we don't have you girls around any male teachers for the first month. Now that you're in the main school and exposing yourself to men, it's important that you stay vigilantly aware of the nature of your feelings."

I nodded, distracted. I liked when Dr. Zsilinska used the word *historically* about me. It made me feel like something important enough to be studied in a book. "I don't think you should be suggesting I expose myself to men," I said wryly.

"That joke was defensive."

"Jeez." Though I guess it was. I was thinking about the boy I saw when I was out in the grass. The one who lived with Mr. Derrian.

Harrison?

"If you're not prepared to talk about it now, we'll pick up this topic later. Do you have any questions about life in the main school?"

"What about the living situation?"

Dr. Zsilinska blinked. "You're living with Carmen. We keep you girls with people you already know, whenever possible. Carmen and Maureen. You remember Maureen, from your first day? She's there to guide you two. She's a model Hidden Oak success story."

"She's a Diet Coke girl," I said.

She cocked her head.

"You know, she's not really sweet. She's chemically sweet."

"Well," Dr. Zsilinska said impatiently, "she's what you have."

The implication was clear:

I needed all the allies I could get.

Chapter Nineteen

Zsilinska decided that my breeding group, whatever that was, could start tomorrow, so I went off to the cafeteria. It was empty, and I used the rare quiet to sneak myself a slice of ham and some salty gravy, a roll, and a few leaves of white-brown iceberg lettuce. I ate them while I read my book, and left just as the first girls were arriving for dinner.

Room 201 was silent and lonely. I sat on my bed and continued to read, occasionally glancing out the window at the low shrubs and sparrows.

After some time, I heard the door open. A blonde walked in.

"Oh, hey!" she said. "I'm Maureen."

I stood up. "I know. You showed me around my first day."

"Right. I wasn't sure if you'd remember."

"Yep. I did."

"So! I see you've set yourself up. Hope you don't mind that bed."

"No, it's great, actually."

"It's going to be a quiet room, because I spend all my time down the hall with my friends. It should be real peaceful for you to study or be alone or whatever. I'm going down the hall now, but I'll be around, okay? Holler if you need anything."

I nodded and watched her back out of the door. "Oh," she continued, "I hate to say this, and it's awkward, but I'm officially a prefect, which means we can be friends and everything, but I'm officially sort of an authority figure. Just so we're clear on that."

"You got it." I gave her a thumbs-up and a weird sort of plasticine smile that creeped even me out.

As Maureen left she crossed paths with Carmen, who was loaded up with notebooks, holding the teetering stack steady with her chin. "Oh," she said, dumping the books on her bunk. "Hi."

"Hey, Carmen," I said. We stared at each other for a moment.

She sighed loudly.

"I've decided that I'm not mad at you," she finally said. "It's not like it's you who pushed me off the roof. And why would you have turned yourself in just to be with me? That would be dumb."

"Thanks," I said. It sounded weak, but I couldn't think of what else to say. She'd already apologized for me. "So what happened to you?"

"Not that much, actually," she said. "I lied and said that I snuck onto the roof because I wanted to see the sky up close. They figured I was just being stupid and dreamy, not misbehaving. I had to be in detention every evening for my first week, but it wasn't terrible. I don't think I ever want to see Juin again, though."

"And what's this new part of the school about?"

"The lessons are terrible," Carmen said. "Well, you saw Biology, I guess that might be okay, but my French teacher tried to impress us by introducing the class in French, and she didn't even know when to use which past tense. Can you imagine?"

"I wasn't really wondering about the lessons."

"Oh. What were you wondering about?"

"What's this Sexy Time, or whatever it's called?"

"Breeding group? Didn't you go today?"

I shook my head.

"It's when they teach us how to behave well. It's not like in the mansion, when all they seemed to do was push our buttons. This is teaching us more like how to hold cups and say thank you."

"For real? Like a lame-ass charm school?"

Carmen nodded.

I threw myself on my bed. "I've already done all that. It's like learning how to be weak."

"They tell us it's to teach us self-discipline, so we'll be productive members of society. It's not so bad," Carmen said, sitting next to me. "Not nearly as bad as the stuff we had to do in the mansion."

"That's probably their whole point by starting us out there," I said. "So we'll be grateful for the new crap they put us through. What's Maureen like?"

"She's okay. Everyone thinks she's nice."

I grunted.

"What?"

"Nothing. I've had some bad experiences with girls like her."

"She's not going to turn all prom queen on us."

"We'll see."

Carmen gave me a look like I was being unnecessarily bitchy. Then she started putting her books away, slotting them into cubby holes alongside the bed.

"I'm glad you're back, Angela," she said, still turned away from me.

"Me too."

That night Carmen and I hung out with some of the girls on the hall, before we headed back into the room in time for bed checks. Maureen busied herself writing some sort of letter on the backs of scrap paper, Carmen (for no apparent reason) read ahead in the Biology textbook, and I lay on my bed, staring out the window.

There wasn't much new to look at, except for at one point I saw Mr. Derrian and the Spanish teacher, Mrs. Alsanz, cross the grass toward one of the far-off ruins. I wondered for a while what business they could possibly have out there late at night but I soon forgot all about it.

Once it got dark, I realized why they had saved this bed for me. As the sunlight disappeared, it was replaced by the bright orange beam from a security light mounted above the window. Even when I scrunched my eyelids shut, they still shone pink. There was no blind or shutter; I pulled my bed a few inches away from the wall, but in the end all I could do to block out the light was crush my pillow against my face.

Every time I shifted in my sleep, my pillow would come loose and I'd wake up. So that's how I came to be sitting up and staring outside my window at one in the morning. The heating pipe near the bed made regular banging noises, like it was trying to talk to me. Outside, the security light cast an orange patch on the ground, and whenever the wind blew, I could see the pine branches of nearby trees dance in and then back out. There were no blinking lights of distant civilization, only the black stare of the wilderness. The security light was so bright that I couldn't see any stars, just a stretch of wall from which my window bulged like a wart.

Down at the first level, a light was on. I had only a slanted view of the room's contents, but could occasionally see a hand appear as whoever was inside moved around. I balled my pillow under my chin and stared at the open stretch of wall until the hand revealed itself again.

It did, followed by a guy's bare back pressed against the window. Chalk it up to being stuck in an all-girls school, or having stared at a plain wall for full minutes, but this guy's back seemed like the most beautiful thing I had ever seen. His shoulders were pressed so flat against the glass that they glowed in a paler two-dimensional plane against the window. His hair, thick and shaggy, was wet with sweat around his neck.

Then, as suddenly as he had appeared, the guy vanished. He was replaced a few moments later by a slimmer figure, a bare arm and the upper part of a butt, definitely a teenage girl. Her arm pulled away and then I saw the guy enter the window frame as well, this time facing me, only his face and neck visible above the girl's shoulders. He nuzzled his lips under her ear, and I could see her toss her head, either in pleasure or the pretending of it. Then he looked up and his eyes met mine.

I wanted to pull away, to barrel under my comforter and pretend I had never been watching. But I held still, staring down at his eyes. It was the guy I had seen from the field outside the school, the one who had stood alone in his darkened room. He watched me, frozen for a moment. Then, slowly, he returned his mouth to the girl's neck, never losing eye contact with me.

My eardrums throbbed and pounded. I looked around my room, and could see, in a stray shaft of light, Carmen fast asleep. When I looked back out the window, I imagined he would be gone, but he was still there, waiting for me to return. Only now the girl had vanished, leaving just the guy's head and chest in the window. He ran a hand through his sweaty hair and smiled up at me. It was an infuriating smile, masterful and sexy.

I remembered the name Dr. Zsilinska had used – *Harrison*. Then, maddeningly, her analysis rolled through my head, her simplistic claim that I had based too much of my self-esteem on guys. I didn't ever think a doctor would actually change the way I thought, but I realized this was a clear case of making myself powerless, watching and waiting for a guy to do something to make me feel better. But what else could I do, if getting this charge from a guy was the only good part of an awful day? I gave him a small nod, letting my shirt fall off one shoulder as I did.

He raised an eyebrow and mouthed something I couldn't make out. He looked like he was about to nod back, when a curtain of blond hair fell over him, and the girl was clutching his back. Turning abruptly, he disappeared farther into the room with her.

I watched the empty window, but he didn't appear again.

I didn't go to sleep until his light clicked off.

Chapter Twenty

When I woke up the next morning, Maureen was already gone from the room. Carmen was dressed in her uniform and hovering by the door.

"Hold on," I said groggily. "Wait for me."

"Are you kidding?" she asked. "I'll miss breakfast. You're not even out of bed."

"Come on, come on. I'll just be a minute."

Carmen watched me stagger out of bed, grab for a towel, and miss. "Jeez. Did you sleep at all?"

"Walk to the bathroom with me and I'll tell you all about it."

"I *really* don't want to miss breakfast."

"You won't! God!"

The bathroom was empty except for us. Carmen waited by the old Heath urinals until I'd gotten into the shower, then moved nearer once I had slid the curtain closed. "So what's going on?" she asked.

"First of all, thanks for saving me the bed right under the lamp. That was real sweet."

Carmen paused. "You were the last to arrive. I didn't know it was going to be *you*."

The Carmen I first met would have offered to switch places right away. Good for her.

"But that's not what kept me up," I continued. "Or at least, that's not *all* that kept me up."

"Sounds interesting."

"You don't know the half of it." I told her about the guy I'd seen.

"There's only one guy our age around here. Mr. Derrian's son, Harrison. He's eighteen and just graduated from the high school in town. He does odd jobs around the school. He's not supposed to talk to us, much less have naked make-out sessions in the windows."

"He was so hot, Carmen."

"Have you seen his face? Ugh."

"Sure I did. He looked fine."

"But did you see his *skin*?"

"I don't care. He's gorgeous."

"You can keep him."

I was confused. It *was* Harrison I'd seen, right?

"Angie, for real. Girls wouldn't give him a second glance anywhere else, but here he's running wild. He makes the rounds, you know what I mean? He's so dirty."

"I wonder who he was with last night," I mused.

"Who cares?"

"She was blond and skinny."

"Ugh. Take your pick."

Actually, owing to our not being allowed hair dye, there weren't too many blonds at Hidden Oak. I could figure it out eventually.

"Look, Angie," Carmen continued. "We've got to get going."

I raised an eyebrow as I turned off the water. I was Angie now? I hated the name, though it was sweet that she was nicknaming me. I saw my towel appear over the rail and took it. I opened the shower curtain before I had finished wrapping the towel around me. If Carmen was going to be my best friend here, I wasn't about to start hiding anything from her. Besides, I liked being looked at.

I was wondering whether I'd see the mysterious boy on my way to breakfast, if I'd spot his rumpled hair peeking up on the other side of the milk dispenser. Even though there was no sign of him, I was in higher spirits than I'd been in for weeks. I actually caught myself whistling a pop song as I got my yellow cake of eggs, and wondered loudly to Carmen how much new music must have been released in the last few weeks.

We sat down next to Rebecca. "Angela!" she said. "You're in with the Golden Ladies!"

"You got me, girl." I'd noticed the gold thread crew had taken on the speaking patterns of sorority girls. They did it ironically. I hoped.

Rebecca was sitting next to a girl I didn't recognize. "Hi, I'm Angela," I said.

The girl nodded. She had a tight afro and the prettiest brown complexion I'd ever seen. "Did you just arrive?" she asked.

"Say that one more time," I said.

"What? Um, did you just arrive?"

"Your accent – Texas!" I said.

"Yeah, Waco. Total pit."

"I *know*! I came in from outside Houston."

"Don't say 'outside Houston' to a fellow Texan. Where?"

We carried on like that for the whole breakfast. As we were leaving and the girl went in the opposite direction, I asked Rebecca what her name was. She shook her head. "She doesn't tell it to anyone. At first we thought she was some kind of celebrity, but turns out she gets these paranoid fits she can't predict, so when she's well she doesn't want to give anyone any information they can hold against her later. We call her Blank."

"Blank." I shook my head. "Okay, whatever." Suddenly, I remembered something, and ran to catch up with Blank before she disappeared into the senior English classroom.

"You said you were a third-year, right?" I said. "Do you know a girl named Pilar Felix?"

Blank thought for a moment. "Nope. Name sounds familiar, but there's no Pilar around here."

"Oh. Thanks, Blank."

Was it possible that Pilar had altered her name, too? I wondered if anyone at Hidden Oak was who he or she was supposed to be.

There were two computers we were allowed to use in study hall. The same rules as before applied about e-mail: It would all be checked, and there wasn't any direct Internet access. Gold thread status only went so far, I guess.

I started with Trevor.

T:
I still haven't heard from you, and while that's not the end of the world, it's weird. I know you've got your own life, and plenty to keep you busy, and maybe you've hit a rough turn or something. I have no way of knowing, though, because you're not writing. Look, I'm not going to be a moron and keep banging my head against a brick wall. It'd be great if you wrote back. But if not, then screw you.
–Angela

Figuring I was on a roll, I moved on to my parents.

Mom:
You and Dad haven't written me yet. I'm not totally surprised, and there are actually other girls here whose parents don't care enough to write, either. We'll kind of joke to each other about it, like "Yours yet? Nope, mine neither."
But it's not something I can really ignore. I know I caused trouble for a long time, that I haven't been the perfect daughter, but if there's one thing I hope I've drilled into your heads during our fights, it's that you guys aren't exactly perfect, either. I always suspected that maybe you simply didn't care about me, and I guess this is my proof. I should just accept it. But even as I write this, I know I'm not

accepting it. You're my PARENTS. I don't care what I've done, if you blame Abuelito's death on me. I feel like other kids in the world get to go through life knowing at least one person is there for them always. But you haven't even checked in. That's bull. I'm sorry, guys, but that really sucks.

I'm here, and I'm surviving, and though this is the strictest school I could imagine, you'll be happy to know that I seem to have been stuck with the good girls.

–Angela

Chapter Twenty-one

Every time I'd ask an older girl about Pilar Felix, I'd get either the slightest glimmer of recognition or nothing at all. One day Carmen skipped lunch to study, so I sat next to Maureen, who was (unusual for her) eating alone. We talked about classes, and the school, and movie stars, and then I dropped all the boringness and asked if she knew anything about Pilar. She got real snippy after that. I put it up to her personality (like all overly sweet people, one in a hundred times she was a rip-roaring bitch instead), but then she got up and went over to the faculty table. I watched, open-mouthed, as she said something to Mrs. Vienna, who promptly stalked over to me, her heels making woodpecker sounds on the floorboards.

"Angela?" she said.

I nodded.

"With me, please."

A collective *ooh* rose from the tables around me.

She took me, not to her office, but to the narrow space behind the Coke machine.

"Listen closely, you little bitch," she said. "I will *not* have you getting everyone riled up over inconsequential issues. You know very well that you're not allowed —"

"It's not inconsequential," I said. "I know Pilar is *here*, but you've got her hidden away, like in a sweatshop knitting scarves or something, and I don't think that's *inconsequential*. Like where are Juin and Riley and —"

"That's it," Mrs. Vienna said. She grabbed my arm and steered me toward the kitchen. She snapped her fingers at the cook, who had been busy wiping a sneeze guard clean. "This student has been misbehaving."

The cook nodded, and Mrs. Vienna shoved me in her direction. I slipped on the steamy tiles. As I lay on the floor, blinking in shock, all the possible tortures a kitchen offered circled my vision — cleavers, tenderizers, and slicing machines. The meaty cook pulled my shoulders and dragged me, my legs kicking over the filthy floor, into a back room. I heard a click and a heavy door opening, and suddenly I was closed into a frigid, dark space.

The freezer barely had room enough for me to stand in, and as my eyes adjusted I saw that was because it was clogged with cardboard boxes and cylinders. I tried sitting on an industrial-size ice-cream tub, but I immediately felt the cold seep through my skirt. So I stood back up, lifting one leg and then the other off the frozen floor.

I was becoming aware of so many parts of my body, because when I touched them they weren't mine anymore —

when I licked my lips, they were corpse-like. It was possible, I realized, that if they forgot about me — or pushed the punishment too far — it would all be over. I banged on the door, but it was so well insulated that I could barely hear my own knocks. I screamed, and tried kicking, but nearly lost my balance.

Eventually I heard a sound on the other side of the door, and a crack of fluorescent light appeared. The cook pulled me out. When I tried to step on my own, I found that my leg muscles had tightened so much that I couldn't move. I lurched out of the freezer and fell on the ground, right into one of the slushy gray puddles left by a milk crate. The cook asked if I was all right, and I was imagining so many obnoxious answers that I couldn't say any one of them. She shrugged and left me there to thaw.

As soon as I could stand, I stumbled out of the kitchen and back into the cafeteria. My skin stung at the sudden warmth. The students had left but, as always, some of the faculty were lingering over coffee. I stalked over to where Mrs. Vienna was sitting.

"You locked me in a freezer," I said. "You guys shouldn't be allowed to do that."

A flicker of enraged irritation passed over her, causing the crepey skin at her throat to wiggle. Then she smiled.

"What a clever idea," she said. "I'm afraid we don't take enough student input into consideration when devising disciplinary measures. But of course, that would be allowing the lunatics to run the asylum."

I turned to Dr. Spicer, the lone familiar face at the table. "She locked me in a freezer," I said. I knew it sounded stupid, but I was so upset that nothing better came to mind.

Dr. Spicer took a deep breath, and I waited for some long and boring philosophy statement to come out. But instead she said, "Yes, she did," and forked a triangle of cheesecake into her mouth.

My indignation wheezed out of me. I stood before the table of faculty, suddenly embarrassed and scared.

"I'm leaving today," I said quietly.

Dr. Spicer sighed. "Come to my office after I've finished eating."

"No," I said. "I'm leaving now."

"No," Mrs. Vienna said. "You're not. The doors and fences are locked. You do not leave unless we allow you to."

"Let me call my parents," I said.

"Absolutely not. We'll inform your parents of your mis-behavior, and I'm sure they'll agree with us that you've demonstrated a need for more restrictive therapies."

"You can't do this," I said quietly. I looked away; I couldn't stare at this group of adults any longer, their judgments and condescension.

"Unless you're hungering for more punishment, I suggest you head straight up to class. You're already late, and don't think for a minute you'll be able to offer these shenanigans as an excuse."

As I left, I saw Mrs. Vienna shoot Dr. Spicer an *I told you so* look.

I wondered what, exactly, she'd been told.

*   *   *

Later on, I couldn't concentrate on my study hall reading; my brain was focusing on dozens of things, all way more important than Mesopotamia. I'd been able to humor Hidden Oak's weird power trips before – like the breeding group; they made me learn how to cross my legs like a lady and how to fake my way through a job interview. Fine. But I'd assumed that, like at other schools, if things got really bad there was some way out. But now I knew I was stuck here. The administration was willing to torture me into submission, had made some of the girls, like Pilar, disappear entirely, and was obviously lying about having our best interests at heart.

Despite my brief show of bravery in the cafeteria, realizing how corrupt the administration was actually made me want to behave better. Back in my old high school, I was able to talk back to any teacher, because I knew that the worst punishment they could throw at me – expulsion – wasn't really a punishment at all. But here, they controlled my communications, so I couldn't call my parents or the police. They could lock me into a freezer and report it as an accidental death.

The lunatics *were* running the asylum.

The moment the bell rang I slammed my books closed and bolted from the study hall, back to my room.

I crawled into my bed and sat with my back against the window frame, staring unseeingly at the floor. And then Maureen came in.

Part of me wanted to say "you nasty bitch" to her, to start a fight and yank out a fistful of her pretty blond hair. But I controlled myself. All I wanted, really, was for nothing to have happened. So I said nothing.

"I'm sorry," she said from the doorway, her eyes downcast.

"I bet."

"I really am." She dropped her books on her bed. "It's just that I've got an official role. And Mrs. Vienna told me to let her know if you kept asking about purple thread girls. I'd have gotten into big trouble if I hadn't said anything."

"That's what Pilar is, a purple thread girl?"

She didn't say anything. "Tell me, Maureen," I continued, "what does being a prefect get you that's so great?"

"It's an honor."

"It means you're better than the rest of us, you mean."

Maureen paused. "More responsible, I'd say."

"You've fully bought into their program, haven't you? They're playing all these perverted games with us, and you're desperate to get on *their* side. *Think*."

"Look, Angela, I'm not going to keep talking about this."

"Why, because we're on camera?"

"They only turn the bedroom cameras on if you're in trouble. You're a gold thread girl, now; you have more freedom. Behave and you'll keep it."

"Look, I'm sorry if I don't act gooey to you – you're a narc and almost got me killed; you're lucky that the thing I want most in the world right now is to be away from you – so just avoid me from here on out."

"They're trying to help us," Maureen said. Tears of indignation stood in her eyes. It was amazing — she really believed in the school. You always heard about it, prisoners who gradually come to idolize their captors. I recognized, then, that my brief urge back in study hall to behave as well as possible was a mistake. I pledged myself to fight it as long as I could.

I had to stay dangerous.

Chapter Twenty-two

"Dr. Zsilinska," I said at our next meeting, "you haven't been honest with me."

"I haven't? How so?"

"This school is evil. Mrs. Vienna locked me in the freezer for no reason."

"There was a reason. Our punishments reflect the fact that Hidden Oak is a last resort. You can't expect the hand-holding you've taken advantage of in the past."

"I know you don't have to take my word on anything, but you should have seen Mrs. Vienna's eyes . . . she didn't regret having to punish me at all. It's like she enjoys it."

"You're right — I don't have to take your word for it. One day, when you're rehabilitated and back in the regular world, you'll be able to accept your reactions and evaluate the actions of others. While you're at Hidden Oak, however, you simply have to accept that we have your best interests at heart. Don't second-guess; don't look for malice where there is only methodology."

"I know what you're saying, I guess. But why would any-one consider it 'methodology' to put me somewhere where I could *die* if they forgot to let me out? And why won't anyone tell me what's happened to the purple thread girls?"

"You've been warned about what cannot be talked about. This session is over."

Dr. Zsilinska wouldn't look me in the eye.

Maureen wouldn't look me in the eye.

Carmen could barely look me in the eye.

Juin, who would have stared me right down, was nowhere to be found.

All of this, I could live with.

But not with him so near. Not with the boy.

I waited until Maureen and Carmen were asleep. Then I moved to the window and watched. Only rarely would I catch him looking back at me. Normally it would be me staring at him through the window while he prepared himself for bed, or talked on the phone, or rocked out on his headphones. But when he *did* look at me. Oh.

He'd lock eyes with me, and maneuver so as much of him as possible was in the window, from the top of his head to the waistband of his underwear. Then he'd mouth words I couldn't make out, or dance a little, or laugh, or mimic my serious expression. Once we'd made faces at each other for a while, it'd turn serious again, and he'd stare. Not moving a muscle, just looking flatly and openly and wantingly. Once he even slowly stripped off his shirt, taking his eyes off mine only for the moment it took him to undo the buttons. This wasn't the boy Carmen had described. He was gorgeous.

I almost felt he wasn't real. He was a ghost left behind from the time this school had been filled with preppy boys. I never saw him anywhere but in the window. I'd even tried to walk by his door – but that hallway was locked.

Keeping them safe from us, I thought. There would be no way inside.

Unless, of course, he invited me in.

Between him, the orange security light, and the banging heating pipe, I had some very active evenings. The pipe noise was something I'd heard about from relatives but had never experienced before – in old buildings heating pipes run through the rooms, and they're filled with steam or hot water or something that makes them bang and moan and hiss. Well, there was a pipe right by the head of my bed, and it would knock in really odd patterns. Some nights it would be silent, others it would rattle or I'd hear these rapid knocks in quick succession.

As a result, I was barely awake for my first Saturday at the main school, groggy even though I only had a half day of classes to worry about. After bio lab there were a couple of hours of supervised study hall, a group meeting, and then time to wander on the grounds.

The campus was made for losing yourself, if you wanted to – the low walls of the ruined buildings were good for leaning against with homework or a doodling book, and you could wander far on the grounds and still get yourself back easily as long as you kept some landmarks in sight, like the freestanding ruined stairwell or the dirt-filled swimming pool. At the edge of campus there was a tiled gymnasium surrounded by piles of dirt and brambles too thick for us to approach, and a couple of haunted-looking old dorms. Rebecca, Blank, and I once boosted one another up to peek into them and spotted a few relics from the '80s — a box of some old-fashioned batteries, a teen magazine with some unknown star on it, and a rack of cassette tapes, all surrounded by swirls of sun-faded paper and broken glass.

Some small part of me hoped I'd glimpse Juin and Riley and the others, even just for a moment, so I'd know where they'd been hidden away. But no one had been in these old dorms for years. I was coming to suspect that maybe the other girls had been sent away — that being in the purple thread actually meant being sent home. It's like you never existed.

I spent a lot of my time out there alone, but I was always glad to know that Carmen would eventually come to find me. We spent one October evening perched on the top of a wall and watching the sun fall under the line of the trees. Halloween was only a couple of weeks away, Carmen pointed out. As if there wasn't enough creepiness around already.

"Hey, do you want to switch beds?" she asked a while later.

"Why do you ask?" I asked quickly, wondering if she had noticed the games I'd been playing at the window.

"You don't seem to be sleeping well. I was thinking it might be that security light."

"Thanks," I said, holding her hand. "But I don't want to switch. I think it's the banging pipe that gets me, but I'm learning to ignore it."

"Banging pipe?"

"Yeah, you know that heating pipe that runs by my bed? It makes noises at night. That's what old heating systems do."

"I know. *I'm* from Connecticut, Miss Texas. But, Angela . . ."

"What?"

"There's no heating on yet."

"Pipes don't make noise when there's no heating on?"

Carmen shook her head.

"*Something*'s banging the pipes."

"What's above and below our room?" Carmen asked.

We had half an hour left until dinner, so we hurried back into the building to do a quick investigation, more because we were bored than out of any hope we'd find something. The room below ours was the Biology classroom, which we had already been in plenty of times. Above our room was a door marked JANITORIAL CLOSET. I pressed my ear to it, heard nothing, and did a scan up and down the hall.

"Do we open it?" Carmen asked.

I tried the handle. It clicked, and the lock released.

We couldn't find a light switch, so we pushed the door open far enough that a triangle of the hallway light was shed onto the shelves. It lit part of a small room, stiff mops against the wall and cleaning supplies jumbled on the floor. The pipe ran along the back wall and was surrounded by a conference of brooms, their handles forming a cone pointing to the ceiling.

"Do you think there's an attic?" I asked.

"Well, there's a handle on the ceiling," Carmen said, pointing.

I pulled a steel ladder from the wall and unfolded it. Carmen held on as I climbed toward the ceiling and tugged on the ceiling hatch. A layer of brittle plaster dusted me as it pulled open. I shook my head and patted my hair back into place.

"Be careful," Carmen warned as I climbed the final steps and stuck my head into the attic.

"Huh," I said, looking around.

"What's up there?"

"Nothing."

"Nothing at all?"

"Well, a box. One of those cardboard boxes with sides that look like wood, like lawyers have. Kinda moldy."

"Boxes don't bang on pipes," Carmen observed.

"No, they don't," I said as I got off the ladder and stood in the attic room. It was very small and coated in dust. I pressed my face against the window, which was so dirty that it let light in but no picture through, like a shower door. "Come on up," I told Carmen.

She climbed the ladder and stood next to me on the creaking floorboards. It was small but cozy, somewhere you could imagine children spending a bored afternoon at

Grandma's house. We sat in front of the box and opened it together.

There wasn't much inside. A couple of old paperback school textbooks without pictures, some empty exam booklets, and a manila folder full of newspaper clippings. We pulled out the folder and opened it between our laps. A slip was paper-clipped to the front:

H: Preliminary research you requested for A Boys' Tradition: A History of Heath. Start with bio of founder? See you at Thurs picnic, Yves

Following it was an article announcing the opening of the Heath Boys School back in 1894, then some more clippings about the school being used for military training in WWI, and its dwindling enrollment in the 1930s. There were announcements of a string of new headmasters in the '40s and '50s, then three articles about the school going coed in 1974, only to go back to boys only in 1975 after some alum threatened to withdraw funding.

The articles traced the boring yearly events of the school, and we kept ourselves interested by picking out the cute boys from the graduation photos, watching them go from shaggy heads to gelled flattops to big waves of moussed hair as the years approached 1990. Then the graduation photos stopped, and the folder finished with a clipping from *The New York Times*, dated January 28, 1991. The other articles had been neatly taped to card paper, as if to keep forever, but the last had been roughly ripped from a newspaper, folded twice, and thrown in.

It began with a half-page photo of the school. Three landmarks were clearly similar — the mansion and the main building and the gymnasium in the background — but the rest was practically unrecognizable. The grounds were trimmed rather than overgrown, and there were many more buildings: additional dormitories, a track, and a swimming pool. Banners hung from some windows, and the bricks were a clean, bright red. It was the fresh creature to which Hidden Oak was a carcass.

HEATH SCHOOL ANNOUNCES CLOSING IN WAKE OF SCANDAL

Alexandra Callahan

HEATH, CO — In a swift move that has caught the educational world by surprise, the prestigious Heath Boys' School closed its doors on Friday, only eleven days after twenty-one students were discovered dead in their dormitory beds, with four more still missing.

Says headmaster Bronson O'Reilly in a statement released to the press yesterday, "There are accidents and there are tragedies — the first a boarding school is well equipped to handle, but the second can prove impossible to overcome. When one-twentieth of the student population is suddenly wiped out, and the perpetrators are still somewhere in the wilderness, we can hardly hope to foster a healthy emotional atmosphere, much less an environment conducive to elite learning. Therefore, upon the advisement of the board of trustees, I have reached the difficult decision to close our doors indefinitely."

Others in the school community, however, have less clear-cut positions. A faculty member, who agreed to speak to the *Times* only under condition of anonymity, pointed out that, in the course of the police investigation, the school was observed to have many fire code violations, including inoperable locks on dormitory doors, asbestos in the ceilings, flammable furnishings, and a lack of fire exits. "I can understand closing the school for a year over a tragic event," he said. "But why should we shut such a venerable institution down entirely? The truth is, this accident revealed that this whole campus is a powder keg. But it's much easier for the powers that be to ascribe what was inevitable to a single, undeniably dramatic incident."

The "incident" is the January 16 deaths of an entire dormitory annex full of boys. Still under investigation, the tragedy is thought to be the result of a prank gone awry, in which four classmates stuffed a boiler with towels in the early morning, hoping to make it explode, but instead only snuffed out the pilot light and caused the dormitory to fill with carbon monoxide. The four classmates suspected have been missing for ten days.

Heath is famously snowed in for the winter months, making approach by snowmobile extremely difficult, and impossible by foot or car. When the accident was discovered, the victims were poisoned but still alive. Their subsequent deaths due to improper ventilation of the dorms, and inaccessibility to hospitals, have led parents to claim that the school is outdated and should be shut down. "Lack of access to proper medical facilities is inexcusable," said one concerned parent of a survivor. "Not in this day and age."

The yearly impasse of snow has added issues to the aftermath of the tragedy; it has simultaneously hampered efforts to find the four culprits and made it highly unlikely they have survived the forbidding conditions [Continued on 4F]

I flipped the article over, and saw only a lingerie ad.

"Where's the rest of the article?" Carmen asked.

"It's not here," I said, scarcely breathing.

"Wow."

"Yeah."

After a short silence, Carmen said, "Maybe they're still out there."

"Carmen. This was, like, almost twenty years ago."

"Okay, fine," she said, still with a note of awe.

"I can't believe this," I said, folding the article and putting it in my pocket. My words sounded angry.

"What?" Carmen asked.

"Well, the campus is too dangerous for preppy boys, but it's *fine* for bad girls."

"I'm sure they fixed everything that was wrong."

"We still get locked in at night, maybe not into our *rooms,* like in the mansion, but into our *hallways.* Look at this dusty attic. Do you think a fire marshal or anyone has been in here in ten years? Like the article said, this whole place is a powder keg."

Carmen nodded. "I didn't know we got snowed in."

"Me neither. Look, we have to get out of here before then."

"Yeah, right. How?"

"I don't know. We'll have to find someone with a car."

Carmen snorted.

I pulled the article back out of my pocket. "Did . . . tell me if this is crazy, but did that anonymous teacher they quoted sound to you like Mr. Derrian?"

Carmen read back over the quote. "I don't know. It could be anyone. Why?"

"It's the 'to ascribe what was inevitable' bit. That's so him. I feel like he's said that exact phrase before. You know, 'we mustn't ascribe evolutionary adaptation to inevitable change,' some crap like that."

Carmen nodded. "Now that you put it that way. . . ."

"If it is him, he might help us."

"Uh-uh. It's one thing to sneak into an attic. It's a total

164

other thing to rebel. And it's a whole, whole other thing to tell a *faculty member* that we're rebelling."

"Yeah, it does sound dumb, suddenly."

"Look, let's think this over for a while. We're going to be late for dinner." She paused for a moment, debating something. Then she said, "It's Saturday, isn't it?"

I nodded.

"Do you think the coven is going to meet?"

I told her the truth — that I wasn't sure that Juin and Riley were still at Hidden Oak at all. I told Carmen it surprised me that she would want to see them again, considering what happened the last time we were all together.

"This is serious, and we need somewhere private to talk about it," she said. "If Juin and Riley are still on this campus, they'll try to make it to the tree house. Either they'll be there, or they won't, and either way we'll have a chance to find something out about what's happened to them."

I looked at Carmen with new respect. "We're still going to sneak out? When did you get so ballsy?"

"The coven is very important," she said, fully serious.

And so our fate was decided.

Chapter Twenty-three

Even though life in the gold thread was less strict, and our room doors were unlocked at night, there were still major challenges to sneaking off. First, now Carmen and I had a roommate to deal with. Second, since the hallways locked at night, instead of the individual rooms, we couldn't fiddle the doors nearly as easily as we used to. Third, we were now at the top of a three-floor building. Fourth, the boarding faculty slept in a wing next to ours, so if we made any noise, we'd be sure to get caught.

We figured our best bet was to go out the window, since we had no way of controlling who might go for a midnight pee and screw up our plastic-spoon-over-magnetic-lock method. Carmen would drape her comforter over the side of her bed, shielding Maureen's bottom bunk from our doings. Then she'd wake me up and we'd figure it out from there.

The first part came off fine, and soon enough Carmen and I were on our knees on my bed, perched in front of the glass like puppies for sale. I cracked the window open; it shuddered in its rails, but didn't make a terrible noise. The breeze that came in rustled the comforter blinding Maureen, but didn't do anything more worrisome than toy with its corners.

"Okay," Carmen said, sticking her head out the window and staring down at the ground far below. "Now what?"

"Hmm," I said.

"You haven't thought of this part yet?"

"What do they do in old movies, tie sheets together?"

"*Angela.*"

"Got a better idea?"

Carmen shook her head and started peeling my fitted sheet away from my bed. We knotted it with my flat sheet and blanket, and then Carmen tiptoed over and fetched her sheets. When we were done, I tied the chain to my bed frame.

"You first," Carmen said.

"Thanks."

The length of blue and yellow knotted sheets fell down the side of the building, dropping past a dorm room and the Biology classroom and ending a few feet from the ground. I'd have to be careful not to disturb anyone on the other side of the dorm window, but otherwise it wouldn't be much more difficult than anything we'd already done in gym class.

I looked over to the boy's room, to make sure he wasn't watching. Or, maybe, that he was watching.

It was dark.

After a jaw-clenching first few steps, I started to enjoy it.

Looking up, all I could see were Carmen's encouraging smile and the clear night sky. I was alone in the cool air, exposed to the whole school if anyone cared to look, and it thrilled me. I released myself arm length by arm length, quickly hopping down the dark dorm window, then more slowly working my way down the Biology class window. (*Will I be able to see my shoe marks Monday morning?* I wondered with a smile.) I was starting on my last sheet when I felt the knot slip. I still had a hand on the next sheet up, and clung to it as the bottom sheet fluttered to the ground like a released ghost.

I hung there, staring down. It wasn't too dangerously far to drop, but it was still a good ten feet, enough to sprain an ankle. I looked up at Carmen, who held her hands over her mouth, plainly worried.

I dangled, my grip on the sweat-slick sheets slipping, and prepared myself to fall.

I heard some commotion from farther along the wall. I tried to pivot to see what was going on, but my movements were limited by my hold. I'd have to drop and run. They'd catch me eventually, but at least when I was nabbed I wouldn't be dangling outside the school like a moron.

As I fell, I scrunched my eyes shut and prepared to feel the hard ground reverb through my ankles. But instead I hit something warm, which grunted as it fell with me.

I rolled with my captor, coming to rest at the bottom of a shallow hill. I felt the warmth of flesh, of breath. I kicked free and bolted.

When I didn't hear anyone following, I slowed and stopped. All I heard from behind me was groaning. Turning, I saw that it was the boy from along the wall. He was holding his face up to the moon, clutching his nose.

Definitely not a ghost.

"Oh, jeez," I said. "You were — did I hurt you?"

"Ow, ow," he said, putting out a hand to keep me at bay.

"You were trying to help," I said, to myself as much as to him.

He nodded. "Bad idea. You were supposed to, you know, crumple into my arms."

"I didn't see it was you. I got scared." I offered my hand. "I'm Angela."

He didn't want to let go of his nose. "I know who you are."

"And you're?" I picked up the fallen sheet and held it to him. "For your nose."

He held it against his face to stem the bleeding. "You know, if you get caught out here, you'll —"

"I'll be kicked out."

"Nope, a lot worse than that. You'll get one of Vienna's specials. It doesn't matter for me, of course, but then again I'm not a student." He held the sheet against his nose and peered at me. "What are you trying to do, anyway?"

"A few friends and I, we go off into the woods sometimes."

"Sounds like fun." He wasn't making fun of me, but there was still something naughty in his tone.

"No boys allowed." Damn it, there was something naughty in my tone, too. I didn't want to be flirting with him, especially not in the middle of the night after I'd shinnied down a sheet ladder. But that didn't change the fact that he was hot. Arrogant, too, and dirty. Looking closer I saw that, yes, he had a pimple or two, which might have been worse at one time. I wouldn't call him *cute*. But take in the whole body and he was definitely hot. He would have been hot even if he weren't the only thing going around, I was sure of it.

"Well, Harrison," I said, realizing he still hadn't told me his name. "I guess you've seen me watching."

"I think I've been watching more. You're killing my sleep," he said.

"Mine, too."

"But I wouldn't stop. I always want to be polite, keep telling myself I'll look away next time, but you're so damn beautiful."

"All right, that's enough," I said, knowing I was being played.

We paused for a moment.

"Um," he said after a while, "shouldn't you be worrying about your friend?"

Carmen! I looked up and saw her peering at me, scared as hell. I beckoned her down. She shook her head. I beckoned again, and she slowly started to descend. It was hard for her, I knew, and she paused every few arm's lengths on her way. As she got to the end of the sheets, she dangled precariously and Harrison positioned himself below her, creeping a foot left or right as she swayed. My lust broadened to something tinged with fondness.

She dropped into his arms, and for the second time Harrison went rolling on the ground. Carmen and he stood, and she had this scared look that soon lifted. She clapped once in pure glee.

"You don't have any more buddies coming, I hope," Harrison said to me. "I don't think I can survive any more of this."

I reached a hand out toward his bare back. The last few moments before I touched, his smooth skin stretched and lengthened. Carmen squinted at me as I clapped Harrison's shoulder. "Do you ever wear shirts?" she asked him in her most academic tone.

"I have one thing to ask for repayment," he said, ignoring her.

"Yes?" I asked.

"I'm coming with you, wherever you're going. Have pity on a guy with a boring life."

"Oh," I said. "Okay."

"Are you kidding?" Carmen said. "No way."

"Come on, Carmen," I said. "He can help us."

"Absolutely not. We're not about to show you our secret location."

Harrison laughed, and I laughed with him. Carmen looked from one to the other of us, wounded. "I'm serious."

I put my arm around her. "I *know* you're serious."

Harrison mock-pouted at Carmen. "I *really* want to come."

"No."

He dabbed a new trickle of blood running down his nose. "Fine. But how were you guys planning on getting back up to your room?"

I paused. "Climb back up?"

"You were going to climb up three stories? And I guess you were also planning on leaving those sheets hanging outside in the meantime?"

I nodded.

"Okay. Now you'll owe me two favors, because I'm going up to your room and taking the sheets up. When you're back, rap on my window and I'll get you in with the keys from my dad's ring."

"Thanks," I said.

"I believe you already know which room is mine," he said.

"Thanks," I repeated. "Just be sure not to wake our roommate."

"I'll be on my best behavior," he promised.

Carmen and I made our way along the forest trail by the stream, and were happy to find, once we arrived at the fallen tree house, that we weren't alone. Rebecca was there, and she had brought Blank along. They leaned against the far rotting wall, their arms crossed. "What *is* this place?" Blank asked.

"It used to be a tree house, back when this was Heath," I explained. "But the tree fell, so now it's more like a cave."

"I think it's awesome," Rebecca said, though she didn't uncross her arms.

Carmen was still hovering. She'd been thrown off guard; I hadn't told her that our coven had broadened to include Rebecca while she was stuck in the main school. "Do you think the others are coming?" she asked.

I shook my head.

This was the final proof that Juin and Riley were gone. I could read her feelings: It felt wrong to meet without them, but it also felt wrong to stop.

I threw open our stash sack and pulled out a blanket and pillows. We set them up and sat at the four corners. Blank lit a clove.

"Where did you get that?" Rebecca cried, pouncing at the cigarette.

Blank passed it to her, and she took a puff. "Traded commissary points to Bertha. Cigs are all I barter for. I don't eat junk food, and your white-girl hair crap don't do me much good."

"You don't eat junk food?" Carmen asked interestedly. "What do you like to eat, then?"

"Soy. Lots of soy."

"Huh," Carmen said. "I think we might have to have you tell your story this time."

"No way," I said. "You haven't gone yet, and it's totally your turn." I looked at Blank and Rebecca and added, "She was one of the originals."

"Who else comes here usually?" Blank asked, rolling her eyes.

"Me and Angela founded it one night with Juin, who you haven't met," Carmen said proudly.

"We try to keep it small, so no one finds out. Only the select few," I said, smiling graciously at Blank, who smirked back.

"So what happened to Juin?" she asked.

"She was with us for the orientation month," Rebecca said. "But we never saw her again."

"So she's purple thread."

"Yeah, I guess – but what does that *mean*?" Carmen asked.

"She's what they call a bad girl," Blank said simply. "They don't think they can make her get better, and don't want her tainting the rest of us."

Blank seemed to know a thing or two more about this than she'd already said. "So where is she?" I asked.

"There aren't too many purple thread girls, and they keep them hidden. I don't know much more. I'd have to *be* one to know more. I heard all of this from Harrison."

"Oh?" I asked, trying to sound neutral. "You know Harrison."

"*Knew* Harrison. A lot of us have 'known Harrison.' He's got a radar for whoever'll give it up for him."

"Ah," I said.

Blank looked at me knowingly and said, "Hey, he's what's around. Don't pass it up. All I'm saying is enjoy it while it lasts, because he'll be moving on. Not 'let's be friends' moving on, but 'done' moving on."

I nodded. I guess I'd suspected that.

But, despite myself, part of me knew it would be different with me.

To change the subject, Carmen brought up the article we had found. I had forgotten to bring it, but we filled them in as best we could.

"Yeah, the school's basically a big dynamite factory," Rebecca said. "But what are we supposed to do, call the fire department? We don't even have a phone."

"The school really does get snowed in every winter," Blank said. "And it's like everything changes after the first snowfall. Everyone gets cabin fever. And if things go wrong, there's no fixing it. Like last year, the juice delivery was a week too late, so we didn't have any OJ until March. Not like that's a huge deal, but you'll be surprised what people find to fixate on when they're cooped up together all winter."

"They locked me in a freezer," I said. "And when I said I wanted to leave, Mrs. Vienna and Dr. Spicer laughed at me and said it was all the more reason I couldn't."

Blank nodded. "That's the way it works here. In my three years, I've seen it again and again. The more you try to leave, the more reasons they have to compel your parents to make you stay."

"But here's the thing," I said. "Some of our parents would listen to reason. But we can't get through to them without our e-mails being censored. We might be able to escape on foot, but soon we won't be able to do even that. And meanwhile, they're bad-mouthing us to our families, convincing them that we're not reliable. Even if we do finally get word out, no one will ever believe us."

"You catch on fast," Blank said drily.

"They could do anything to us, and we couldn't stop them."

"Look," Blank said. "You got locked in a freezer. It's not the worst punishment going around, believe me."

"It's not just that they put me in there, it's what I saw in their eyes afterward. There was no remorse, you know? The faculty table's like a table of little serial killers. Mrs. Vienna *enjoys* it, I swear."

"She is totally evil," Rebecca agreed.

"Find your friends on the faculty," Blank advised. "Go for the old-timers. Derrian's good, and so's Mrs. Binghamton — most of the old Heath faculty are. On the psychiatric side, Zsilinska will hear you out. She won't do anything to help, but she'll hear you out. Are you guys all with Zsilinska?"

Rebecca and I nodded. Carmen said, "I've got Hammond."

"Oh. Good luck." We laughed. Hammond's breath smelled like frying pan grease.

"You know what . . . listen up, guys," I said. When they all snapped to attention I couldn't help but feel cool, like I was the chair of some important political committee. "We have to find Juin. If the purple thread girls really are somewhere on campus, I want to break her out so she can join us."

"Okay," Blank said slowly. "Beyond the fact that we'd get our asses beaten, we don't even know where they keep the purple thread."

"Are they still in the mansion?" Carmen asked.

"If they are, they're hidden really well. I never hear anything when I walk by."

"Angela's heard what we think is someone banging on our pipe," Carmen said. "Maybe it was one of them."

Blank looked skeptical.

"Or there's the abandoned dormitories, the ones we peeked into the other day," Rebecca offered.

"Well, I think we know what we have to do for next week," I said. "Carmen and I'll do a search of the main school, Rebecca can check out the abandoned dormitories, and Blank, can you see what you can find out about the mansion?"

She nodded. Rebecca nodded, too, but said, "You know at least one of you is coming with me. I'm not going there alone."

"Fine," I said. "Maybe we'll all three go on Monday afternoon, since Carmen and I don't have a C period class. But for now, Carmen's going to tell us what got her here."

Carmen seemed surprised. I held the sack out to her.

"Go on," I said. "Choose an object."

I could tell she was uncomfortable. I knew she wanted Rebecca or Blank to go first. But her reluctance only made me want to press her harder.

It was about time I knew her story.

177

Chapter Twenty-four

Carmen reached into the sack and picked the busted pen. Her hand was shaking so much it looked almost like she was using it to scribble on the air. If she hadn't seemed so vulnerable and so serious, I might've laughed. If Juin were here, I bet she would've . . . but then again, if Juin were here, I don't think Carmen would have gone where she went next.

"I've been best friends with Ingrid since I first moved to Connecticut. My dad was born there, so we went to live in his big old family house when he got his New York job. I was twelve.

"The town we moved to was posh, full of old money. Right away I knew I'd never fit in. My mom offered to take me shopping for some fancier clothes now that Dad had his new job, but I wasn't really interested. All I wanted to do was sit out back and read or walk my dog. Her name is Josephine. Well, she was my grandparents' dog, but they'd died, so she was mine. My mom started getting on me about my weight –"

"Are you serious?" I said. "You're not fat."

"I was heavier then. Or maybe not. Whatever – I felt bad. I couldn't run because it made my boobs hurt, so she made me go to the community pool every afternoon. I got myself this fifties-style one-piece, one of the kinds with the frilly skirts, and brought a book, and as soon as she drove off I'd be settled on the folding chair by the bathrooms, reading. I'd do a lap right before she picked me up, to look wet.

"Well, let me tell you, you get to know the other people at the community pool really well. There was the old lady who was super tan and wrinkly and kept patting her hair and hitting on the crippled younger guy. There was the old man with the big heart-surgery scar, always doing laps. And there was Ingrid.

"She was always in the same spot, in the shallow end in front of the jets, her arms hitched over the side, her hair in a ridiculous bun – ridiculous because she was my age – reading a book that she'd propped up on the concrete, the lower half of the pages huge and waterlogged. Her shoulders were always burnt, but she never covered them or anything; she concentrated on her reading.

"I'd glance at her whenever I walked by. Sometimes she was reading books I'd already read, and sometimes they were books way beyond me, adult books with cloth bindings while I was reading, you know, Narnia. So one day I picked a random impressive-looking book off my parents' shelf and brought it to the pool and stood near to her, reading. It turned out the book was some history of Austria, and I could barely make myself read a page. So that helped me pluck up the courage to talk to her, just to give myself something to do.

"It ended up that she lived around the corner, and her mom was the librarian at the local library, and she was my age but was in a grade above because she was so smart. We talked together all day, buying ice-cream sandwiches with my salad money. When my mom picked me up, I got in trouble because my dad's book had gotten totally waterlogged. I'd left it by the edge and forgotten all about it."

My mind wandered down some of the various directions Carmen's story could take. I chuckled, imagining a couple of nerds jacking a library shipment.

Blank gave a loud, bored sigh. Carmen broke off, glanced at her self-consciously, and restarted her story at twice the speed.

"We spent every day together, that summer and beyond. We talked about serious stuff at recess, or joked around at each other's houses or watched a movie a billion times in a row until we knew every line by heart. We thought we were so beyond our classmates, that we were deeper than they were, and we told each other that all the time, even without saying it in those words. But at the same time we were *behind* our classmates, too. We never talked about makeup or dating or boys. Instead we'd talk about goblins or flowers. We kept doing the stuff that our classmates grew out of. Making up board games, stuff like that."

Carmen wouldn't look at any of us, but it wasn't because she was self-conscious anymore – she was totally living inside the memory, blissfully imagining her life at home, doing lame stuff with Ingrid. I'd never seen her smile so goofily. I felt a pang of jealousy, and almost wished she'd stop.

"Ingrid and I never thought we were behind the other girls – that's just how my mom phrased it to me. My dad will love me whatever I do, but she was always judging and worrying about me, for whatever reason. She was friends with all the society moms, and I think she wondered why I didn't hang out with their popular daughters. She'd make sure I got invited to their parties, but of course Ingrid was never invited so I was miserable and lonely and just waiting to see her afterward so I could tell her how ridiculous everyone else was.

"My mom called Ingrid's mom and told her she was concerned that Ingrid and me were too close, and Ingrid's mom heard my mom out and then hung up the phone and told us exactly what she'd said. We all laughed, because my mom said things like *luncheon* instead of *lunch*, and Ingrid's knew true friendship was rare enough that you didn't mess with it. I liked being there way more than being at home, and after spending a weekend at their house, I'd come back smiling but cry from loneliness within minutes of being back in my big old room.

"So eventually – and this is a few months ago, now – my mom sat me down and told me that I was forbidden from ever seeing Ingrid outside of school. She said if I was too

181

close to her, other girls would be intimidated to be friends with me, and I wouldn't meet any boys. 'You don't arrive at the party with your own dessert,' she said. 'You go and sample the food and let yourself try new things.'

"Honestly, I tried to understand what she was saying. But I didn't really get it. If I was happy with Ingrid, why *wouldn't* I spend all my time with her? And being forbidden from seeing Ingrid made our friendship seem all the more precious. I'd be so desperate to see her that when we finally stole away I couldn't let go of her hand. I'd kiss her whenever she said something Ingrid-like."

"Whoa, whoa. Are you a lesbian?" Rebecca asked.

"Come on, don't ask her that," I said. Though I had been thinking how close Carmen's feelings for Ingrid were to how I used to feel about Trevor.

"No, it's okay," Carmen said, finally looking at us. "I don't think I am. I mean, I haven't met a boy who's really fired me up, so sometimes I think I am. But with Ingrid, I wasn't having sexual thoughts about her or anything. I loved her, so much and so simply. I wanted to be part of her. I wasn't *attracted* to her, not in that romantic way, but if she'd said she wanted to make out with me, I would have done it in a split second, only because it was what she wanted. So I don't know how to answer. I wanted to spend my life with Ingrid. Maybe that's enough to make me a lesbian. I don't know. I don't think so."

I found myself unfazed by the possibility that Carmen was into girls — I'd considered it before, and it's not as though any of us were getting any play, anyway, so the whole issue of sexuality was pretty much a big nothing — but instead I got that jealous feeling again. Not just of Ingrid, but of the two of them. I'd never met anyone who I wanted so much. I wondered if that was my fault, or if I just hadn't met the right person.

"Regardless, my mom thought it was enough. She got more and more strict about me not seeing Ingrid anymore, until she came in my room one day and said it was weird and wrong, and having my mom call the most important relationship I'd ever have wrong was enough to send me into this fit of misery that was really deep. I was making animal sounds and sobbing so hard that I was half passing out. She tried to comfort me, but by the time I regained my senses, she was standing by the door to my bedroom and had lit a cigarette, which she was smoking nervously, her eyes rimmed red, just like mine. I guess she hadn't really realized how deeply I was feeling until then.

"We didn't talk about Ingrid or my crying fit for a week or two, until my mom and dad came into my room one morning and told me to pack my suitcase because I was leaving for the one boarding school they found that was willing to fix me. And that was it."

"You seemed pretty calm when I met you," I said quietly.

"I'd finished crying by the time we got to Indiana."

I know that my parents could actually make a pretty strong argument for sending me to Hidden Oak. But there was no way Carmen belonged here. She really and truly hadn't done anything wrong. In fact, she was punished for living more deeply than most people did. I took her hand.

"What do you work on with Dr. Hammond?" Blank asked.

She shuddered and then the tears, which she had been holding back from the start of her story, began. "He's . . . trying to fix me."

I put my arms around her and rocked her. The shoulder of my uniform was instantly wet. "Shh. You don't need fixing. Shh."

"I . . . miss Ingrid so much."

"I wish you had told me."

"It's not allowed, remember?" she said, hiccuping.

"We're getting out of here," I said, newly determined.

Blank and Rebecca nodded solemnly, though neither had made any real attempts to comfort Carmen.

"Remember our assignments," Blank said. "Angela and Carmen, keep checking out the main school. Me, the mansion. Rebecca, abandoned dorms."

When Carmen and I rapped on Harrison's door, we must have gotten him out of bed. He looked at us groggily, then opened his window and hauled us in. He asked us where we'd been, but I smiled mysteriously and put my arm around Carmen as we sneaked upstairs.

Chapter Twenty-five

Each girl was assigned her own laundry time slot, and if you wanted a uniform that didn't smell of armpit (a distinction a large number of girls were willing to overlook, unfortunately), you had to make your time. I had the last slot before hall checks on Sunday night, and carted my mass of uniforms down to the basement. The washer and dryer were some huge industrial machines that were apparently German, because there were no directions in English. You pressed buttons and hoped. Whatever. It's not as though it would have been a huge tragedy if my socks turned plaid, too.

I'd brought my textbook down to study, but my ambition to finally be a good student had started its inevitable drop-off. I never opened it. Instead I stared around the laundry room, sorting through my thoughts.

Carmen's story had taken my urges to flee the school and deepened them — it wasn't enough to get out; I wanted to get the whole place shut down. The cruelty I'd seen in Mrs. Vienna and Dr. Spicer, the school's unsafe history, its callous treatment of a girl who was as obviously well as Carmen — they were clearly keeping her here for the tuition money — it all made me think that Hidden Oak was irredeemable. The classes were jokes, and breeding group was actively useless. I'd do better educating myself, running away and hanging low until I turned eighteen and got a GED and applied to college by myself.

The washing machine shook violently when it entered the spin cycle, which made the overhead light swing and cast shadows on the wall. The room went creepy. The iron grate cast thick floral shadows on the tiles and walls, and it seemed like there were creatures moving behind the black bars. "Hello?" I whispered, immediately embarrassed for having let my imagination run so far.

There was no answer, of course. I turned my attention back to the washer, prepared to transfer my clothes once it finished its cycle.

The dryer vented off somewhere deeper in the basement, and there was this wrought-iron plate in the wall next to where its silver spaceman air tube went. As I opened the dryer door, I caught some stray motion, looked down, and saw a hand slide along the ground on the other side of the grate. It pushed a piece of paper through, then disappeared.

Stop trying to find me.
—Pilar

"Pilar?" I called, getting on my knees before the grate. "Pilar, come back!"

But there was no answer. And I realized, if she'd passed a note rather than said something, maybe for her safety I shouldn't yell into the grate. I ran into the basement hallway, and wrote on the back of the card using the pen attached to somebody's door.

Tell me how to help you.
—Angela

Then I thought better and ripped away the part with my name on it, in case the note was intercepted. I slid the rest under the grate and waited for an answer. None came by the time my laundry slot was over. The slip of paper shone at me in the dim light.

As I sat waiting, I saw a heating pipe running the length of the wall, down into the dark region past the grate. I realized it had to be the same heating pipe that ran up to my room, that I heard clanging throughout the lonely nights.

Carmen and I planned to help Rebecca investigate the abandoned boys' dorm the next afternoon. As we cut across the grass, I told them about the note and Pilar's phantom hand.

"Wow," Carmen said. "Did you try to pry the grate off?"

"You've seen it – it's totally welded on."

"You know what?" Rebecca said. "This Pilar might not be in the purple thread at all. She could be in her own trouble and locked away somewhere."

I shrugged. "Sure. But either way, she's bound to be able to give us some sort of clue."

"It's terrible," Carmen said. "She's caged up somewhere, banging on the pipes on the off chance someone'll hear and realize it's her. Then when we try to find her, she's so terrified she tells us to stop."

"She could be in a different dorm, and isn't allowed to talk to us. It doesn't have to be some horrible thing," Rebecca said.

None of us really believed that – nor, honestly, did we want to.

I wondered how she'd found me. Had Mrs. Vienna punished her for my questions, and let slip that there was an Angela Cardenas at the school? Or had one of the other students gotten word to her? Blank? Maureen?

Maybe it hadn't been her at all. Someone had been playing a prank.

But it felt like it was her. I didn't know how to explain it to the girls, but I was sure that Pilar was in some kind of trouble.

I tried to put her out of my mind as we began our investigation. The old boys' dorm was sealed up pretty tight. After checking that none of the outside attendants was watching, Rebecca lifted me to her shoulders, and as we lurched around the building I peeked into every window I could. There were rotting mattresses, splintering desks covered in rat droppings, jumbled and faded posters for '80s bands, and wide water stains on the floor. When we got to the far side of the building, we found that one of the broken windows was low enough and shattered enough for someone to slip through.

"Guys," I said, "I think I can fit."

"Are you sure?" Carmen asked nervously.

"Go on," Rebecca said. "I'm ready." I sensed her bracing below me.

I gripped the two wooden sides of the window frame and, careful to avoid a nasty triangle of ragged glass on the bottom, eased myself through.

I landed in an old classroom. A cracked map of the United States still clung to the wall, teetering from a pushpin. I heard the skitterings of fleeing creatures from some distant room. I peered back out the window. "Anyone want to join me?"

Carmen shook her head. "Be careful," she said.

"We've got ten minutes until we have to be back for H period," Rebecca reminded me; she probably knew that I'd explore every corner if I had the chance. "So hurry."

I nodded, then headed out of the classroom and into a dark hallway. A faint moaning echoed throughout the building anytime a breeze whistled through the broken windows. I shivered.

The wood floors had rotted in places, and while they never gave way entirely, they bent like sponges wherever my feet fell. It looked like the dorm had been cleared out in a hurry, with all the sets of matching furnishings, dozens of beds, dressers, and desks left behind, as if the building were waiting for the class of '91 to finally arrive.

Since the stairs to the second floor looked rotten and yellow-black with fungus, I took the concrete steps leading into the basement. At the bottom I heard heavy pawings from some distant area of the floor. Then they stopped. Probably a raccoon. The room before me was nearly black, lit only by occasional envelope-sized windows near the ceiling, most of them clogged by leaves.

I took a few steps into the darkness, then paused. When the door had closed behind me, it cut off most of my light. I couldn't see any way to prop it open. I knew it was foolish to wander through an abandoned basement in the dark, but I took a few hesitant steps. I banged into something metal and saw the dim outline of a boiler, perhaps the same boiler that had once killed twenty-one boys on the floors above.

I tried to feel them here. When you died like that, you must leave something behind. Not beds or desks – a part of your essence, part of what you lost. You had to leave more behind you than just silence.

The pawing sounds began again. They didn't seem to be any closer, but still my heart pounded. I had once learned to announce myself to a wild animal, so I wouldn't startle it. "Hello?" I called. The noises stopped again. Then I heard, from far away, a whisper carrying through the dark basement.

"Yes."

I moved closer to the voice, until I was at the edge of the scarce light coming from the stairwell.

"Who are you?" I asked.

From far away: "Please keep quiet, please."

"Who are you?" I repeated, as softly as I thought would carry. I craned my neck and concentrated on listening.

"Angela . . . is that you?"

I couldn't move.

"Yes," I whispered. The voice sounded more familiar now.

"It's Riley, Angela. Riley."

I still couldn't tell where the sound was coming from. Below me? Behind one of the walls?

"Riley, where are you?"

"Please help us, *please*." I stepped a little closer to the sound. "Stop," she warned. "They can't see you. I — oh, I have to go. Don't come back. But help, please."

"How?" I asked.

There was no answer. "Riley?" I whispered. I didn't dare raise my voice any higher.

There was still no answer. Imagining what would happen if Riley had been overheard, picturing some subhuman guard barreling through the basement toward me, I sprinted upstairs, back to the geography classroom, where I hurtled through the broken window, gashing myself on the ragged shard of glass as I fell into the arms of Carmen and Rebecca.

"They're kept down below," I said as we stalked across the grass, back toward the main building. I held one of Rebecca's red socks against my arm, pressing until the bleeding stopped, figuring no one would notice if it got bloodstained.

191

"Who?" Carmen asked.

"Riley, at least. And Pilar. Probably all the girls that were left at the mansion, and who knows how many older girls."

"But why would they do that?" Rebecca asked.

"I don't know. But give me your other sock." I'd bled through the first, and was feeling light-headed. We ducked behind a ruined wall as Rebecca hopped, working her second sock off her foot. It was pretty disgusting but, with no other option, I pressed it against my arm.

We parted ways once we got inside, and I was on my way upstairs to wash my scrape when the HH called to me from the front desk.

"You've got an e-mail," she said, holding out a piece of paper. I didn't want to read it in her presence, so I waited until I was in the bathroom to unfold it.

hey its trevor. sorry i havent written but sometimes life gets away from you you know? anyway, look, things in my life have moved on and i think its best if you stopped emailing. not to be a dick or anything but we should both be able to move on if one of us has. that makes sense, right sour apple? miss you and sry.

I skipped dinner, asked Carmen to grab me a roll, and sat on my bed with the printout wadded up in my fist. She asked me what was wrong, but I said "nothing" and she knew better than to press me.

The dorm was noisy during mealtimes, because plenty of super-anorexic girls always found excuses to hang back.

Maureen, for example. I had fully settled into my misery when she came into the room, chirping about the length of her braids or some other nonsense. She'd been especially sweet ever since she'd ratted me out, which just made me hate her more. I brushed by her and left, deciding to hang out at the top of the faculty stairwell where no one would bother me.

At first I'd convinced myself that the e-mail was faked. Maybe Zsilinska had concocted it late at night to make me forget about Trevor. But I couldn't deny how much it sounded like him. The e-mailing without caps, like it was a text message (because he probably sent it from his friend Lawrence's phone), and calling me sour apple. Had I ever mentioned that to Dr. Zsilinska? I searched through all our sessions in my brain. I didn't think so.

Trevor didn't want to be with me anymore. It's not as though I thought it could never happen – things had never been peaceful for us for very long. He'd be hot for me for a couple of weeks, then the heat would turn off, and I'd freak and get clingy, and Trevor would get more distant because of it, until we wouldn't see each other for a week, which was when he'd start calling all the time, and it would be hot for a couple of weeks, and then off . . . I guess I knew we'd eventually break it off for good. We hadn't ever really discussed how things would work with me going away to boarding school, and I'd never pretended to myself that he wouldn't be seeing other girls.

The problem was: I still thought of him as my fallback,

who'd appear one day to rescue me. Now that chance was gone. I'd miss the reality of him far less than I'd miss the idea of having a savior.

I was sitting there, not getting anywhere with my thoughts, when I heard footsteps on the stairs. Harrison appeared and sat a few steps below me.

Normally I would have gotten flirty or tongue-tied, depending on my mood. But today flirting with Harrison seemed pointless.

"Hey," he said. "I didn't see you in the cafeteria."

"Yeah," I said. "But you're not usually there, anyway."

"I went today. I looked for you." He paused, as if waiting for me to realize how important that was. I nodded, offering him as little as possible. "But yeah, you're right — normally I eat in my apartment."

"Does it suck living at a girls' school?" I asked, because it seemed expected that we keep talking. As much as I wanted to be alone, there was something in his voice that comforted me. Maybe it was just that it was the voice of a guy who wasn't trying to teach me history. But it might have been something specific to him, too. He was play-ing with me, sure — but he didn't have to. The fact that I had his attention meant something, even if it wasn't very much.

"Nope. I've got my car, so I can get away as much as I want — or at least until the snows start. So. Why are you sitting up here all by yourself?" He leaned back, as if lounging in bed. He was one of those guys who dress so casually, and act so casually, that you realize it's actually a master plan, that they're formally casual, working really hard not to put much effort in. I hadn't ever gotten a chance to see him up close in a full set of clothes before. His body was perfect for me – I knew that, and tried not to get lost on the inch of abdomen exposed above the waist of his jeans. And he had these amazing brown eyes, all the more beautiful for being placed in the center of such a struggle of a face. His skin was dull and white from some intense acne treatments, and was studded with red bumps on the hairline and chin. But he was beautiful; there was no denying it.

"I think too much sometimes," I said. It seemed like an attractive way to say I was moody.

"Yeah," he said. "Me too." I wasn't so sure he did. "This have anything to do with you and your roommate sneaking out on Saturday?"

I shook my head.

"When are you going to let me join you guys?" he asked, grinning and easing himself nearer to me.

I said, "I'll bet that you're not supposed to be talking to us inmates."

He looked surprised. "Really? Why would you bet that?"

"Our safety. Your safety. We're *very* dangerous."

"I know. But tell me, Angela – would you be dangerous to me?"

I nodded. "Very." I couldn't help it – I was closing in, leaning right where he wanted me to be. "I'll steal your car." *Closer.* "I'll break into your house." *Closer.* "I'll kidnap your children." *There.* "And I'll hold you hostage."

This was the closest I'd been to anyone since Trevor. Breath close. Skin close. Kiss close.

"You know," he whispered, "I can be very dangerous, too."

I had him. And I knew I'd have him even more if I chose this moment to pull away. "I've had experience with your weapons," I said, leaning back, eyes locked on his the whole time.

He chuckled. "Why do I feel like nothing I could tell you would surprise you?"

I smiled slyly. "I don't know – because you're predictable?"

He faked a wounded look. "And here I was, thinking we were soul mates."

I started to gather my things. "All right, Romeo, you go on thinking that."

He sat up, the game suddenly over. "Look, why are you being such a bitch to me?"

Because look what it's doing to you.

I leaned back, body on display. "Because you think you can play me. And you can't."

"Who left you so cold?"

Suddenly this wasn't fun anymore. I stood up. "Thanks for coming up to console me," I said. "You've done a hell of a job." He stayed in my way. "Let me pass."

He shook his head, grinning again. "I'll let you by if you promise me one thing," he said.

I held fast. "What?"

"Okay, two things. First, stop being a bitch to me,

196

because I don't deserve it. Second, if you sneak out again this Saturday, which I know you will, don't climb down your sheets and kill yourself. I'll sneak you a hallway key at dinner. Deal?"

I nodded, then slipped by him, making sure my shoulder brushed against his.

I couldn't stop thinking about him as I headed back to my room. Why did every interaction I had with a guy have to turn into a contest? He was a player, sure, but wasn't I playing just as much? Was that wrong, or just the way things had to be?

I tried to stop thinking about him. But a reminder soon came from the strangest possible source.

When I got to room 201, Maureen was standing in the doorway.

"Hey," she said, "I noticed you with Harrison."

"What do you mean, 'noticed'? We were off in the faculty stairwell. Were you spying on me?"

"I happened to hear. And he's right, you know. You *are* being a bitch."

"Look, *narc*, I'm not about to stand here and listen to your crap. Unless you want me to do something that'll land us both in the headmistress's office, step aside."

She surprised me by doing exactly what I asked. As she moved to one side, her blond hair floated after her and the image clicked into place with another in my memory.

Suddenly I knew exactly who I'd seen in Harrison's window a week before.

Chapter Twenty-six

It was as if the Hidden Oak faculty somehow knew that we were up to something, and decided to bury us with work. All Carmen, Rebecca, Blank, and I wanted to do was sneak out and search around more — but we spent our afternoons shackled to assignments and our nights working on "group projects" or "breeding exercises." I had no desire to do any of the work . . . but I also didn't want to call any attention to myself. The fact that nobody had mentioned our infiltration of the old dorm told me that we hadn't been detected — but there was no guarantee that we'd be as lucky the next time. Mrs. Vienna was always watching. I had to play along. I desperately wanted to return to Riley, but I also had to take her warning into account — if I made the wrong step, I could be jeopardizing more than just myself.

As a result, Carmen, Rebecca, Blank, and I had to keep our investigative work on the down-low. Our week of espionage bonded us tight: We clung together in the hall-ways, never mentioning what we'd discovered or our planned return to the tree house on Saturday night. We couldn't get enough of one another's company, our nerves causing us to laugh too readily or let the threads of conversation slip away and leave us in giddy silence.

Finally, Saturday rolled around, and our anticipation of sneaking out again was electric. At dinner, though, we received the first sign that tonight wouldn't go as we'd planned. We went into the dining hall and there was Harrison, sitting at the edge of the faculty table, occasionally giving one-word answers to his dad but mostly staring over at the table where I sat down with Carmen, Blank, and Rebecca.

Since Harrison was facing the same way as Dr. Spicer, I had to stop myself from shooting him any glances or signals. I was glad for Spicer's presence, actually, because she forced me to keep cool. I'd been good the whole week — I'd switched my alignment on my bed, so he would get a good view only of my feet, and had told Dr. Zsilinska, in all honesty, that I had taken her words to heart about not being able to maturely relate to boys until I found my own self-worth. It really made sense . . . except I found myself not at all interested in eating my potato casserole, with Harrison over there smirking at me.

"Any sign of a key?" Carmen whispered.

"Do you really think he's going to help us?" Rebecca asked.

Blank stayed quiet.

"No sign," I said. "And I have no idea if he's going to help us." It wasn't like we'd parted in the hallway on positive terms. Odds were pretty good that his offer had been revoked when he'd called me a cold bitch.

Unless, of course, he wanted to make a peace offering.

Mrs. Vienna was on dinner patrol, so I could hardly pass by the faculty table to ask Harrison about it. And he, on the other hand, couldn't strut over to a tableful of girls. I risked a conspicuous shrug in his direction. He laughed too hard at something his dad said and winked. Then he muttered something and headed toward the food area, taking a long route by the soda machine — and us. As he passed me he whispered out of the side of his mouth, "Go for the clear Jell-O in five."

"'Kay, slut," I whispered back into my carrot sticks, watching Dr. Spicer watch us.

Once he had gone into the food area and come out, I headed for the dessert section.

Clear gelatin has to be the worst culinary development of the last century. Half the time it's unflavored, which means eating pure gooey bone, and the other half the time it has a chemical coconut taste that sits on your tongue for hours afterward. All of which, of course, made it a very smart choice for subterfuge — no one was going to swoop in and crowd around the clear Jell-O.

The same three bowls of filmy cubes had sat for weeks on a shelf above the ice-cream freezer. In fact, they'd gone untouched for so long that they had developed a toenail-yellow skin and ceased to wobble. I took them down one by one and examined them.

The last one had a note and a key at the bottom, magnified and made permanent through the clear cubes, like a paperweight. The note read: *Wish I was coming with you guys. Luv always, H.* ☺

"Having trouble choosing a dessert, Cardenas?"

It was Mrs. Vienna, standing at the salad bar and fixing me with a severe look. I remembered what she'd done to me last time we were in the cafeteria kitchen together, and felt an involuntary flash of fear.

"No, Mrs. Vienna," I said. "I think I've found one."

I could see her search for wrongdoing. Luckily, my hand covered the note and the key.

"Very good," she said after a further moment's examination. "Eat it quickly, because we'll be cleaning up in a few minutes."

"Yes, Mrs. Vienna."

I could feel her watch me as I left. As I walked out, I stepped only on the black tiles. It was the only way I could think of to send a message back and not get in trouble for it.

I bet his eyes were on me.

It was cloudy and drizzling, and by the time we assembled the coven, we were wet and cold. Blank had brought a notebook that we ended up burning page by page. We thought it would provide warmth, but you couldn't really feel anything from a single page burning. Still, it was pretty, and I looked forward to when it would be my turn again to light a corner and hold the page as it flamed and fell.

"Rebecca," I said once we had caught up on what we'd found during our investigations. "You're up."

I held the bag out to her. She picked the old bus ticket.

"First of all," she said, "I don't know what my real last name is. I say it's Rothko, but that's only because I got to choose. You see, my dad dumped my mom, and then she dumped me into the system. Foster care means living with one family and then another, and you take what you get, because you're a little kid and don't think you can complain about things. My first foster mom was fine, a little moody, but a good woman. I stayed with her until I was eight. Then I got placed with the Chainanis, and that was when things —"

Juin stepped through the window. She was soaked through, her hair stringy against the sides of her face, her eyes submerged in blue-black puddles, and her wrists ringed in the same color.

"I see you started without me," she said, unsmiling.

Chapter Twenty-seven

We all shot to our feet.

"Juin," I said. "What's happened to you?"

"Systematic abuse," she said. "Anyone got a towel?"

No one did, so she dried herself with the bag. We sat her down and burned the rest of the notebook trying to warm her.

I couldn't believe I was actually seeing Juin again. I guess I thought it would never happen — that she was meant to be a quick flash in my life that disappeared forever. Now that she was back, I was afraid she'd be mad that I'd moved on and kept on living without her, that I'd taken over leadership of the coven. But if she wanted to take control back, that was fine by me.

With a start, I realized Juin was following my thoughts in my face. Since she'd never met Blank, I used the excuse of introducing them to break her stare.

"So you're a real live purple threader," Blank said, offering her hand.

"For now," Juin said, taking it. "I'm out of this place."

"You're breaking out?" I asked. "How?"

"*We're* breaking out. And I don't care how. Walking."

"There's a fence. And if you make it past that, it's still hours to civilization," I said.

"That's why we wait for the right moment."

"What have they been doing to you?" Carmen asked.

Juin looked at her harshly. "Why don't you ask what you really want to ask? I knew they wouldn't punish you too hard after you took the fall," she said. "Good girls never get punished too hard. Or maybe you switched over to their side."

That's when Riley arrived. She stepped through the diagonal windowway and approached us, landing heavily next to Juin. She looked crazier and skinnier than she ever had, like a street cat that someone had dunked.

"You got anyone else coming?" Rebecca asked, peering outside.

Riley had a long scratch on her neck, which looked, in the half-light, like a stream of night. Something had broken in her, and she had gone from glitteringly hostile to dependent kid sister. "We're . . . we're not actually leaving tonight," Riley said.

"Riley's got some craziness in the head," Juin informed us. "She thinks we need to collect evidence so we can get the school shut down, but she needs to realize that, with them controlling e-mail and phones, we'd need to escape to let anyone know. So we're leaving."

"Just not tonight," Riley whispered. "You know what they'll do. To the others."

"Fine," Juin said. "You got it, freak show."

"Where do they keep you?" Carmen asked.

"You want the full story?" Juin asked.

We all nodded.

"There aren't many of us. Twenty. We live in the old gymnasium at the far end of campus. But there are steam tunnels connecting all the buildings belowground, so sometimes we're below you and around you. You might hear us. We certainly watch you."

The idea of it . . . the whole time, they'd been right there. Trapped in the darkness, while we went about our lives above them, completely oblivious.

"And what do you do all day?" I asked. "Because I know you don't take classes."

"We technically have a couple of tutors, but they're only with us for a few hours each day. Mr. Derrian and Mrs. Alsanz. They come over to our building after they finish with you guys. The rest of the time we're doing stuff like what we did in the mansion, only more hard-core. Dr. Spicer is there sometimes, as well as this bitch named Vienna. We're put on lockdown, we're force-fed drugs, which Riley and I've been holding under our tongues and then spitting out. They make us run until we puke, however long it takes. We're given a five-course meal one day and nothing at all to eat the next. Once they made us bury ourselves, and we were only allowed out of our graves once we promised we were 'ready to live.'"

She held up her bruised wrists. "Recently, they've kept one of us in handcuffs at all times. We have to vote on who it is, which keeps us nasty to one another. I think it's to make sure we don't unify and rebel. It's usually me in the cuffs. Bitches. Riley hasn't gone in once yet."

Riley smiled slyly.

"But Riley's first day was spent standing, missing all meals, with a sign around her neck that said 'I can't control myself.' So she can wipe that cutesy smile off her face."

"I don't get why they'd do those things to you," Carmen said quietly.

"The mansion month is when they make their decision about who can be rehabilitated," Blank said. "And the gold thread girls are the ones that show they can bend or fix their behavior. If a girl's too far gone, she goes purple. Which means the school's given up on her getting better, and are only trying to pacify her."

"*Pacify?*" Juin spat. "You sound like one of them. Who the hell are you, anyway? It's not about *pacification*. It's about total control. It's about breaking us down completely so we'll never be able to leave."

"I don't get why any of your parents haven't come to get you out," Carmen said.

"Why haven't *your* parents gotten *you* out, sweetheart? Are you really having that great a time?"

Carmen stammered a little.

Juin nodded. "I didn't think so."

We all fell silent, sunk into our various miserable histories.

"How are you going to get the truth out about the school?" I asked.

"We've got to get to the headmistress," Riley said. "She doesn't see anyone, but she somehow has to be reasoned with —"

"Fat chance," Juin said.

"— or she has to be taken down."

"Do you mean . . . kill her?" Carmen asked.

"No," Juin said, though Riley stayed silent. "We have to get evidence from her office, something on paper that we can take to authorities. Or, there have to be master recordings from all the security cameras, probably in the main office. If we get our hands on those and then get out of here, we'll have enough."

"Just don't mess with the boilers," I said, and told them what Carmen and I had discovered about the Heath School.

"Hey, if killing twenty of us is what it takes to get attention . . ." Juin said.

I laughed, waiting to see if she would join in. But she didn't.

"We have to do all this before the snows start," Juin said. "Which gives us a week or two at the most."

"So what do we have to do?" I asked.

"It's up to you gold threaders," Juin said. "We're basically in prison. You guys have some freedom, at least."

"But why not leave now?" Blank said.

Juin could barely conceal her distaste for the question, and the questioner. "Because, as Riley was good enough to point out in her own insane way, if they sense that we're missing for even a second, they'll take it out on everyone else. They've made that perfectly clear. Even if we managed to get out, they can still take us down. There was one purple girl who escaped a few years ago – and they called the authorities to have her locked up in an asylum so fast that there wasn't any chance of her being believed. They showed us the videos to prove it. And they also showed us what they did to the other girls to make sure no more escapes were attempted. It made handcuffs look like friendship bracelets."

I suppressed a shudder. "So how did you get out tonight?" I asked.

Juin looked right at Blank. "I'm not sure I trust you all enough to tell you. Let's just say it was an opportunity that doesn't come up very often. Which is why we have to rely on you – and get the hell back now."

"So y'all are depending on us to risk our own necks to get you out," Blank mused. "Huh. That sounds a lot like trust to me."

Juin looked at each of us. "Why do I not feel good about this?" she asked.

"We're going to do it," I said.

I just didn't have any idea how.

Chapter Twenty-eight

Juin and Riley vanished almost as quickly as they had appeared. I was shaken, Carmen was scared, Blank was angry, and Rebecca looked like she regretted ever joining the coven. It seemed ridiculous to ask her to continue her story. The past didn't matter now. The present and the future loomed so much larger.

"I don't think I can hang out here much more tonight," Rebecca said.

None of us disagreed.

We kept low and silent as we trucked across the wet, dark grass back to the main school, avoiding the exposed ridge where the security lights would have left us in stark silhouette. I looked for footprints in the grass leading to the far-off purple thread building, but Juin and Riley hadn't left a trace. *Like ghosts,* I thought. *Like the dead.*

Eventually we got to Blank and Rebecca's hall, and I

slipped Harrison's key in the lock to let them in. Then Carmen and I headed to our wing. As I passed through the hall door, I was grabbed from the side, one hand over my mouth, the other around my waist.

"Shh!" Harrison said as Carmen started to scream. He moved his hand away from my mouth and clutched her arm. He was wearing a stained tank top and smelled like sex and sleep.

"Vienna's up," he whispered.

"What?" Carmen said, her voice shot with fear.

"Some pipe broke in the library bathroom. They called my dad, but he's not on duty tonight, so she's up there dealing with all the water. You can hear her cursing every once in a while."

The library bathroom was right at our entrance.

"What about the other end of the hall?" Carmen asked.

"This key doesn't work for that side," I said. "Besides, if she's got a view of the hallway, she'll see us sneaking into our room."

"So what do we do?"

"You stay chez Derrian until morning," Harrison said.

"Yeah," I said. "You're going to sneak us around your dad?"

"Nope. I've already told him."

I pulled out of his grasp, furious. "Tell me you're joking," I said, locking eyes with him. "Tell me you're not that stupid."

"Look, you can trust him. He's in this for you guys, not Hidden Oak."

"Even if he is," I said, "he's still a *teacher*. No teacher's going to want us sneaking out."

"Well, I told him already. So come in." He pushed open his front door. Inside was dark, except for a tight circle of light shed by an exposed bulb in the kitchen, shining on stacks of dirty dishes. The little white dog stood alert, watching us suspiciously. "And hurry up, because I'm freezing out here in the hallway."

"Absolutely not," I said. "We'll spend the night outside instead."

It wasn't just the idea of Mr. Derrian turning us in. Or even the idea of getting him into trouble. I wished I had cared about that, but I didn't. The reason I didn't want to stay was all about Harrison. It didn't matter whether I didn't trust him or I didn't trust myself — ultimately, that came down to the same thing. I didn't trust the situation. This was a test I was destined to fail.

"Angela," Carmen said timidly, "if Mr. Derrian already knows, there's no more harm in going inside."

"I don't care. Come on, Carmen."

"I don't want to sleep outside," she said, crossing her arms and looking like a rebellious child.

I sighed and took a step into the Derrian apartment. "Fine."

At least I'm not the one who decided. So whatever happens, it's not my fault.

Harrison led the way and I followed, trying not to focus on the loose waist of his dingy scrubs, slipping farther and farther down with each step.

The place was a loving shambles. Stacks of open books topped with bowls of long-hardened cereal. A lamp converted to a coat rack. The television draped by a sweatshirt.

"The couch folds out," Harrison said.

"Couch?" I asked.

"Yeah," he said, swiping DVDs and books and underwear off what I had thought was a low table. "The couch."

A motel smell of old sleep rose from the thin gray mattress as Harrison set up the bed. Carmen and I stood by the door, murmuring forlornly to each other, like refugees. She scratched the dog between his ears. After Harrison finished pulling out the bed, he announced he was getting sheets. When he opened the door to the next room he revealed his father, standing in old-man pajamas.

"Hello," he said awkwardly. "Angela, Carmen."

"Hi, Mr. Derrian," Carmen said politely.

We had been in his class the day before, observing paramecia under the microscope, and now we were in his living room, surprising him in the middle of the night. I blinked heavily. "I'm getting sheets," Harrison said, patting his father on the shoulder as he passed into the narrow hall.

"Thanks for taking us in, Mr. Derrian," Carmen said.

"Yeah, thanks," I mumbled.

"Are you girls staying safe?" he said, squinting and running a hand through his thinning, ruffled hair.

We nodded. We had no idea what he intended.

"You know you'd have been severely punished if Mrs. Vienna had caught you tonight. You might even have gone purple."

"Yeah, about that, Mr. Derrian, we have a couple of —" Carmen started saying, until she thought better of it, most likely because I'd elbowed her. I liked Mr. Derrian fine, but this could still very easily be a trap. There are different ways of getting a girl to talk, and kindness is one of them.

"Ahem. Do you want coffee?" he asked, heading into the dim kitchen. "I think I have some crystals of something. I'm a tea drinker myself, but I know you girls love coffee and don't get it in the cafeteria. Here, let me see."

We both said "no, thanks," but I don't think he heard us as he distractedly puttered around his cupboards.

"You know," he said, his voice loosening now that he didn't have to look at us, "I've lived in the school for years. Back when it was Heath, the boys had such freedom. I was going to write a history of the school, but then it unexpectedly closed. I guess I've always fixated on the old days because of it. Those boys were sneaking out all the time; it's good to see their spirit lives on. . . ."

He got distracted, holding a can of stewed tomatoes and staring into its label. I figured he was thinking back to the accident, because he said, "Be careful, girls, be careful," as he put the tomatoes back.

"Mr. Derrian," I said slowly, "I'm sure the Heath School was wonderful. And we both think you're a great teacher. But we're not sure Hidden Oak . . . is the best school . . . for anyone."

He sighed. "You're not alone in that."

"I guess," I said, looking at Carmen for confirmation. She obviously knew where I was going, and looked pissed that I'd elbowed her for starting to say the same thing. "I guess I'm – we're – wondering what we can do to either make it better, or..."

"Well, you'd have to convince Cynthia," he said.

"Cynthia?" I asked, surprised. "Do you mean Mrs. Vienna?"

"No," he said, momentarily irritated. "I mean Cynthia. The headmistress. But good luck. There's nothing here she's not aware of. Nothing. Probably even your spending the night here. Everything usually goes according to her plans. Why would she ever sit down and discuss changing the school? Not that you'd get to see her, anyway, unless you got yourself in *real* trouble. Regardless, I long ago gave up trying to reason with her."

"But surely you could do *something* to help?"

"Dad's got tenure from back when this was Heath," Harrison said, returning with a pair of limp sheets, then bending over the bed. "And no one who was at Heath before the accident can find work anymore, even now. So you can see how he's reluctant to make waves." His tone sounded apologetic, like he'd confronted his dad on this issue before.

"Well, we still need your help," I pressed.

Mr. Derrian looked up, surprised. "To do what, exactly?"

Carmen started to speak, but in case she was going to say "shut down the school," I cut in with, "To get some reforms made."

Mr. Derrian shook his head. "Hidden Oak might be devilishly run, but it's an intricate machine. Any meaningful reforms would require a full re-envisioning of the school's mission. They would, in effect, require the school to be shut down and started fresh. I have to send our dear Harrison to college in a year; I can't lose this job. It's enough risk that I've taken you in tonight – if anyone asks, you told me that you couldn't get your door open. If a lie gets uncovered, I'm afraid it will be yours. I'll be a sympathetic ear always – but don't count on me to help you in any of your shenanigans. And I'm sorry, but I don't think I have any coffee."

"Can you at least look out for our friends in the purple thread?" I tried.

"Which ones?"

I debated whether I should answer, then realized what it would look like if I didn't.

"Juin and Riley," I said.

"Ah, yes. June Carpenter. Very bright girl. Lively. I'll keep a close eye on them both," he said. "Now, it's time for bed."

Harrison helped us get assembled on the foldout couch. I helped him stretch the bottom sheet over the mattress, and as we touched shoulders, I whispered, "I thought Maureen might be here."

He grinned widely at me, like it was some especially witty joke. "Yeah, right."

I shook my head and let it go. There was no winning – if I showed I was hurt by his having slept with her, all it would do was make me seem needy.

Once the lights were out and Carmen was snoring, I slipped out of bed and stood in the kitchen. I couldn't sleep, yes, but that was because while Mr. Derrian was rummaging through the cupboards, I'd seen a phone behind the cereal boxes. Why they kept a phone in the cupboard, who knew. Boys. As I eased the cupboard open and pulled the phone down, I saw that the cord barely reached to the counter, and no one had ever bothered to buy a longer one. I'd have to get up on tiptoe to dial.

The first person I thought to call was Trevor, but there was no answer. Rather than leave him a message, I dialed my parents instead. I didn't know anyone else's number.

"Hello?" said a groggy voice. My mom.

"Hey, Mom, it's me. Angela."

"Angela? Do you know what time it is?"

"Yeah. I do. Look —"

"Is something wrong? What's gone wrong?"

"Well —" My voice caught, and I tried to get its wavering under control. "Yeah, something's wrong. You've sent me to a prison. It's not right, I'm not allowed to call you —"

"How are you calling me, then? Angela, what's wrong?"

"I'm telling you!" I whispered urgently. "It's an unsafe building, there was a huge accident here years ago, the administration is heartless, they have some girls on, like, starvation and drugs, and they're barely getting educated, even, and it's not much better for the rest of us."

I could hear my dad waking up, sleepily murmuring, "Who is it?"

"They warned us this would happen," my mom continued. "That you'd try to contact us. Angela, I'm so disappointed."

"What? I need your help, Mom. Get me out of here."

"They sent us the video of you sneaking out. They told us that you've been breaking into old buildings, that you're not making as much . . . psychological progress as you should. That you might be placed under stricter control. That we should expect you to call and lie to us. I'm sick of being lied to by my own daughter. Sick of it, do you hear me?"

"Mom!" I cried. "I'm sneaking out because they're evil. I'm trying to get away."

"Stop trying to get away," she said stonily. "And that will take care of it."

"Please," I said, but the line had gone dead.

I suppressed a scream and slammed the receiver down. Returning to the couch, I saw Mr. Derrian standing at the door of his bedroom. He had the oddest expression on his face, not angry or torn, but more like he'd been checking me out. He went back to bed without saying a word, and I returned to the pullout couch. I was grateful when Carmen put her arm around me protectively and told me to stay quiet.

The rest of the night, I expected something to happen. Mrs. Vienna to barge in. Carmen to freak out. Harrison to hold out his hand and take me to his room.

But nothing happened. Not even sleep.

Chapter Twenty-nine

I woke Carmen up before daybreak, and we sneaked back to our room. As I tossed around in my bed, I watched Maureen sleeping peacefully. It amazed me that, for everyone but me and Carmen, it was just an ordinary morning. Didn't the rest of the world know that everything was changing?

We acted as if nothing had happened, and in Mr. Derrian's class, he didn't show even a flicker of recognition of what had happened the previous night. Clearly, I wasn't the only one who could project lies so cleanly that nothing else showed through. As for Harrison, he was completely out of sight, but I imagined him everywhere. Our paths were truly linked now, for better or worse.

I called a meeting of the coven that afternoon during outdoor exercise. We met in the shallow end of the old Heath swimming pool, clearing away enough leaves and debris to sit against the wall.

"I called my parents last night," I said, "and my mom said they've sent her footage of everything wrong that I've done here. Do you guys see what they're doing? They're making us seem crazy, so we're powerless to ever speak out against them. We can't appeal to our families. Maybe even the police wouldn't believe us."

"They don't have anything on *me*," Blank said. "I've been the best behaved girl you could imagine. And how did you call your parents?"

"I'll tell you later. And our good behavior is the *point*," I pressed. "You're well behaved because of all the punishment they're threatening to put on you. You're totally playing into their power system."

"Isn't that how all schools work?" Rebecca asked.

"Yeah, okay, but at most schools the punishments don't involve starvation, freezer burn, cuts, and bruises. And they don't make it so that the students have no one to turn to. As soon as the snows come, we're totally stuck. They can do whatever they want to us."

"If things get really bad, then we'll band together," Blank said.

"They're bad now," I said. "When's 'really bad'? We have to stop it now."

"So what do you want us to do?" Rebecca asked, exasperated.

"What we *said* we'd do! Find a way into the administration offices and get our hands on files. Or find a way to talk to the headmistress."

"Look," Rebecca said, "I know you like Juin, and maybe you even like Riley, for some reason, and you want to see them get out of the purple thread. I get it, and I support it. But part of me says, you know what, Juin and Riley did this to themselves. If they'd behaved a little better, not even 'good,' but 'better,' they'd be with us and fine. If they simmer down for a few weeks, I'm sure Vienna and Spicer'll move them into the gold thread."

"That's why you're all in the gold thread," I said flatly. "They decided in that first month who was too meek to make trouble, and took us one by one into the main school. We're being *herded*. Doesn't that freak you out?"

"Hey," Blank said, standing, "don't forget you're *in* our wussy thread. Do you think you're the only one of us with a backbone?"

"Don't forget I was the last one assigned to the gold thread," I said. "Vienna didn't even think I belonged, and vowed to get me sent purple. Seeing all this spinelessness, I kind of wish I *was* with them."

"Don't say that," Carmen murmured.

But Blank was of a different opinion. "Go for it," she said. "No one's stopping you."

I rubbed my temples. I hadn't slept at all at the Derrians', and the showers hadn't been running hot that morning, so I'd skipped mine. I felt gross, powerless, and alone, and suddenly worried that maybe I was wrong about the school, that I was just being difficult. But I knew I could trust the horror I felt whenever I interacted with Vienna. I knew I'd seen the scratches and bruises on Juin and Riley.

"Carmen," I said tiredly, "what is everyone not getting?"

She took a while to answer. "I guess I wonder whether trying to help Juin and Riley wouldn't get us *all* sent to the purple thread. And what good would that do?"

She might as well have punched me. "Carmen? Really?"

She nodded, keeping her gaze away at first but then looking me in the eye. Blank and Rebecca were nodding.

"Okay," I said. "I won't bother you bitches anymore."

I dusted my hands, brushed dead leaves off my shirt, and headed toward the school.

"We still meeting on Saturday?" Rebecca called after me.

I didn't answer. My fists clenched and unclenched as I walked. If I couldn't count on any help from the others, there was only one way for me to get to the truth:

Be as dangerous as possible.

Chapter Thirty

I spent the Sunday study hall sitting in the darkest corner of the library, next to a grate that smelled like a shower drain, thinking about ways to be bad. I'd never made acting up a project before, and I found it surprisingly hard. Misbehavior came most easily, after all, in the pursuit of good behavior. Now that I had turned to the dark side, I was the polite kid sitting by herself in study hall, lost in her thoughts and not bothering anyone.

I knew how punishments worked. If I wanted to get sent to the headmistress (and to have access to both her and her office) I'd have to do something unprecedented enough that there wasn't a pre-established punishment. That's when they bring in the big guns.

I made a list of things I remembered students getting sent to the top for in my old schools:

Hitting a teacher

Sex with a teacher

Sexual exposure in general, actually

Drug dealing

Arson

Fighting, provided there was blood or tooth loss

Cheating, if it implicated the whole class

Poisoning the star of the school musical (esp. if there was
   no understudy)

Suicide attempt

Murder attempt

I considered getting it on with Harrison in some easily discovered place (he certainly would have been game), but I was proud to have resisted him so far, and didn't want to give in after all that effort. We had a test in English the next day, and I thought about pulling my book out in the middle and copying from it. It would certainly be flagrant.

But the problem was that these were all so typical. A school specializing in dangerous girls would have established punishments for just about anything. To do something unprecedented I would have to try to kill myself and someone else, maybe at the same time as I was having rough sex with a teacher and toking on a bong. I doodled a sketch of it.

All this thinking about being bad made me strangely reluctant to do anything about it. Maybe this was how good kids functioned, I thought – they meditated on wrongdoing long enough to lock themselves out of it. There's something improvised about being bad, unless you're actually evil.

And that was it. I'd have to do something blatantly premeditated, something that wasn't just acting up, but showed I was a girl with a destructive plan.

Searching for inspiration, I took the nearest book off the shelf and flipped through. It was a collection of old short stories, some of them with black-and-white engravings. One page showed a woman in a bonnet, looking sadly at the ground. Below it was written: *She wanted to scream, but she didn't dare.*

Screaming.

This was definitely something I was ready to do.

I chose Derrian's class. I'd considered the cafeteria, because it was more crowded, but I was afraid I'd start laughing if too many people looked at me. Derrian's class also had the benefit that I sat next to Carmen, who hadn't yet apologized for disagreeing with me. It would serve her right to stew and worry about my behavior.

Originally I planned to do it right at the start of the period, but then my nerves got to me. Some girls had a really natural screaming range, but I hadn't gone all out and yelled since I was a child. Would I be able to keep it up?

So I let the lecture sludge by, twisting my fingers. I bet Carmen figured I was busy worrying about Juin and Riley – although she never said anything, she gave me a shyly encouraging smile whenever I glanced at her. When the period bell rang, and everyone started getting their books together, I didn't move.

When Carmen asked what was wrong, I stood and let out a clear river of a scream, vigorous and cold.

Carmen dashed to her feet. Everyone stared at me, except for Mr. Derrian, who kept busy fiddling with the stereoscopes for the next period's lab.

When I reached the end of my breath, I took another one and continued.

It was loud.

Very loud.

And while at first it was upsetting, as I went on, I found a strange kind of power in it.

Finally, I was causing a real disruption.

"Angela? What's wrong?" Carmen pleaded. I saw the other girls saying things, but I couldn't make out their words over my own screams.

Soon Carmen was shrieking, too, and while my face was impassive — I wasn't enough of an actress to really pretend to be upset — she was streaming tears, her body quaking. I looked around, staring at everyone, my scream gushing.

Listen to me. LISTEN TO ME.

Girls from the surrounding classes began to swarm into Mr. Derrian's room. Blank and Rebecca appeared outside the door, Blank staring in fear and Rebecca shrugging and playing cool. "Shut up, you bitch!" I heard one girl say loudly, just as Mrs. Vienna walked in the door.

"Indeed," she said. "Ms. Pope, Ms. Cardenas, what is all of this about?"

I looked at her flatly and continued my piercing cry.

"Harold," Mrs. Vienna shouted, "were you aware that there are two wailing girls in your classroom?"

He looked up from his work and squinted at us. "Oh. I suppose I was."

"Stop it this instant," Mrs. Vienna said, summoning every bit of her already considerable authority, her little shoulders quivering.

I kept on screaming, staring right at her.

She grabbed Carmen and me in her familiar arm pinch and steered us to the classroom door. We proceeded down the hall, students making way for us in amazement, my scream an ambulance's wail.

She led us down a set of stairs and into the steam tunnel that had originally led me from the mansion to the main school. Hurling open a rusty iron door, she threw Carmen inside. She dragged me a few feet farther and thrust me into the solitary chamber that I remembered from the first time around.

I broke off long enough to say, "I want to see the headmistress."

"I'll be back in eight hours," Mrs. Vienna hissed as she clanged the door shut.

I was on my way. I hoped.

Chapter Thirty-one

The chamber's one tiny barred window was so high on the wall that I couldn't see much out of it. It was cracked, though, and let in a strong draft. It must have also let in quite a bit of rainwater over time, as the floor was covered in a slick layer of green algae. No way would I sit down on it, so I leaned heavily against the door, shivering in the draft.

I felt terrible, of course, for involving Carmen in my downward spiral. If we'd planned this together, then fine, I'd call getting solitary an okay thing. But she'd been punished without knowing what I was trying to do. The very fact that she had feelings for me had gotten her into trouble. That was messed up.

I would have told her I was sorry, but the wall between us was too thick.

As I stood there feeling bad for myself and what I'd done, I saw the window start to glow white, then get ringed in crystals. I pressed my nose as close as I could get.

No — not yet.

The snow had begun.

Soon my feet started to hurt, so I let myself sink lower and lower against the door. Finally I was squatting against the floor, and then I gave up and sank onto the foul concrete. With the grossness seeping into my pants, I felt my anger grow. Our chances for successfully escaping were slimming. If screaming wasn't going to get me sent to the headmistress, I quickly came up with a few other methods that would guarantee it.

It could have been eight hours that passed, but it felt like far more. The layer of snow in front of the window was a thick, bright white before I finally heard the door unlock again. I stood and prepared myself.

Let it be Mrs. Vienna, I thought.

And it was.

When I slugged her, she had just opened the door and was trying to twist her key out of the lock. Trevor had once taught me to keep my thumb outside my fist and punch in a straight line, and I reared back and bashed her solidly on the chin. It wasn't too hard, really, except that she was so short she kind of flew. Her head hit the iron door with a loud gong.

She wasn't stunned, though, not even for a moment. In a flash she had me on my knees with my arm wrenched behind my back. She smashed my head against the wet concrete once, and then again. I tried to resist but she had me tightly. It was as if she had been prepared for this, anticipated an attack at any time. I grew light-headed as the green concrete struck me again and again. She was weak, but she was still hurling my head with all the force she could; I heard little cracklings in my head and smelled blood in my nose.

"You're so sued," I slurred.

"Try it," she spat.

"I want . . ." I willed myself not to pass out. "I want to see the headmistress."

"Is that what this is about? You little idiot. I was coming to bring you to her."

She lifted me off the concrete and stood me up. I held a hand out to the wall to steady myself. The skin on her cheek had been roughed away where it had struck the wall, and was surrounded by a network of broken vessels. "You little idiot," she repeated. She was smiling, slightly. "Follow me."

I tailed her down the tunnels, turning twice, then three times, until I was totally disoriented. Then we started to go up a stairwell. "Cynthia won't even know about this latest . . . incident," Mrs. Vienna mused as she gently probed her cheek with her fingertips. "But it's not you who will be punished for it, anyway."

Distracted by all that had just happened, it took me a moment to make the connection.

"Don't you dare do anything to Carmen," I said. I was approaching a scream again, genuine this time. "Do you hear me?"

"It's a little late for concern for others, you selfish little bitch. And here we are." We had reached the top of the stairwell, where there was a simple wooden door. As she rapped on it, her huge wedding ring wiggled. "She'll let you know when she's ready for you. It may be a few minutes. I'll be waiting at the bottom of the stairs until you go in, so don't even think of escaping. Once you're safely inside, I'll be sure to personally send your regards to Ms. Pope."

It took all my self-control not to slug her again.

Chapter Thirty-two

I waited in front of the door, twisting my shirttails in my fingers. Part of me wanted to follow Mrs. Vienna down the stairs, back to where Carmen was, to help defend against whatever she was going to do to her. But Mrs. Vienna would be waiting until I got in to see the headmistress, and outside of knocking her out and taking her keys, there was nothing I could think of to do. To be honest, if it came to an actual brawl, I was pretty sure Vienna would win.

I heard a voice, thickly muffled but somehow familiar, call to me from the other side of the door, telling me to come in.

I pushed on the door, and was surprised to find it unlatched. Inside was a small turret room, decorated in '70s furnishings, all wood and chrome. Behind a paneled desk was a tall executive chair, facing away from me and toward a window that was as narrow as an arrow slit. "Please have a seat," said a voice that I was on the verge of identifying.

As I sat, she swiveled. I heard the clack before I saw her.

"Dr. Zsilinska," I said, dumbfounded.

"Call me Cynthia here, Angela."

I stared back at her.

She sighed. "Perhaps I should start by explaining. It's a small school, and I have to wear many hats. My work as headmistress is hardly full-time. When I founded Hidden Oak, I thought it better that the headmistress remain invisible. The group dynamic of girls in your position is such that they'll unite to face down a superior enemy, and I didn't want them to have any one adult to point fingers at. And besides, I came into this field as a psychologist, and I didn't want to give that up. I knew that a girl would be unlikely to open up to someone she also knew was the headmistress. So it's a necessary deception. In any case, tell me, do you think you know why I've called you here today, Angela?"

I nodded.

She looked surprised. "Really? [clack] I'd like you to write the reasons down, please." She opened the desk drawer and rummaged around. "I'm sorry, I so rarely have the occasion to use the headmistress office. These are all the furnishings of the old Heath headmaster – I barely know my own way around. Here we are." She handed me a legal pad and a pencil. "Reasons, please."

I stared at the pad. I knew my best bet was to go along with her until I could press my case, to build up whatever trust I could before I started breaking everything down. It had never occurred to me that the headmistress would be someone I'd known all along. I couldn't figure out if this worked to my advantage or not — it all depended on what, really, Dr. Zsilinska thought about me. She'd never told me she was on my side — but she'd never seemed to be on anyone else's side, either.

I had no idea how to play this.

I looked down at the legal pad. She'd said "reasons," so I figured I was here for more than sabotaging myself. But did she really expect me to list every wrongdoing, to just give myself up? I pushed the pad back toward her.

"I'm sorry," I said, "but I don't get what you're asking me to do."

Dr. Cynthia Zsilinska looked disappointed. "I think we know each other better than that, Angela."

"Go fish."

"Perhaps I can jog your memory along. You attempted to dismantle a school video camera. You encouraged other students to share their histories, though they refused. You broke the ban on discussing purple thread girls. You smoked on school premises. You snuck into the attic, where you aren't allowed. You snuck into areas of the basement where you aren't allowed. You snuck into the abandoned dormitory, where —"

"— I'm not allowed."

"You screamed without provocation, disrupting the learning environment. And Mrs. Vienna just radioed me that you *struck* her."

She remained curiously impassive throughout, even when she mentioned Mrs. Vienna. I wonder if she knew I'd made her bleed.

"Looks like that brings us up-to-date," I said.

"Hardly. I've only started with those things you must have already suspected I knew. To continue. Against my express proscription, you've fraternized with Harrison Derrian. You understand, of course, that you're hardly the only girl on campus to have done so, or to be currently doing so?"

I nodded, wondering what *fraternizing* meant. Though I definitely got the gist.

"We allow Mr. Derrian's son to remain on campus as a sort of litmus test for you girls, so we can see your progress, those of you who have a history of sexual impropriety."

"How do you know what I've been doing?" I asked.

Dr. Zsilinska pressed on. "We also know, Angela, that you have been leading other girls in sneaking out on Saturday nights. We know precisely how you do it, and we know whose aid you enlist. You realize you're endangering many people at this school? Any teacher, say, who was found to be assisting you would be instantly fired."

"It's not their fault," I said, once I could find words. It threw me off balance to hear that she knew about the coven. The one thing I thought had been private and outside the school's control, and they'd known about it the whole time.

"The point," Dr. Cynthia Zsilinska said, her voice rising above a monotone for the first time, "is that it's incredibly dangerous for you to be sneaking off at night. Who knows what danger you could fall into in the open forest — you realize that four boys died in a tree house in the woods, right before Heath was shut down? The same thing could happen to you, especially now that the snows have begun. Visibility is near zero out there."

I watched Zsilinska register the surprise on my expression. I did rapid calculations in my head. She must think I was shocked to hear about the deaths. My real surprise, however, was the realization that she presented the tree house as something I didn't know about — she might know we sneaked out, but she didn't know where we went. The fact that those boys died in our headquarters was a shock of an entirely different variety, a cold and creepy shock, and one that I would save tight in my fist to process later.

If she didn't know where we'd been going, then none of the coven members was the informant.

And if she didn't know Carmen and I had spent a night at the Derrians', that probably eliminated Harrison and his father.

Unless, of course, she was holding back some of what she knew.

"If you knew we've been sneaking away — which we haven't been, of course — why didn't you stop us?"

Zsilinska removed her glasses and rubbed her temples with open palms. She closed her eyes when she did so, and I could stare freely at her frumpy sweater, her terrible cone of fake hair, the worry lines on her face. For her to close her eyes in front of me was so trusting. Some mixture of pity, fear, and sympathy made my lip quiver.

"I would have stopped anyone else, Angela," she said. "But not you."

I smiled. I hated myself for smiling, for warming so easily at being thought special. By the time she'd opened her eyes again, I was back to my frown. I was terrified she'd continue with what she had to say, and terrified she wouldn't.

"Why not me?" I asked, once I couldn't wait any longer.

"Angela, you've undoubtedly noticed that there are specific criteria we use to determine who should be categorized into the gold thread, and who should be sent into the purple. Have you determined what these criteria are?"

This was an easy question, right? I said, "It looks like the more dangerous girls are in the purple thread, and the wimpier girls are in the gold thread."

"Close. But what if I told you that Natalia Grant-Rodriguez, the girl you know as 'Blank,' has a criminal history to rival almost any girl in the purple thread? While Riley Proctor, who is in the purple thread, has no criminal history whatsoever. You, in fact, have a suspected murder on your record, which goes far beyond most of the purple thread girls."

"I didn't kill my grandfather," I told her.

"Let's bracket that issue," Zsilinska said coldly. "I'm sorry I brought it up prematurely, because I have much more to say on that matter. For now, let me correct your hypothesis. You haven't been separated based on dangerousness. You've been separated based on hope of rehabilitation."

"As in?"

"Correctability."

"I know that. We're not dumb. But why do you keep the purple thread girls at all, then? Your school's supposed to help us get better. You and Dr. Spicer talked a big talk about that at the beginning. But you what, just throw in the towel if you decide we're not worth the effort?"

Dr. Zsilinska sighed. "You've broached the aspect of Hidden Oak that makes it different from any other educational facility. You're right – most schools, if they felt they had no hope of rehabilitating a student, would reject her candidacy. But you have to understand that Hidden Oak is the last chance for the students who come here. The alternatives are grim: foster families, juvenile detention, or life on the streets."

"Doc, sorry, but I find it hard to believe that you've *ever* told anyone's parents that their kid isn't worth fixing. You soak in the tuition money, lie to the parents, and keep the undesirables locked away."

"Despite your incredibly childish recent actions, I've generally found you to demonstrate a striking maturity. Don't make me question that analysis."

"I don't think I'm being childish at all, Doctor. I mean, *Headmistress*."

"I worked in standard therapeutic boarding schools throughout my early professional life, and I watched it happen time and time again: Half the girls got better, while the other half declined further into their neuroses, no matter how many therapies or medications we threw at them."

She pushed back in her chair a little and looked at me hard before continuing. "Indian Yogic philosophy says that 'man is a god, man is a demon.' Both are true – we are dualistic creatures, with competing urges between moral, rational behavior and unreasonable, selfish behavior. This idea is nothing revolutionary. Our dispositions are naturally closer to being either godly or demonic, and succeeding at behaving well is easier for some than others. Some of us lean toward virtue, some lean toward malevolence. Most of you girls lean toward malevolence, but we seek to aid you in pushing toward virtue."

I wanted to laugh. Did she really think that transparent mind games and "breeding group" were enough to turn us into submissive little saints?

"But what have you done that's helped us?" I challenged. "I don't think I've been taught any virtues, or anything."

"Moral education is not like teaching history or science. We are moral by inertia — the very fact that you are in a strict environment, prohibited from engaging in grand mischief for four years, is enough to steer you toward a better path. We don't need to have you in morality classes, outside of breeding group."

"Thank god."

"Some girls, Angela, aren't destined to win the struggle toward virtue. It's not entirely their fault: Too much happened too early in their lives, or they are too weak to fight against the biochemical realities of their minds. At some point, we have to stop blaming them and accept that they're not going to get better. Living a life in which you're constantly vilified and judged can only exacerbate an already unfortunate situation. Yogic thinking also says that lunacy is the result of fighting too long, and too vigorously, between one's virtuous and demonic urges. The purple thread girls are those we judge as being at risk of lunacy if pushed too far in a futile struggle."

"So you train them to be evil?"

"We leave them to their own dispositions."

"Huh," I said. "That sounds kind of nice."

"It's not. These are tortured girls. Tortured by their own minds."

"With a little help from Hidden Oak."

"I'm sorry?"

"I've seen Juin and Riley. I've seen their cuts and bruises and scabs."

"You can't really say those are caused by the school. The purple thread operates differently, as you'll find out."

"I'm sorry?"

"That's what you've wanted, isn't it?" Dr. Zsilinska said archly. "To be with the purple girls, the gritty ones? Angela, your behavior has been obvious: screaming for no reason, striking Mrs. Vienna. These acts aren't in your nature, and I know that. It's clearly self-sabotage."

"Sounds like you've decided it is, whether it is or not," I said.

"I don't think you know what you want."

And you have no idea that what I want is to get this school shut down. You have no idea who you're dealing with. Being able to keep my real goals hidden, Dr. Zsilinska, is one of my virtues.

"You're truly a borderline case. I've maintained since the start that you belong in the golden thread. Two of the primary qualities of golden thread girls are genuine self-awareness and a capacity for improvement. You show both. Dr. Spicer argued that your obvious willingness to lie to me during sessions, for example, about your true role in the death of your grandfather, and your blatant willingness to flout our rules and scapegoat Carmen all point to entrenched borderline personality disorder. If when you first met Mrs. Vienna she seemed surprised to find you in the golden thread, it was because Dr. Spicer had already convinced her of your unsuitability. I had overridden her recommendation. I do this very rarely, Angela.

"As for why we haven't put a stop to your misbehavior, the reason is that I've treated you as a potential purple thread case. I can only judge what you're made of by giving you the latitude to act as your natural inclinations lead you. My diagnosis remains that you're a good girl with terrible priorities. But your actions since you've arrived say that you're a bad girl, over and done."

There was something about the way she said *over and done* that scared me. I'd failed her; I could see her sympathy dying.

"I've rarely seen a student with such nerve, which speaks for your potential to go far in either direction. I've been on the fence from the start, but since you're obviously bent on joining the purple thread, Mrs. Vienna will escort you from here to their quarters. Someone will fetch your uniforms. I'm afraid you won't be able to say good-bye to any of your gold thread friends." She smiled. "But there's always your 'secret' Saturday night slumber parties, if you manage to sneak out to go to them."

"I can't even see Carmen?" I asked. "She didn't do anything, so you better not punish her."

"Carmen will be punished, as she ought to be," Zsilinska said. "Rules must be adhered to. But Carmen's well-being should no longer be any of your concern. You have larger issues to worry about."

"What are you going to tell my parents?"

"To be honest, Angela, I'll add your recent transgressions to your record and send a copy of the whole file to them. I'll explain that you've been sent to our more secure facility. I've never had a parent put up a fuss."

"Can I have a second to think this through?"

"You've made your decision. I won't be troubling you with counseling sessions anymore. I can only advise you to remember one thing: Once you join the purple thread, the faculty is hardly your greatest enemy."

"Are you going to tell *that* to my parents, too?" I said.

But Dr. Zsilinska wasn't listening to me anymore.

"Mrs. Vienna will take you away now," she said. "I'm sorry about this, Angela. And if you don't know why I'm apologizing, you will soon."

Chapter Thirty-three

When I left Zsilinska's office, I found Mrs. Vienna waiting in the hallway. She didn't hear me at first, and I caught her in a bored moment — she was standing next to the window, staring at her nails. I have to say, she wasn't too heinous-looking right then. Her fluffy shirt, which normally fell on her body in weird angles, was smoothed flatteringly this time, and her expression — well, she looked really vulnerable. Like she wasn't sure about anything, like being this school's head bitch might be a drag for her, like she wasn't sure if she was doing any good. I know that when you're drafted to be the one to lead and make hard decisions, it can be really lonely. Like with Trevor — he was such a slacker that even a pseudo-slacker like me had to be the nag, the one who had to say we couldn't keep playing pool if we were out of money, or that if we didn't leave the mini-golf place we'd miss his DMV appointment, that random stuff. Anyway, I only saw inside Mrs. Vienna for a second. As soon as she noticed me I watched her ass-hole shield go up.

"I assume you've heard the good news?" she said, barely containing her malice.

"I'm going into the purple thread," I said sullenly, mainly because I thought any tone of excitement or wonder would be punished.

"That's right," she said, grabbing a bag full of the striped-overall uniforms and handing it to me. "Your third home in so many months. A Hidden Oak record."

"Super."

We had arrived at the bottom of the stairs, and stepped into the network of steam tunnels. I picked one pipe running along the wall and followed it with my eyes, trying to remember its twists and turns and odd patches of rust, like Hansel marking his way through the forest.

"I bet I'll still be seeing you, won't I, Mrs. Vienna?" I said.

She laughed. She'd always been one to appreciate the jabs of students, provided they were sly and not fully offensive. "You won't be seeing the faculty much at all, I'm afraid, Cardenas. For three hours each afternoon, you have to obey us. The rest of your time, how you live is up to you. Or, rather, it's up to your classmates."

"That doesn't sound like great education," I said, trying to squeeze the fear from my voice.

"You had your chance to get a 'great education' back when you were in the gold thread. Now you're getting what you actually deserve."

"What the hell are you doing working at a school, anyway, if you hate us all so much?"

We were turning a bend, and she paused before continuing, casually leaning against a pipe, like we were chatting in a crowded bar. "Very few people really care about damaged girls, Angela. Not the police, not the department of education, not most teachers, not your parents or lovers. The ones who care are *us*, those who founded the only institution left with the inspiration and capacity to help you. And we're treating you as well as you allow us to. Which, in your case, admittedly, won't be that well at all." She started walking again.

"I hate this," I said.

"No, you hate *you*. And finally, you'll be in an environment that's no better than what you believe you deserve. We're here."

She'd come to a nondescript door, one of dozens along the winding underground hallway. She unlocked one, two, and three locks, then slid a steel bar across. "After you," she said, yanking the rusty door open.

I passed unused boilers rusting on their sides, and a fire hose unfurled and lying in a flat coil like a bludgeoned snake. I mounted steel steps that led from the hallway to another door, and waited until Mrs. Vienna caught up. "This is the entrance to the purple thread," she said. "I'm afraid I won't be joining you. We have a pact with the girls in the thread — complete self-government except from two to five in the afternoon."

"Is there anything else I should know?" I asked.

"No rules, and no appealing to us based on anything that happens in here. If we find hard evidence of wrongdoing, only then will we administer punishments. In matters for which there's no evidence, you're free to police yourselves. Tutoring and delivery of raw food supplies occur during the afternoon hours. You're limited to this one space. You're free to stay in this room or roam the steam tunnels, but you may not leave the tunnels – indeed, you will find your way securely barred. I suggest you always stay in full view of the other girls. Whenever you allow yourself to be out of view, you risk an assault that cannot be verified by anyone else. I won't be back until tomorrow afternoon. Good-bye."

I waited until I heard Mrs. Vienna leave and finish relocking the steam tunnel exit before I pulled the door. It cracked open and then stuck on the uneven steel floor. I gave it another heave, and it screeched wide.

The purple thread's home had clearly once been a gymnasium. Frayed climbing ropes hung from the ceiling, and a couple of peg-boards were mounted on the walls. The rest of the space, walls and floors together, were covered in shiny and discolored white tile, illuminated by caged industrial lamps suspended from the ceiling.

Hammocks had been hung in the corners, out of which emerged the occasional arm or leg of a dozing girl. The floor along the edges of the gymnasium was covered in twisted bedsheets, bits of food, strewn clothes. In the middle was a pile of large odds and ends – empty crates, an old bike frame, limp pillows, a stack of cardboard – that some girls were lounging on like it was living room furniture. In the far

245

corner were the entrances to the locker rooms, which girls guarded, dozing against the tiled wall. In the nearest corner was a hoard of food — bags of cereal, crates of wilted lettuce, and damaged boxes of cookies and snacks, crushed and strewn along the floor in swirly patterns. Behind an unplugged fridge stood a couple of water barrels sitting in shallow puddles, bent tin ladles chained to their rims.

The screech of the door seemed to have frozen all the activity in the room. A girl with a shaved head looked up from picking cheese curls out of a pile of spilled snack mix. The girls in the center paused their game of homemade cards. A muscley girl climbing a rope, and the small audience watching her, all turned to stare. Nearest to me was a dozing girl with a freckled face, severe black bangs, and a huge ass. She snorted, got up, and stood in front of me. Her olive green uniform made her look like a drill sergeant.

"They send someone new?" she asked. "This late in the year? What's your name?"

"I'm Angela," I said. "Is Juin here?"

"'Is Juin here?'! Uh-uh, you're with me. I'm Calista. Come on, I'll get you set up." She grabbed my arm and led me toward a set of hammocks.

"Ha!" I heard a girl next to the rope climb say. "Calista's got herself another troll."

"Don't listen to that, you're no troll," Calista said to me, confidentially. "You're just gonna stick with the one who can protect you."

Calista stopped in the middle of a set of three hammocks. "This is our spot," she said. "Those're Teresa, Shayla, and

Isabella." Girls' greasy faces appeared from the hammocks, staring at me balefully.

Calista got on her hands and knees and lifted one of the hammocks with her shoulder, rummaging around beneath. The girl resting inside cursed weakly. Some stray light illuminated her face, and I saw Teresa from the mansion. I guessed all of her stunts — capped by the hoarded medication — got her thrown directly into the purple thread.

"We don't have another hammock set up yet, but I've got a spare sheet," Calista said. "We'll get you strung up; hold on."

I wasn't sure I wanted to be strung up.

Teresa kept protesting. "Shut the hell up," Calista said, punching her thigh through the hammock. "This morning they doubled Teresa's dose of painkillers, so she's gonna be a space cadet for a while. What the hell? I have another sheet here, I know it."

"What do you think you're doing?" came Juin's voice. I turned to see her standing at the center of the gym, beaming fire at Calista. "Like hell Angela's staying with you sluts."

"Don't you dare cross over here!" Calista shrieked.

Juin gestured broadly at her feet. "Do you see me crossing the line, bitch? Come over here, Angela. Now."

Though irked to be ordered around, even by Juin, I crossed the gym to her. Juin slung her arm around me and guided me toward the wall, ignoring Calista's yelled curses. "Sorry for the tone," she said breezily, "but getting by in this hole's all about showing authority. We've got a little turf war going on."

She stopped at a similar bank of hammocks. "There should be a hammock at the bottom of that bag Vienna left you. Calista's been here so long, she probably forgot they send you in with one."

Sure enough, there was one in my bag. As we worked on setting it up, Juin grilled me.

"So what did you do to get sent here?" she asked. "Rob the commissary? Poison Vienna?"

"Close," I said. "I punched her. But it turns out most of the administrators thought I was meant to be in the purple thread, anyway. I guess I didn't really need to hit her — but I really wanted to."

"Attagirl," Juin said. "Best to go violent before they've really decided about you. If I punched Vienna now, they'd kill me. Fully serious. It's not as though they haven't killed girls before."

"What do you mean?" I asked.

Another voice chimed in. "They're monsters." I saw Riley standing against the wall, quiet and staring. She'd been watching me the whole time.

"Who'd they kill?" I asked. Honestly, I found it unlikely. Zsilinska might be wrongheaded and willfully negligent, but I didn't see full-on murder as part of her master plan.

"Are we really going to get into this now?" Juin sighed. "Fine. That girl you kept going on about, what's her name, Pillar?"

I sucked in my breath. "My cousin? Pilar Felix?"

"Yeah, that's the one. Was she always that sickly? It's like she was allergic to air, and last week they sent us this bread

248

that was made from almonds or some crap she wasn't supposed to eat. She went into shock, right here in the middle of the floor. No faculty was scheduled to come until hours later, so she kinda stopped breathing while we stood around her. Her lips were blue when they arrived."

I didn't say anything; it's like I stopped living for a second, and only slowly revived. "There's no . . . like no safety alarm or anything?"

Riley shook her head. "This is purgatory," she whispered. "And we get sent down to hell one by one."

Juin punched Riley on the arm. "Riley's our resident cheerleader, aren't you, Riles?"

Pilar was dead. I remembered the last time I had seen her, years ago, sneaking an extra piece of wedding cake at one of the rare family weddings she actually attended. And she had died a week ago, right here in this crummy barracks of a dorm, because of this criminal, willful *neglect*.

"Whoa," Juin said, watching me closely. "How are you feeling?"

"I can't believe this," I said. I tore down the hammock, wrapped myself in it, and sat on the floor, punching the tiles until they were smeared with blood from my fingers. "I can't can't can't believe this!"

"Wow," Juin said. "You *are* purple thread." She sat next to me and nonchalantly draped an arm over my shoulder. "Don't worry, we've got a plan."

"You've replaced her," Riley whispered, her voice and mind equally cracked. "They only have twenty of us here at a time. Pilar's dead, so you're the new Pilar."

"Don't be so creepy," I told her.

"Hey," Juin said, "Riley's on our side here. No infighting. It's tough enough with Calista's ogres over there."

"It's the truth," Riley said. "You've got to take the truth."

"Is that so, spaz?" I asked.

"Riley's got a neurological problem," Juin said. "But turns out it was having to go to classes that made her nervous. She's doing better here."

Riley stared at me, glittering.

"Can you guys leave me alone for a few minutes?" I asked, still huddled in the hammock fabric. I kissed my bloody knuckles.

Juin looked around, grinning. "Um, hate to break it to you, but there ain't no alone anymore."

Chapter Thirty-four

By cursing long and hard enough at the shaved-head girl guarding the food, Riley got her to allow us a few rolls and a hunk of meat. Juin led us into the steam tunnels. "We usually take our dinner underground, don't we, Riles? Walk and munch. Our daily constitutional. I was hoping Vienna would have left that entrance door open after she airlifted you in. I keep waiting for her to screw up, so we can really cause some trouble."

I was so glad to be out of that gymnasium, not to be exposed any longer to the hostile stares of the other purple thread girls. We passed through vacant chambers and dark tunnels, our sneakers making sucking sounds on the damp concrete. Juin and Riley strode along with total confidence, like they'd evolved into new and alien creatures here, agilely ducking under pipes and swinging around corners.

"So what's this plan you have to get us out?" I asked.

"You fought to go purple, and now you're ready to fight to get back out, huh?" Juin said, unfolding a cloth bundle and handing me a roll and a slick chunk of turkey. "That was quick. Well, first thing we do is get some evidence. And the best evidence has got to be those video recordings you told us about."

"I saw them playing in Zsilinska's office," I said, remembering when she'd played the footage of me dismantling the camera.

"Yeah, they *play* there," Juin said. "But where are the masters? Gotta be the headmistress's office. You see anything while you were there? Discs or hard drives?"

I shook my head. "No, but I was pretty distracted. And even if we get evidence, how do we get away? There's no escaping on foot, not with all the snow. That's how those boys died, long ago."

"I've got an inside with a faculty member," Juin said, smiling cryptically. "I'll ride out with them, and then get the word out. Then the school will be done with. All of us free girls."

Riley shuddered. "Never free. We will be free."

I stared at her. Juin raised an eyebrow that told me not to ask about any of Riley's oddities. "Who's this faculty member?" I asked.

"Can't say. If anyone finds out, we're all done for."

"You drama queen! Tell me. Or do you not actually have one?"

"Oh, I have one." The pleasure behind her smile was unmistakable. She had someone under her finger, all right.

As we walked farther away from the gymnasium, I realized there was a sprawling hidden side of Hidden Oak, a dark underground layer running beneath the daylight world. The air chilled as we walked. When I wrapped my arms tightly around my chest and asked where we'd wandered to that was so cold, I saw we'd arrived back at the gymnasium door. Juin rapped against a pipe running along the wall. It rang out hollowly. "Welcome to the purple thread nights. No heating, just whatever warmth we catch that's in transit to the girls who matter." Juin paused, her back against the door. "Get ready," she said.

I tensed, wondering what I had to be ready for. Juin pushed open the door and fell into a defensive position, back tensed and fists raised.

All that came from the gymnasium was a cold wind, the creaking of hammocks and the sound of quiet conversations. "All clear," Juin whispered as she straightened up. "Jumping us on the way back from walks is Calista's favorite trick."

"Be a jumper. Jump or be jumped," Riley said to me severely.

Juin scruffed her hair good-naturedly. "Good one, Riles."

"What is *wrong* with her?" I asked Juin as we passed into the gymnasium. But she didn't answer me. As for Riley, she didn't even react, just played with the ends of her hair.

I didn't sleep much that night. Chilly gusts passed straight through the hammocks' netting. When I wasn't dozing I could see, elsewhere in the gym, other restless eyes gleaming in the scarce moonlight that passed through the high barred windows.

I snoozed more once dawn came, once the gymnasium was slightly warmer and no longer as dark and unknowable. I was woken, though, by a horrible bashing noise right by my head. Juin and Riley rolled over and ignored it, but I sprang out of the hammock. A girl was standing over the water barrel right near my head, striking the surface with the metal ladle.

I watched her, wondering what the hell she was doing. Then, as I saw sprays of frost, I realized she was breaking through the ice layer that must have formed on the surface. She slurped some water from the ladle and returned to Calista's side of the gym. Suddenly thirsty, and ready to stretch my sore legs, I placed one foot and then the other on the cold floor, then crept over to the barrel. I had nearly gotten the ladle to my mouth when I heard a voice, right at my elbow, telling me to stop.

I spun around. It was Calista. She had clearly just gotten out of bed – her greasy hair fanned behind her in erratic waves. "Were you planning on slurping your germs into *our* water? We'd take that from one of our own, but not from one of Juin's bitches. Go get a cup."

"Fine," I said. "Where are the cups?"

"Oh! That's too bad – they've all been taken."

I recognized this as the insecure game that it was – Calista wanted to control something, to feel she had some power over her world, so she exaggerated this gang concept to feel important. But knowing what was going on wouldn't stop it from ruining my life. I was pissed about how dumb and predictable it was, and I guess my face said so.

"What, Miss Prissy Chica, you don't think you need to play by the rules, here?" Calista taunted. "You too good for all this?"

"I just don't think we need to be all divided," I said. "We should be going after the assholes who put us in here."

"You know," Calista said, suddenly switching course and placing a hand on my shoulder, "you're totally right."

I didn't believe it for a second. "Screw you," I said. Then, never removing my gaze from hers, I lifted a ladleful of water to my mouth.

She grabbed my hand and smacked the ladle hard against my cheek. I tasted blood. The water spilled down my shirt, a freezing shock.

"You're going to pay for that," I said, and lunged at her. We crashed onto the cold cement. My arms were instantly around her head, my fingers lost in the oily mass of her hair. I reared up to smack her skull into the floor.

But then hands were on me, and I was pulled away. A couple of girls I couldn't see held me in the air. Calista was still on the ground, leaning against the water barrel. Teresa moved from her side and approached me. She placed her palm against my nose and then pressed. My cartilage creaked. "No," she said into my ear, then gestured to the others that I should be released.

"You're going to love where this just got you. Just wait and see," Calista said, standing and shaking the floor crud from her clothes.

255

I stood by my hammock as Calista and her gang returned to their side of the gym.

Clearly there was one thing about me that Hidden Oak hadn't changed: I was still good at making new friends.

"So much for cooperating with Calista's side," I said to Juin and Riley once they'd woken up and we were back in the steam tunnels. We were standing around one of the biggest pipes, absorbing the heat.

"Uh, yeah, Mrs. Care Bear. I already told you that."

"I thought at least I could get a couple of her bitches to cross over to our side. And, yeah, call me Mrs. Care Bear, Mrs. Snoring-Away-While-Angela-Wrestles-the-Ogre."

"Hate," Riley said, crossing her hands in satisfaction, like she'd just explained everything.

Later that day I went to the bathroom and glimpsed, as I turned to lock the stall door, Teresa lurking around my hammock. Once I returned I discovered that she'd put rat droppings in my socks. But that was fine, actually, because I was in the process of dunking Calista's hammock (stealthily ripped down by Riley) in the nasty toilet that no one used.

Our feuding went on from there. In the middle of the night Juin plopped down on our side's toilet and found the seat had been ripped away, so she sat against filthy brown-white, cold porcelain. That next day, having been tipped off that Calista's squad was planning on following us into the tunnels and jumping us, we spent the morning before tutoring sessions loosening screws on a steam pipe. When the bitches came after us, they passed near the pipe. Juin and Riley and I shook the far side of it, making it burst and spray steam. Shayla had been in the lead, and wound up with a red welt on her face that looked just like Maine.

It all felt . . . not like a nightmare but like a gray horrible zone, the early part of a slasher movie when it's not scary yet, but all tense and unpleasant. I guess it could have been far worse. There was an obscure honor code to our mischief: Calista made our lives miserable, but never did anything lethal; when we fought back we left her side bruised and crying, but never bleeding (too much) or broken. Zsilinska's dire warnings about trusting no one were overstated. As I met more of the purple thread girls, I discovered that they had done what they could to save Pilar, all of them. Some splashed cold water on her blue face, some beat on her chest with their fists.

Which is way more than we could say for the faculty, who had locked us away without hope of rescue or even medical attention. Really, who were the evil ones? Why were *we* considered hopeless?

I was pissed about it, don't get me wrong, but I guess I wasn't that shocked to have been given up on. Most other kids grow up with some essential trust of adults — they know that even if their parents are strict or mean or plain wrong, they still have good intentions at the core. Or even if your parents abuse you, or whatever, some other adult will step in and save the day. But what had brought our particular group of girls to Hidden Oak, and to the purple thread in particular, were childhoods in which that faith had been ripped

257

away. We relied solely on ourselves, and occasionally one another, and had no illusions that someone would put out a safety net if we started to fall. This neglect of the purple thread made me angry, sure, but not indignant or surprised. I knew that I hadn't ever received much better, and probably didn't deserve it, either.

The tutoring sessions with Derrian and Alsanz were haphazard. Some days both would come, some days only one, and many days neither. Some days we'd meet in groups, some days individually. We never had tests because no two of us seemed to be learning the same material at the same time. They didn't seem to know what they were going to teach when they came, and just kind of winged it. We took what we got, and gave the teachers as much grief as we could, but still looked forward to the distraction of their arrival.

Juin always had solo sessions with Mr. Derrian. I was jealous — I actually wanted to have more time to talk about biology, anything academic that would confirm there was still a world outside the gymnasium. I also wanted to work my way further into his compassion so that I could get an answer about how Carmen was doing, and whether Harrison cared that I was here. I wanted to take that tortured sympathy I saw in Derrian's eyes and use it as a wedge to get the things I needed. But all I could do was stare pleadingly while he prattled on about bivalves or the evolution of donkeys or whatever. Finally, one day when I turned in a worksheet, I wrote *please ask to see me alone* at the bottom.

I watched him grade the worksheets while we were doing our reading, saw him get to mine and read the note without even reacting. The next day when Juin and I went to look at the posted schedule, we saw that it was me listed as meeting solo with Derrian, not her. "Thank god," I said. "About time you shared the wealth."

Juin looked surprisingly angry. "What does he want to meet with *you* alone for?"

"Gee, thanks." That was all I said. I couldn't exactly say why I didn't trust the truth with her, but I didn't.

Derrian and I met in the old Heath coach's office at the back of the locker room. A lot of the girls would hang out half-naked in there, so before Derrian and I could meet, I had to go first and call out to warn everyone a man was coming in. Telling Derrian it was all clear made me feel a little protective of him, like he couldn't get by without my help. I picked up some stray dirty clothes from the floor to clear him a pathway.

Once we'd arranged ourselves in the cramped and pink-tiled room, and Derrian was pulling out his books and placing them on the creaky desk, I asked him to tell me what he knew about Carmen's whereabouts.

He looked surprised. "Carmen? She's fine."

"She's back in the dorms?"

He squinted through his heavy glasses. "Where else would she be?"

Derrian clearly didn't know that Carmen had ever been in Vienna's dungeon. Which meant she couldn't have been in there long. Suddenly my concern for her turned to irritation. Why was she allowed to go free while I got stuck in this pit? She probably promised she'd never have anything to do with me, that she knew I'd been a bad influence all along, and she was relieved to have me gone. Maybe she actually meant it. Maybe she was on their side now. I couldn't think of any other reason Vienna would let her go, except to use her.

"And what about Harrison?" I asked.

"What is this, Angela, social hour?"

"I just wanted to make sure everyone's okay."

"Well, he's fine. Pull out a half-sheet of paper, please."

I did. "Actually," Derrian said slowly, watching me curiously as he relented, "my son asks about you more than he probably should."

"Oh?" I said. Calmly.

"He's even tried, once or twice, to come with me to see you."

"How funny," I said, hoping Derrian couldn't see my pulse thumping in my veins.

"Of course I said he couldn't."

"Right. That would be weird."

He laid a hand down on the tabletop. His fingers were a gummy gray color, with purplish creases at the knuckles. "Angela, I don't know what might have happened between you and my son, but whatever you think you're hiding from the administration, you're probably not. You understand that any misbehavior you got into, or manage to get into, will implicate Harrison. And having my son implicated puts my own job in jeopardy. Getting me fired would be very stupid, Angela, because I am one of your very few allies. You do understand that, right?"

"Of course."

His hand lingered on my shoulder as he stood and crossed behind me. "I'm glad. Now. Cellular respiration."

I wasn't going to learn anything else from him.

At least, not today.

Chapter Thirty-five

That evening some new food was rolled in, and Juin and I joined the swarm of girls picking over the supplies. Four crates of stale crackers and four burlap sacks of dried beans. "Where's Riley?" I asked. She was the best at getting to the supplies first, with her wiry body and animal daring.

Juin pointed dismissively at the far side of the gym, then continued to stuff beans into a pouch she'd made in the fabric of her shirt. Riley was standing against a wall of folded bleachers, rocking her head against the wood.

"What happened to her?" I asked.

"Slowly but surely going from crazy-fun to crazy-psycho."

"Should I go talk to her?"

Juin discovered a bruised pear at the bottom of a box and held it up to the light, inspecting it. "Nuh-uh. She's turned into one of those slaughterhouse pigs that go bonkers and start trying to eat their own tails. Talking's not going to help. She just has to get out of here. We all have to get out of here; Riley's just the one showing it first. If we want to keep her sane, the clock's ticking. I'd give her a couple days."

We periodically glanced at her as we rummaged through the food. The bleachers gave a rattling bump every time she knocked her head.

Once I had as much food as I could carry, I started across the gymnasium. Calista and some of her bitches detached and positioned themselves between me and our side.

Calista pointed to Riley. "Your crazy friend wandered over to our side. We'll let you know when we're ready to send her back over."

"The bleachers aren't on your side. They're totally middle ground," I said. I regretted it immediately. I shouldn't have even been talking to her.

"Hey, you've actually got tits today," Calista said to Juin, behind me.

Juin rummaged a tangerine out of her shirt. "This?" she asked, and launched it. It flew between Calista and Shayla and clattered into the bleachers.

"Good one," Calista said.

"No worries, plenty more," Juin said, and launched another.

Teresa caught it and sent it back, hitting me in the gut and spraying me with orange mist. I dropped all my food and got ready to hurl the bits of fruit back when I saw Riley silently steal over to Calista.

"No no no," Juin quietly seethed.

Riley fitted her fingers over Calista's throat and began to squeeze. Calista spun and tried to scratch Riley away, but Riley was relentless, shrieking, and soon had Calista kneeling on the floor. Teresa and Shayla and Isabella were pulling on Riley, yanking out fistfuls of her hair, but she didn't let go. She just held on and closed her fingers tighter and tighter.

Riley was scratched and bloody by the time we broke through to her. Girls formed a taunting ring around us as Juin and I tried to coax Riley off. She wouldn't relax her grip, though, not even by a bit, and Calista's desperate coughs kept getting weaker and wetter. Her eyelids made fluttery motions. Shayla yanked on Riley's hair so violently that a piece of scalp came away, which made Juin let go of Riley and launch on Shayla instead. They rolled together, screaming and hitting. I scooted over so I was staring right into Riley's eyes. She was smiling grimly, and looked more alive than I'd seen her in weeks.

When Calista finally went limp, Riley let go of her and looked up at me proudly. Out of all the room, she chose me to concentrate on, with this expression like she'd done something great, like she expected to be rewarded.

Calista took a huge, swooping breath.

Calista's bitches were all over her, babbling to her and slapping her and trying to get her to stand up. I just stood there, paralyzed by the weirdness of the eager cultist look Riley was giving me.

"Let's go, ladies," Juin said in the calm tone she got when what she was saying was urgent.

"We've got to make sure Calista's okay," I said.

"That's exactly it, sweetcakes. She's standing up."

Calista had stopped sputtering and had lurched to her feet. I grabbed Riley by the elbow. We were all safe on our side of the gymnasium, with plenty of our own bitches backing us up, by the time Calista could get her side assembled.

"You're dead!" she screeched hoarsely. "The minute you fall asleep, you're all dead!"

Riley yelled something incomprehensible back and made little scratching motions in the air. At the sight of Riley's bizarre gesture, Calista finally cracked. "You're not going to do *anything*," she warned. Then she ran to the exit and banged her fist against the locked door. "Mrs. Vienna! Mrs. Vienna! They're trying to kill me!"

The whole gymnasium fell silent. Calista had broken an unspoken rule: We might have made enemies of one another, but the administration was the Enemy.

"Mrs. Vienna!" Juin called, and made baby-sucking-on-tit noises.

Calista whirled around, her sweaty hair whipping in her face. "Shut up!"

I looked closely at Calista's side. Isabella was awkwardly laying her hand on Calista's neck, Shayla was staring at her feet, embarrassed, and Teresa was regarding her leader with something that I was pretty sure was contempt.

"She's got some link to the administration," I said to Juin.

"Don't I know it," she replied, looking at Calista curiously from across the gymnasium. "And doesn't everyone else, now."

Chapter Thirty-six

But what could Calista's link to the administration be, really? I never saw her talk to them. Dr. Spicer and Mrs. Vienna were rarely present, and even when they were they never really said much, only observed and took notes and whispered things to each other with their noses pointed over their shoulders. I certainly never caught them having private conversations with any girls. They walked through us like they were in a zoo filled with exotic and dangerous animals.

The day after Riley nearly killed Calista, Juin and I met with Alsanz. She was trying to bully us through a short story when Dr. Spicer appeared behind the gymnasium stairwell. "Angela, you need to follow me," she said.

"What'd she do?" Juin asked.

"Now." I headed toward my hammock, so I could put my notebook away. "Don't bother with that. Just follow me."

Spicer and I headed out the locked doors and down the steam tunnels toward the main school. "Can I ask where we're going?" I said.

She didn't answer, but I could see I'd fired some charge of energy within her; she sped up and walked a few paces ahead. When I tried to catch up, she sped up even more.

We passed up a stairwell and into the administration offices. Zsilinska was waiting in the hallway. "Hello, Angela," she said. "I trust everything is well?"

"Screw you."

She looked genuinely hurt. "If you're having problems, I want you to tell me."

I didn't know how to answer. I hadn't even seen her in more than a month — how the hell did she expect me to tell her about any problems?

"Angela, I need to remind you of a few things," Dr. Spicer said.

"Don't," Zsilinska said, putting up a hand. "She doesn't need coaching."

"What's going on?" I asked.

"You have a visitor," Zsilinska said.

Chapter Thirty-seven

Trevor, I thought, excited despite myself. *Trevor's made it.* *He got my e-mails, and that last one from him was a fake.* I felt excited but all jumbled up by the idea of seeing him. Like it was the morning of my birthday, when I was perfectly aware everyone'd forgotten it. I was glad he'd come for me, even if he was still a dickhead.

Zsilinska opened the door to the conference room before I could decide if I'd be scowling or smiling, but it didn't matter because seated at the other end was a woman dressed like she was going to church. She had the face I recognized, slathered in foundation two shades too light, those small porky eyes that only showed love once or twice a year, the patent leather pocketbook whose purchase had consumed far more attention than she had ever devoted to, say, picking an appropriate educational facility for her child. I thought I couldn't have cared less about her, but the sight of her made me choke up.

"Mom?"

She stood up and mouthed my name, but no sound came out. She reached out her arms to invite me into a hug, but Zsilinska laid a hand on my shoulder. "Mrs. Cardenas, as you know, I already have strong reservations about having you meet with your daughter. Physical contact is strictly out of the question. Have a seat, Angela."

I was shocked to hear Zsilinska speak to my mother in the same tone she'd use for one of us, and it made me feel more angry than anything I'd felt for my own sake. If my mom had seemed wounded with what Zsilinska said, I probably would have started fighting. But she looked cowed by her. We sat down at the table, me and Mom at either end and Zsilinska in the middle, her cone of yellow hair at a slant.

"Your mother came to visit you at great expense and difficulty," Zsilinska said admonishingly.

"Thanks?" I said.

"She came because she was called by another family member about the incident involving Pilar Felix. As you both know by now, ten days ago Pilar was rushed to the hospital in anaphylactic shock, but was unfortunately delayed because of the snows. [clack] Your mother wants to make sure you're safe, Angela."

"It's terrible here," I said in Spanish. "Please please get me out."

"I feel obligated to inform you," Zsilinska said, "that I speak Spanish."

"I've been starved and punished, they're not teaching me anything. Pilar died because she was locked away, and they only watch over us for a few hours a day, otherwise it's just these brutal girls beating on each other —"

"You'll notice," Zsilinska said briskly, "that your daughter's capacity for exaggeration has not diminished."

My mother stared at the space between the two of us, her face a mask.

"You have to believe me, Mom," I said. "They're running this like a prison."

"I will *not*," Zsilinska said, "let this become an accusation session. That is precisely the kind of indulgence I cannot tolerate. If, Mrs. Cardenas, you believe your daughter's ravings, take her away now and leave me to educate the others. And, Angela, if you notice there are prison-like elements to Hidden Oak, then I might remind you that, as a school of last resort, your next alternative is indeed prison. Yes, we're not Exeter. But you're not an Exeter girl."

"Mama," I said in Spanish, my voice cracking, "I'm going to die here. Do you know twenty boys died here years ago? In these same buildings? They're *killing* us."

"The only similarity between Hidden Oak and Heath is the campus, Angela."

"That's exactly it. We're locked in. If a fire broke out . . ."

"Yes, Angela, Mrs. Vienna has clearly noted your propensities toward pyromania in your record."

I stared at her and blinked. Pyromania? They might be able to check off every other box, but I'd not so much as lit a match while at Hidden Oak. I opened my mouth to speak, then was shocked dumb when I saw my mother nodding.

"Mrs. Cardenas," Dr. Zsilinska said, "I arranged this meeting so you could see that your daughter is alive and well. And she is, as you can see, as spirited as ever." She pushed a thick manila folder across the table. "This is a catalog of only the highlights of Angela's misbehavior while at Hidden Oak. You have, of course, seen some of it before – but there are some things I haven't sent you. You might find it informative as you make your decision on whether to withdraw her. But in the meantime, I ask that we not continue this meeting any further. We've already set Angela back in the therapeutic process by letting her see you at all."

"Are you saying that I am a bad influence?" my mother asked. She was so clearly the woman I remembered from my old life: the same old feisty confusion, the quickness to take things personally, her caring most about how she came off. I was nostalgic for it all, suddenly.

"No. What I'm saying is that Angela has not reached her potential in her old environment. The only way to give her a last chance is to sever all ties to her old life while she remains here. You were informed of the school's philosophy on the matter when you enrolled her."

"Angela," my mother said, "do you truly, truly want to leave?"

I didn't hesitate. "Yes."

Zsilinska set her palms down on the table and stood. "Fine. I'll remind you that the year's tuition is nonrefundable, and that the school's official exit recommendation will be for a semi-incarceration facility. If there are none near

Roanoke, you'll need to find a boarding school appropriate for delinquents. With her disciplinary record included in the transcript, you'd be lucky to find a school that will take her."

"I have not said I'm withdrawing her," my mother said.

"You didn't need to. I'm a psychologist, Mrs. Cardenas. I can read what you're feeling."

Zsilinska might have been a psychologist, but she should have known not to take too severe a tone with my mother. Mom sniffed, adjusted her pillbox hat, and stood, beckoning me to follow her. We headed out of the office, my mom muttering curses in Spanish.

"The suitcase you arrived with is in storage, Angela," Zsilinska said. "Mrs. Vienna has offered to escort you to get it. I'm afraid you'll have to wait here with me, Mrs. Cardenas, for your own security. We don't allow visitors into the main campus while students are present."

Vienna was waiting at the end of the hallway, staring at us stonily, her arms crossed. I wanted to walk out of the doors and forget about my suitcase. But my mom crossed her lace-gloved hands and said she'd wait. When I looked at her, pleading for us to just leave, she gestured me away, toward Vienna. At that moment, I couldn't argue. She was my savior; I would have done anything she suggested. I allowed Vienna to escort me for the last time.

Chapter Thirty-eight

Vienna led me across the snow-covered grass. I expected her to say something harsh, that I was selfish and weak to abandon my friends, or that I'd better not spill any of Hidden Oak's secrets to the outside world. But she seemed moody and abstracted, like she had forty other things on her mind.

We stopped outside the abandoned boys' dorm. They hadn't bothered to give me a coat to put on. I couldn't stop shivering, and I could feel the snow seeping into my sneakers. Vienna unlocked the main door and flicked a light switch. Most of the lights stayed dark, but a couple of the old lamps slowly blinked on. "Your suitcase is in the end room on the left," she said. "I know exactly which one is yours, so don't try to nab anyone else's. Here's the key to the room."

I bit back a hot response. Now that I was almost free, I wasn't about to fall for any of Vienna's bait.

Vienna might not know, of course, that I was already

familiar with this hallway, so I took my time heading along, pretending it was all new. The ancient wooden floorboards creaked under my feet, and I shivered as the realization came back to me that I was back in the same place where all those boys had died. At the end was one of the sealed rooms I had passed that afternoon when I'd first heard Riley in the tunnels. I fitted the key into the lock and pushed the door open.

It was full of our suitcases and backpacks, those remnants of our old lives. I slid between the cases until I reached mine, wiped the dust off the top, and hauled it toward the door. When I saw the red dust caked around the bottom, I remembered the day months earlier when I had lugged it up the dusty hill. I had been almost hopeful, then: What if Hidden Oak could have helped me? What if I had failed the school, rather than the other way around? I hated the place, but sometimes I still doubted.

I put the case down and pulled out the handle, the plastic hard and slick under my palm. As it clicked into place, I realized the air in the room wasn't as still as it should be — I wasn't alone. I whirled around, but I didn't see anyone else in the room. Had Vienna followed me in, untrusting to the very end? Or was it Harrison, having heard about my withdrawing and coming to say his final good-bye? Before I could turn and find out, I heard the flick and hiss of a match. Something flashed at the edge of my vision.

I spun and saw Calista in the doorway. In her hands was a plastic pail full of greasy, smoking rags.

"You're not going anywhere," she said.

She pitched the contents at me. I wasn't about to catch

anything Calista threw at me, especially if it was on fire, so I dodged, and the smoldering rags landed all around the room.

Flames. Everywhere.

Blood pounded in my head. I was being set up.

Calista bolted. For a second I followed her, then I stopped and turned back to the flaming rags. Some had fizzled out, but others, exposed to the dry air, had erupted. I stomped on the pile nearest me, and the fire seemed to dampen. But as soon as I lifted my wet sneaker, it was back as strong as ever. There was no way I could stop all the fires in time. Black smoke was already curling at the corners of the room. I began to feel it in my lungs.

I dashed down the hallway, my suitcase swerving and bouncing behind me. "Get back here!" I yelled. But Calista had vanished entirely.

When I got to the main door I reached to pull it open — but it was locked. I pulled and banged on it. "Open the door, open the door!" I could smell the tendrils of foul smoke creeping down the passage. "Please!"

I pressed myself against the wood. The fire was casting its own light in the hallway now, sending out yellow reflections that blended with the white fluorescence of the ceiling lights. I fell to the floor as smoke flooded the hallway. My throat was going hoarse from screaming. I was going to die there.

Then I remembered the broken window I'd once used to get inside.

I dashed to my feet, and was about to run down the hallway when I heard the door unlock. I squeezed the handle and threw it open, falling through to the ground.

"Angela," I heard Mrs. Vienna proclaim with artificial innocence, "what have you done?"

I breathed against the snow for a few seconds, then looked up. Vienna and Zsilinska and my mom, all shocked and shivering, were staring at the abandoned dormitory. I staggered to my feet.

The storage room was fully in flames, red and orange and even green bursts sprouting from every opening. The window frames were melting, dribbling globs of metal onto the ground. Plumes of smoke — black piped in gray — emerged from all the windows, spiraling together into evil-looking tornadoes that soared into the overcast sky.

"What have you done?" Mrs. Vienna asked, her voice rising. "Angela, what have you done?"

I stared at her in astonishment. She stood next to my mother, whose hand was over her mouth. Zsilinska had already run inside the main building, presumably to call the fire department.

"What is this," Vienna said, disgusted, "a send-off prank? Your final revenge?"

The thought of Calista's stupid grin, those piles of rags . . . why had the front door relocked, anyway, if not to make it look like I'd spent a suspicious amount of time inside? I screeched. "I didn't do this, Mom. They've set me up."

My mother looked at me blankly. What could I say to her? How could I explain why an administrator would arrange to have a student set fire to her own school?

No one was going to believe me.

Chapter Thirty-nine

The fire trucks eventually made their way through the snow, but not before the blaze had gutted the abandoned dorm. My mother and I had been directed into the administration building long before then, and I watched through a small window as the gold thread girls lined up outside the school to watch, bundled in overcoats and chattering excitedly, their rapid breaths pumping white puffs into the sky. I tried to find Carmen in the crowd, but didn't see her.

I caught occasional glimpses of the firefighters passing in and out of the school while my mother and I sat with Zsilinska. The headmistress was rubbing her temples and shaking her head. As I watched her, it struck me that she might not have been in on this at all, that the staged fire could have been Mrs. Vienna's inspiration.

"You have to know I wouldn't do this," I said. "Why would I?"

"I can't answer that," Zsilinska said wearily. "Though your mother and I would both surely agree that your past behavior has been erratic. Maybe you wanted to make a statement, and thought you would be out of here by the time the fire caught on. Maybe you were simply, as I've said time and again in our therapy, thinking about your present hostility and not your future well-being."

"Mom," I said. "They framed me, to make me have to stay." I paused. "I don't even have a lighter or matches!"

My mom and Zsilinska looked at me, frankly disbelieving. I glared hard at Zsilinska, but she didn't blink. It became even clearer that she might not know about what had actually happened — that it was all a vendetta hatched by Calista and Vienna.

"Believe me, Angela," Zsilinska said gently. "It wouldn't be in anyone's best interest to keep you here against your will. Especially now that you've committed arson. It simply doesn't make sense for us to keep you here."

"They don't want me to spill the secrets about what really happens at Hidden Oak," I told my mother. "Let me show you where they make me live, Mom. Talk to some of the other girls, and you'll see."

"Angela," Mom said slowly. "Angela, my poor child."

"No!" I said. "You can't do this. If you don't take me away, Mom, I'm running away."

"You can't," she said. "Have you seen the snow?"

"It's out of the question, Angela," Zsilinska said. "And frankly, I think the time for protestations has run out. My first reaction to what you've done is to *expel* you from Hidden Oak, not compel you to stay. Frankly, I agree entirely that it would be best for you to leave. I could hardly want you to remain, after the capacity you've just demonstrated. Self-destructiveness is one thing, but you could have hurt any number of people. The fire chief is coming to see me once the fire's fully put out — it will be up to me to let him know whether any criminal activity has taken place. Mrs. Cardenas, I'm sure you don't want to see Angela charged with felony arson. Nor do I, because I see in her the potential to be a productive member of society, as long as she continues to get the proper education.

"So long as we keep her in our most restrictive learning environment, I'm willing to tentatively offer Angela a continued place at Hidden Oak. Honestly, having her remain here is the only way I can see to avoid pressing criminal charges. I'd explain to the fire chief that she is under psychiatric restrictions, and it was a bureaucratic error on our part that led to putting her in a position to set a fire. If she wasn't going to stay at the school, I couldn't make the same argument, as she would no longer be under my care. So you see our options, Mrs. Cardenas." She said all of this with a tone of such wearied goodwill that for a moment I found myself almost thankful.

"You're saying it's either Hidden Oak or prison," my mom said.

I was on the verge of saying "I'll take prison," but I stopped myself. Would I really? I had friends at Hidden Oak, at least. I had the coven.

"What do you say, Angela?" my mom tried.

"I didn't do it!" I said, and watched some light inside her, already flickering, further dim.

"I think she should stay," my mother said quietly.

Zsilinska sighed and nodded. "I'll have to add extra psychiatric fees to the bill, I'm afraid. She'll require substantial supervision."

"Of course. Thank you for giving her this extra opportunity."

"This is the last fresh start I'll be able to offer Angela, I'm afraid," Zsilinska said.

"I understand," my mother said. "And so does Angela. Don't you?"

I stared through the window at the smoldering dormitory, realizing all over again that I had always been entirely alone.

Chapter Forty

The gymnasium door stuck as Vienna pulled it. For an irrational moment I hoped that maybe it would never open, that I'd never have to go back. But, with a shredding metal sound, it pulled free, and she and the HH pushed me through.

Scattered around the gymnasium, the purple thread girls stared at me with red, gummy eyes.

"Angela," Harrison had said in the brief moment we'd had together, his eyes searching mine for clues to what I'd been through, "you look like hell."

Vienna clapped her hands sharply. "I return your precious Angela to you, ladies."

There were only a few mutterings and scratchings as the girls shifted positions.

"And," she continued, "I know you'll all be interested to hear what she's just done."

He sprinted across the field as soon as they walked me out of the administration building, hurtled over a fence to get to me. Vienna had called out that he should keep back, but he'd grabbed my hand, anyway. When I finally made myself look at him, I saw his face set against a backdrop of smoldering embers and a haze of smoke from the abandoned dorm. It was strange to see him so concerned about me. Didn't he know I was worthless? Hadn't he figured out that I was doomed?

My mind was racing, and I couldn't stop my eyes from darting around. "Angela," he'd said.

Vienna threatened to sack his father if Harrison didn't back off, so he had no option but to obey. I didn't look back at him as we marched to the gymnasium.

When Vienna pushed me to the floor, I didn't resist. I just lay there and wondered if, by concentrating very hard, I could sink into the concrete and disappear.

"Angela," Vienna announced, "set fire to a dormitory."

A few scattered grunts of approval.

"The same dormitory that contained your belongings. They're all destroyed."

The girls stared at Vienna distrustfully. "She won't try to deny it, will you, Angela?" she said. "She'll just take your gratitude, in whatever manner you choose to offer it."

And she left.

I peered up, and then just held my head in my hands. I was surrounded by the enemy. And I couldn't even make myself move.

Juin got to me before Calista did, thank god, and led me to the safest place we could think of – the back of a locker room. We took over a bench and barricaded ourselves in with old barrels.

Juin and Riley didn't say anything as they set up the barricade. We were soldiers in conflict, beyond language.

"Are any of the others around?" I asked before I let myself fully open my eyes. I'd curled myself between a bench and the wall.

"No," Juin said curtly. "They're pissed, but they're not out for blood. At least not at the moment."

"You have no idea how glad I am you're here," I whispered.

"Tonight's the night. We're getting out no matter what," Juin said. She was shaking, from what I first thought was cold but I soon realized was an anger so intense it was almost psychotic. I had never seen her rattled before, and it really unsettled me that she had lost her composure. She unzipped the top of her sweater, revealing twin blue hand marks on either side of her neck, like moth wings.

"What happened to you?" I asked.

"Calista and her crap-mongers. She got all enraged when she saw you going off with Vienna – she thought you'd turned into her new favorite narc, I guess. Took down me and Riley. They ripped pipes from the walls and went after us. Shayla had me in a choke hold. Then Vienna came in, I guess because she heard the noise, and carted Calista away."

"Yeah, and I know exactly where she took her." I told Juin how Vienna and Calista had framed me. As I did, I saw that Riley had, like me, pressed herself into the corner. She'd curled up so tightly that her nose was between her knees.

"Riley, did Calista's gang get you, too?"

Riley didn't say anything back, didn't even look at me. To all appearances, she'd become lost in her own body. "Riley hasn't talked since you left," Juin said.

"But is she okay?"

"No idea. She drew blood on some of the girls. She's 'okay' enough to have done that much."

"She needs help."

Juin shook her head. "From who? If Calista doesn't kill us, Vienna will. Or now, any of the other girls would probably do us in. You're everyone's favorite, Little Miss Arsonist."

"I didn't set that fire," I said.

"Who the hell cares if you did? I'd give you props either way. Even if you incinerated my suitcase. And everyone else's. You crazy bitch."

"Are we still aiming to get the school shut down?"

"Something like that," she said, shaking her head vaguely. We sat in silence as she rubbed her chapped hands. Lines of dried blood striped her knuckles. "But we're starting with Calista."

Chapter Forty-one

The lights in the locker room didn't click off at night, so we had no easy way to find out when everyone had gone to sleep, except by opening the door to the gymnasium and checking. The cracked door sent a rectangle of light out into the dark. As it shone on the unsuspecting sleeping girls, the beam of light traced our focus as we checked out the room. A couple of girls were awake, and as we opened the door wider, their eyes shone back at us, like wild animals. They didn't react as we slipped into the gymnasium. We closed the door and waited for our eyes to adjust to the dark.

I manned the light switch while Juin took a couple old shirts and crept away to douse them in the water barrel. Once she'd done that, she disappeared from the light. I heard a scuffle from Calista's area. When Juin gave her whistle, I flicked on the overhead lamps.

It was a horrifying vision. Juin had tied Calista to her hammock using the wet rags, and as Calista struggled to free herself, Riley loomed over her, looking creepy and bonkers, all stringy hair and hollow eyes and body shaped like a crescent moon. At first she wasn't doing anything, just peering at Calista with this unhinged, demonic energy.

Seeing Riley, Calista immediately started thrashing. Some of the girls yelled for her to shut up, but most got out of their hammocks and came over to watch. Riley reached her hands toward her menacingly, and that's when Calista really started screaming — "You dare touch me, you whacked-out bitch, and I'll have you snuffed out so fast that you won't even know what happened."

Shayla, Isabella, and Teresa stood behind Calista. They watched her curiously. None of them moved to help her.

"You hear me? Let me go, you and your pathological Frenchie and demented spic friends. You hear me?"

"Why should we?" Juin said, her teeth gritted as she strained to keep the wet shirts tight over Calista. "What could you do to us?"

"You know exactly what I can do!"

"Say it!" Juin said as Riley brought her hands even closer.

"What? That I nearly burned her to death, and I'd do it again in a heartbeat? Do you really think I wouldn't do it to you, too?"

"What was that?" I called from my side of the gymnasium.

Calista craned to see me, and as she did saw the unfriendly faces of the other girls, more of whom had rolled out of their hammocks and padded over to watch. She had her mouth open to speak again, but nothing came out.

Riley placed her hands over Calista's throat. Calista began to sob. "Let me go!"

Juin released the wet rags holding her to the hammock, and Calista hurled Riley off and got to her feet. She spun and took in the gymnasium full of unfriendly faces. "Shayla, get over here," she said.

But Shayla didn't move.

"Isabella, Teresa!"

Isabella didn't move. Teresa didn't move.

Calista bolted for the door. Riley made to stop her, but I yelled to let her go.

Calista pulled out a key and jiggered open the exit door. She had it open, slipped through, and locked it again in a split second. Riley had almost caught her, and howled in frustration.

But it had all gone according to plan.

Lucky for us that some bitches are so predictable.

Chapter Forty-two

Now we had everyone's attention.

"We all know where Calista's gone," Juin started. "She's Vienna's little monkey — and soon she'll be back with her master." She'd obviously worked for some time on that line, and beamed proudly.

The crowd's reaction, though, was less than enthusiastic.

"Who cares?" someone yelled.

"Who cares?" Juin yelled back. She wrapped the wet rags she had used to restrain Calista tightly around her fists. "Who said that?"

No one came forward. Riley strutted forward and paced in front of Juin, like some guard dog. I put a hand on Riley's shoulder. She calmed down a little, but I could feel the blood pounding in her veins.

There was a rustling as some girls complained and went back to bed. But the rest were alert, watching. None of them made a noise.

"We've got Calista on the defensive. We've got Vienna surprised. This is our chance!" I said.

"Shut up," someone said. Her tone told me exactly what she meant — who was I to say anything?

"Our chance to do what?" Shayla asked.

"We're breaking out," Juin said. "Tonight."

"With what? How?" she asked.

When she yelled to the crowd, Juin's already slight French accent slipped entirely away. "You been skipping math sessions, Shayla? There's twenty of us versus only one Calista and one Vienna. Unless you idiots are still going to back up the narc."

Shayla shook her head. Teresa and Isabella stayed motionless.

"So we're at least four. Who else will join us?" I said.

Shayla came to stand beside me, Juin, and Riley, but no one else moved.

I glanced at Juin. I remembered the force with which Vienna had bashed my face into the floor. Four wouldn't be enough. Not for everything we'd have to do.

I could hear girls going back to bed all around me. Hidden Oak had served its purpose. They'd been broken.

A few lingered, though. "If we did get out, where would we go?" Isabella asked.

"I've got transportation lined up," Juin said. I looked at her, startled. She did? I tried to keep my face impassive. It was probably a lie — whatever it took to get the girls to help. "We'll get to town, then to Denver. From there it's wherever you want to go."

Isabella dove in first. "Okay, I'm in."

Where Isabella went, Teresa followed. They brought some other girls along with them — ironically enough, most of our new allies were from Calista's side. We got ten, total. We'd just grouped by the door, and Juin was starting to lay out her plan, when we heard a key rattle in the lock.

"Get ready!" she whispered.

They caught us off guard, so Calista and Vienna got fully inside before we could form our semicircle around them. Because we'd left only one overhead light on, Calista and Vienna immediately focused on it — at the far side of the gymnasium. From the comfort of the darkness, we watched them stare in the wrong direction.

Vienna looked tired and cranky. Her shirt was back-to-front. "Where are they?" she snapped at Calista.

Calista looked nervously around. I saw her expression change as she saw our shadows. "They're right here," she said quietly.

Vienna narrowed her eyes and squinted around. "Show yourselves, right now."

Not one of us moved.

"Do you hear me? Right now."

Juin stepped into the light.

"Juin, you need to come with me."

The rest of us stepped into the light.

Once she'd seen our expressions, Vienna's jaw trembled. She made one step backward, then dashed for the door. Her key was back in the lock before any of us had time to react. "Now!" I yelled.

I was nearest to Vienna, and so I should have been the first to grab her. But I couldn't bring myself to touch her. It just seemed logically impossible, that I'd break some unwritten law of the universe, and the rest of the world would unravel. Calista, however, I could easily bring myself to tackle. I pinned her in my arms. She tried to stomp my foot, but missed, and I took the opportunity to hurl her to the floor. I might have been small, but I had a low center of gravity; she went down hard. I heard scuffling, but was too concentrated on keeping thrashing Calista under control to see what it was.

By the time Isabella helped me restrain Calista and I had time to look up, I was treated to the astonishingly cool sight of Juin's arm locked around Vienna's head. Vienna was spitting and cursing, until Juin hurled her, as well, to the floor. She smacked her head against the ground and went quiet. Vienna wasn't knocked out or anything, but scared into submission. She stared up at us. Teresa and Shayla kneeled on her arms, but I knew it was unnecessary. Vienna wasn't going anywhere.

Juin pulled the key off Vienna's neck and stood. When she addressed us, I saw that the crowd had grown. The rest of the girls had gotten out of bed, and stood in gloomy clumps, watching us. "We're moving on! Angela and I are getting everything set up. We'll be back for you. Anyone who actually wants to beat it out of here needs to be ready in half an hour."

I waited for someone to resist, to say they wanted out right now. But Juin's voice made it clear that nothing was up for discussion. And by taking down Vienna, she'd made herself our undisputed leader.

"You all have to keep them barricaded in the locker room. They don't get let out for any reason. And no one enters the gymnasium but us. When the rest of the faculty comes for Vienna, you need to keep them occupied until we can return with reinforcements. Do you hear me?"

Plenty of the girls nodded.

Juin jiggered the key in the lock. "Two down," she murmured to me, "and a helluva lot to go."

Chapter Forty-three

"Now, let's think," Juin said as we glided through the tunnels. We hadn't dared to turn a light on, so we passed through the darkness like spirits. "I'm sure Vienna was just the first to come check on us, and there will be plenty of —"

We stopped. Footsteps in a parallel tunnel neared and then receded.

"— others," Juin finished as we started moving again. "The faculty will realize Vienna's been captured, but since the purple girls aren't going to let anyone else in, the headmistress might not realize that *we're* gone. And we'll be long out of here before they do."

"And back with the transportation, right?" Juin hadn't mentioned it yet, and I wanted to make sure we really were springing out the other purple thread girls.

"Yes," Juin said. "So our biggest priority is to avoid being seen. Which means we can't do what would be easiest."

"Taking the tunnels to the main building."

"Yep."

"But where else do the tunnels lead?"

"One other place, where they won't expect anyone – at least not anyone living."

Back into the fire.

As we passed farther along the tunnels, a cold wind started to course through. Then the air became clean and scentless. Eventually, when I squinted into the distance I could see that – amazingly – it was snowing *inside* the tunnel. Swirls of broad flakes, struck as bright as stars by the outside light, vanished as soon as they settled on bits of charred wood on the tunnel floor.

"You did a number on the old dorm," Juin said admiringly. We may still have been in the tunnel, but we were now also under the open sky. When we looked up, a few blackened walls led up to the sky. The blizzard was in full force; I couldn't stare for long until flakes clogged my lashes.

"What now?" I asked, wrapping my arms tightly around my chest. My coat, of course, was neatly stashed away in the gymnasium. It was like Zsilinska always said: I didn't plan for the future.

"Come on," Juin said. "Not far to go, now."

I didn't push for an answer – it was typical dramatic Juin. We pushed a burnt dresser to the wall and climbed up the drawer handles into the snow. The world was bright and clean and clear. I couldn't see much, but caught enough stray glimpses of school buildings to realize that Juin was leading us toward Derrian's apartment. She put a hat on. Too bad she hadn't thought to grab me one. I pulled my hair flat against my stinging ears as we trudged against the cold wind.

We arrived at the dorm's side exit, the same door Harrison had once used to get Carmen and me back inside after the coven met. When Juin pounded on the door, though, it was Mr. Derrian who answered. He looked surprised to see snow on the ground, to have been waiting by the door at all, and to see us, even though it was clearly us he'd been waiting for. Totally senile. "Oh! Come in."

Mr. Derrian didn't know whatever trick Harrison had used to disarm the alarm, and a tinny siren rang out down the hallway. Seeing my nervous look, Mr. Derrian said, "Don't worry, checking on that alarm is the last thing on anyone's list right now."

There was something different about the hallway today. You couldn't feel the pulse of everyday life. It was like school wasn't in session anymore, or all the girls had gone far away. "Where is everyone?" I asked.

"Off checking out the commotion at the purple thread," Mr. Derrian said.

"Everything lined up?" Juin asked.

Derrian nodded embarrassedly, as if Juin had just asked if he watched porn. He doddered off down the hall, followed by Juin, who was walking with a peculiarly jumpy step, like a pent-up racehorse. I tailed farther back.

I would be seeing Harrison. My face felt oily, and my old

polo shirt had begun to smell like me, instead of my deodorant. I'd have to answer dumb questions about the fire, and I wasn't sure my answers would satisfy him. The truth wasn't ever enough, with boys. They expected something more glorious than that.

I hurried to catch up to Juin and Derrian. *I am being lame*, I told myself. *My life is about far more than boys now.*

They'd already gone inside. Harrison was sitting on the stairs across from the apartment door, smoking. He didn't see me at first, and I had the luxury of watching him take a big drag and stare at the cigarette intensely, like a parent killing time outside an ER. I didn't move or anything, but he felt my presence, anyway, and looked up. On a normal day, he would have said "hey" right then. But he didn't say anything.

"No smoking in the school building," I said. Of course I meant it ironically, but it came out sort of pissy.

He just stared at me.

"Has Juin told you what's going on?" I asked.

"What the hell are you doing?" he asked. "Do you really think you're busting out of here in the middle of a snowstorm?"

"Don't tell me you expect me to stay." My ears buzzed. What right did he have to get all unsupportive when I was in the middle of the hardest moment of my life?

"At least you're *alive*, here."

"Partially. You haven't been living in the purple thread. If I could stay in a nice little apartment with my dad, maybe

I wouldn't feel the need to bust out, but I don't, and I sure as hell don't need you getting all judgmental, especially not right now."

He stubbed the cigarette out on the banister and stood. "I'm not getting all judgmental." He bit back words and waited for me to go into the apartment. He didn't have the emotional skills, but he wanted to say, "I'm just worried about your safety." I was sure of it.

As we entered the apartment, I experienced a flood of sensations: the stale smell, like hard cheese left in a cupboard, the reassuring mess of two guys (a pair of Harrison's boxers was pinned between a couple phone books), and then Juin and Mr. Derrian, standing shoulder to shoulder over the kind of indecipherable squidgy map you'd see posted outside a state park.

"Okay," Juin said, "Harold and I are getting our wheels, which means you have to get your hands on the security camera recorder."

Harold? Who did she think she was, Mr. Derrian's buddy? "I don't know how to do that," I said, taking on the sulky child role.

"Well, you're going to have to figure it out. I can't do everything."

"As Juin already suspected, the recorder is in the headmistress's wing," Mr. Derrian said gently. "With all the recent commotion, you shouldn't find it too hard to slip inside."

"Are you in?" Juin asked Harrison.

"Of course I'm in," he said.

"Sorry I had to ask. We can't count on anyone for certain anymore," Juin said tragically.

Harrison rolled his eyes and slipped his arm around me. As we steered toward the door, I tried to will my nerves to subside. There was no going back, so there was no point in getting nervous. Too bad it didn't work; I couldn't stop the trembling. He held me tighter.

"Meet at the garage. You have an hour," Juin called after us.

"The queen is dead. All hail the queen," Harrison muttered as we turned the corner.

"Wait," I said. "Where are we going?"

"The headmistress's office. Where else?"

Our actual next step had been so obvious to me that I couldn't believe Harrison hadn't been thinking the same thing. "Nuh-uh. We have to get Carmen first."

"Carmen? What's she going to do for us?"

I punched him on the arm. "Don't be such an ass. She's my best friend."

I knew it was a risk — I still didn't know how she'd gotten out of Vienna's grasp. They could have gotten to her; anything to do with Carmen could be a trap.

But I had to take the risk, in order to live with myself after.

"I don't know," he said with mock seriousness, "she's not in Juin's *plan*."

Neither are you, I thought, but would never say.

My old floor was as lifeless and abandoned as all the others. As I stood before the door to 201, it seemed very unlikely that anyone would be inside. But when I knocked, I heard shuffling.

Carmen might be mad at me, since she got locked up, I told myself, *but I'll just have to explain what happened. She'll understand.*

But it wasn't Carmen who opened the door.

It was Maureen.

Chapter Forty-four

If I had seen it in a movie, the rapid transition from boredom to shock on Maureen's face, the jaw that dropped so fully that I was left staring at the silver fillings in her molars, would have been funny. But in this situation, it was just terrifying. I watched in slow motion as her chest expanded and she prepared to yell.

Then she saw Harrison.

She released the air in her lungs in a whoosh. "What are you doing here?" she asked. It was both shocking and unsurprising that she moved so quickly past me, basically an escaped convict, and focused instead on the hot guy.

Harrison held his hands out, palms up, as if he was talking to a terrorist. "Don't freak out."

"Are you *helping her*?" Maureen asked. She turned to me with renewed energy. "Do you realize what you've done? All our stuff is burned to a crisp, and now you've, what, got your henchmen to kidnap Mrs. Vienna?"

"Isn't it awesome?" I said, grinning. She was so righteous. I couldn't play into it.

"Look," Harrison said. "Is Carmen in there?"

Maureen closed the door partway so we couldn't see in. "Maybe she's asleep. What are you guys trying to do?"

"Nothing you'd want any part of," I said.

"Hold on," Harrison said. He put his hand on my arm but stared intensely at Maureen; the disconnect was upsetting. "Do you want to come with us?"

"Like hell she's coming with us!" I said.

"Hush," he said, squeezing me but still talking only to Maureen. "We're getting out of here. Do you want in?"

"Harrison!" I said.

I saw Maureen weigh it. Getting out of the school, and with Harrison . . . but that would also mean getting into trouble, big trouble. She shook her head.

Harrison let go of me and leaned into her sexily, the same way he'd leaned into me so many times before. "Okay. Come find us if you want to join in."

She nodded. I saw precisely what he'd accomplished — he'd turned her from an observer (and potential narc) into a collaborator. What weirded me out was how easily he'd done it, and with moves I'd seen before, up close. Real close.

Harrison let his voice rise a notch. "Carmen? Are you in there?"

Someone shuffled in the background. "It's Angela," I called. "Let's go."

The shuffling paused. Then I saw fingers reach around Maureen and grip the edge of the door. Maureen gave way, revealing Carmen.

"Come on," I said.

Maureen didn't do anything to stop us, just stood there limply, like a wife watching her husband sail off to sea.

"Man," Carmen said, grabbing us coats before we raced down the hall, "you get me in so much trouble."

"Was it awful?" I asked.

She shrugged. "Maybe. But we're getting out now. Come on."

"Down to the courtyard, up the back stairwell," Harrison said. "And no talking from here on out unless absolutely necessary."

With surprising speed for normally pokey Carmen, she swung around a banister and followed me and Harrison through the school. The courtyard was eerily quiet, as well. Everyone must have been off trying to deal with the purple thread rebellion.

Harrison made it to the back stairwell first. I recognized the area — we were at the very steps I'd taken to meet with Zsilinska in her headmistress role. Harrison held up a hand to stop us. "This is not good," he said.

"What?"

He peered up. "April is up there."

"Who?"

"The school secretary. She's talking to Zsilinska . . . wait, now she's – *hide*."

We frantically looked for a hiding spot. The only real possibility was behind the stairs themselves. We crouched.

The stairs began to shake as the Hostile Hag descended. Through the gaps between the steps, I watched her crepe-soled sneakers and support-stockinged ankles thud down. Then she was at our level. She didn't even pause to look around, just rushed toward the school entrance. She was wearing a heavy coat and carrying an industrial flashlight.

"She's heading outside. Probably to look for you," Harrison said.

"Well," I snickered, "she's not going to find me."

Harrison gave me a terrible look, as if he couldn't believe my selfishness. "No, but she'll find Juin and my dad."

Of course. I was such a bitch. I put a hand on his shoulder.

"I've got to go warn my dad," Harrison said. "You guys are gonna have to do this alone. Listen up. Upstairs, there's a hallway, and you definitely don't want to go in the door at the end –"

"I know. That's the headmistress's office."

"Take the door to the left instead. Here's the key – they gave me a copy a long time ago, since I'm the only one who's any help with the computer network. You should hear the room humming. If there's a light on inside, that's normal. There's some sort of DVD machine, and you have to try to get the discs out. If you can't, yank out the whole thing and get out of there."

"Hey," I said. "Good luck."

"Don't get caught," he replied, and dashed away.

The stairwell turned quickly, so I didn't have the chance to stare after him. Carmen and I climbed slowly, listening for any footsteps that weren't our own. Once we passed the spot where Vienna had waited for me, Carmen stopped us.

"You should go up alone," she said.

Was she serious? No way I was going up there without company. I guess it showed in my face.

"You're way faster," she explained, "and you know your way around up there. If we get caught, I'd just slow you down. This way I can stand guard, and if anyone comes along I'll run up and warn you."

It made sense to post a guard, but it also seemed to me that Carmen was wussing out, and just happened to have found a good excuse to do it. All my suspicions came back.

"You're coming up with me," I said.

"No, I'm not." She bit her lip.

"Why were you waiting in the room with Maureen, when no one else is around?"

"Because Rebecca and Blank heard about Vienna getting kidnapped, and I figured if you needed help, you'd come find me in our room. And when I told Maureen I wasn't going to check out the commotion over at the gymnasium, she was suspicious and wouldn't leave me alone. What, do you not trust me?"

"So you've been hanging out with Rebecca and Blank

without me? Life just goes on, huh?" I was being pathetic, but I didn't know where to put the feeling that no one seemed trustworthy anymore.

"The coven's been meeting, Angela."

"It has?" I asked, surprised to feel my heart sink.

"Don't look like that. We spent most of the sessions strategizing how to get *you* out."

She had such a pitiful, tender expression — the thought of losing me had set her world on the brink. "Of course I trust you," I said. "I'm just — we really don't have time to talk about this. Wait for me. I'll be back soon."

Carmen nodded in relief. "Okay. Thank god you're not mad. I'll give you fifteen minutes, then I'm coming up to find you. I'll be listening. If Zsilinska catches you, try to keep the rest of us out of it, and I'll go warn the others."

She made me suspicious all over again by saying that, but I got it. No point having everyone get caught. I gave Carmen a long look and headed up the stairs.

Most of the lights were off on the headmistress's floor, except for the startling glare of a safety bulb. Two doors were dark around the seams. But, just as Harrison had said, light shone from the left one. The door was one of the steel ventilated kinds that you see guarding electric equipment, and gave off a hum of fans and energy.

Beneath the buzz, I heard voices.

Spicer.

And Carmen.

I crept to the stairs and peered down. They were two floors down, so I couldn't make out their words. But I saw

Dr. Spicer shake Carmen's shoulders roughly, and Carmen meekly nod. When her hand pointed up the stairwell, Dr. Spicer let go of her shoulders and stared up — directly where I was crouching.

I pressed back against the wall, my breath coming in rapid gasps.

Not. Possible.

As Spicer started up the steps, I jumped. There was no exit from the hallway, except the very stairwell she was climbing. Unless . . . there was the window at the end. I ran to it and looked out. The burned-out dorm was there below, like a war ruin. The still-falling snow had obliterated the rest of the campus.

The ground was three stories down. I'd be lucky to survive the fall.

I opened the window, anyway. I'd rather risk the jump than let myself be caught by Spicer. Or even if I couldn't actually bring myself to do it, I'd at least be able to use the threat of jumping to keep her at bay.

The stairwell gave little shakes every step Spicer took closer to me.

But she never arrived. The stairs stopped shaking, and I heard the snap of her high heels on the floor below me as she strode away.

Carmen had sent Spicer to the wrong floor.

She hadn't betrayed me. She'd saved me.

But there was no time to thank her. We had already wasted far too much time.

The door clicked and creaked open as I unlocked it. Inside was a small room, stiflingly hot and filled floor-to-ceiling with electronic equipment. The bright halo of an architect's lamp cast its glow over a computer monitor displaying views of the campus. As I glanced at it, I saw that everything looked surprisingly normal. I couldn't see the outside of the gymnasium, but in the main school, at least, there were no girls running panicked down the halls. On the outdoor cams, there was no sign of Juin or Derrian.

Next to the screen was a blinking recorder. It didn't have anything that looked like an eject button, so I yanked it away from the wall. It was surprisingly heavy, with sharp metal edges, and once I'd unplugged all the cords, I realized that I'd barely be able to carry it, even using both hands. But I had to try.

I waddled toward the door, then paused. A shelf above the doorway had a series of boxes it, labeled by month and year. I set the recorder on the ground and stood on it in order to reach them. After I pulled down the most recent box, I saw that inside were various discs, labeled with ranges of dates. I yanked out a few and jammed them into the waistband of my skirt, then heaved the recorder back into my arms and staggered my way out the door.

I was halfway to the stairs before I realized I wasn't alone. "Angela," came a familiar voice, "stop."

I halted, then slowly swiveled.

It was Zsilinska, minus the ridiculous cone wig and wearing a frayed bathrobe. Her face was slick with some ointment.

She looked not angry or authoritative, but sad. Disappointed. With that same condescension that disappointment always comes with, that message that if she were me, she would've done better.

I ignored her and lurched toward the stairs.

"Angela," she said again. "The least that you owe me . . . I deserve an explanation for what you're doing."

"You don't," I said, stopping at the first stair. My voice came out sounding hysterical. "You don't deserve a thing. Who told you I'd be up here?" Any number of people could have ratted me out. I felt nauseated, suddenly.

She gave a tired smile. "I'm impressed April gave her name to you. She never tells it to anyone. She must really trust you. No. I came this way because I heard you drop that recorder you're stealing."

I stared down at the box, as if surprised to find it in my hands.

"I assume you're planning to get out of here and lug that machine miles through the snow to civilization?"

I nodded.

"Angela, four boys died trying to escape from this campus years ago. Don't. I can't see you injured."

"Injuring me is all you've been doing since I arrived." A familiar feeling came over me as I said that, and I realized I was using the same tactics I'd always used with my mother, picking any word she said and turning it back on her.

Zsilinska gripped her robe tighter. "I've been the only person in your life who's bothered to try to understand the center of you. And if that hurts, perhaps it's supposed to.

You seem intent on demonizing me, but all I've been doing is trying to get you happy."

"Framing me for arson doesn't 'get me happy.'"

"What are you talking about?" she scoffed.

"Calista tossed me a bucket of gas-soaked rags inside the old dorm."

"What?" She seemed genuinely confused. "There are very serious implications to these allegations, Angela. I don't take them lightly."

"And you wouldn't take the word of a dangerous girl, anyway," I spat.

She sighed. "Generally, you're right. But I'd take your word. Or I'd at least consider it."

I realized what she was trying to do — it was just what Harrison had done with Maureen. She was getting me to see her as an ally so I wouldn't betray her. Seeing through her ploy only doubled my conviction not to feel bad for her. "I'm sorry," I said, and bolted toward the stairs.

I would have made it, too, if the stupid power cord hadn't been trailing after the recorder. Zsilinska stepped on it and the machine jerked out of my arms, its rough edges cutting my fingers. I fell, scrambled to my feet, and turned on her, ready to fight. But she reeled the recorder in, kneeled over it, and clutched it to her. I wondered if that was going to be the last sight I had of her — staring down into the recorded history of the school.

I dashed down the stairs and nearly bowled over Carmen. "Oh my god," she said. "I heard you guys, but I didn't know what to do, because Spicer's still around —"

I didn't slow down. "Come on!"

"Where's the recorder?" Carmen asked as we ran.

"She got it. But I've got discs," I said, patting my waist. "Where do we go?"

"Um, um . . ."

"Carmen!" We'd bolted down the stairs to the very bottom, stopped at a T-junction in the steam tunnels.

"I can't think, I can't think."

"Neither can I. Damn it."

"Juin said the garage."

"Where's the garage? Next to . . . we need . . . the faculty parking lot!"

We skirted through the tunnels beneath the gymnasium, rounding corners so fast we slammed into walls, listening for the sounds of pursuit even as our own footfalls reverberated back against us from the concrete walls.

"We're there," I said. The tunnels had sloped upward, and above us was a hatch. A chain hung from it, sawed through by some blunt tool. I put my hand on it.

"Wait," Carmen said. "If Juin's been caught, then they'll be waiting for us there. Only one of us should go at first. That way the other one can still get away."

Wow, Carmen was coming through with the cold and clinical decisions. "Okay," I said. "I'll go first."

"Give me half of the discs," she said. "If one of us gets caught, the other will still have something for proof."

I nodded, handed a few to her, and then pushed against the hatch. It was heavy with accumulated snow, and I had to strain to lift it enough to slip through.

The hatch opened, not directly into the snowy grounds, but to the edge of a garage. Seeing no one around, only a line of vehicles, I pulled myself out and took shelter.

The snow was falling stronger than ever, and it was nearly impossible to see anything. I nestled myself between a couple of vans and waited for Juin to arrive.

For some reason, I couldn't get Zsilinska out of my mind. Every time I pictured her kneeling on the floor, I felt this confusing swell of feelings. It was hard to keep thinking of her as the absolute enemy when I was also convinced of her essential goodwill — she was entirely misguided about how to treat me, but did want to see me get better.

Regardless of how I was feeling about her, she'd undoubtedly informed the rest of the faculty that I'd escaped. She'd probably called the cops, too. It was only a matter of time until someone came by the garage and caught me and Carmen. Actually, it was one of the likeliest places for them to start their search.

Where was Juin?

Then I saw her, rushing into the shelter from the far side, her face flushed and her frozen hair pinned under her heavy wool hat. She kept glancing behind her, like she was being pursued, so I instinctively crept farther in between the vans.

She stopped beside some machine draped by a cloth and pulled her gloves off. She and I both watched someone approach, at first only a black smudge, then clarifying into Mr. Derrian. He was wearing this ridiculous stocking cap and an ankle-length coat.

At first, she stared at him coolly. Then she reluctantly

folded him in her arms and kissed him on the lips. I watched, stunned, as she ran her hands over his slack face, his gray temples. He pulled her head away, but allowed himself to stay in her arms.

"All set?" he asked, quivering with nervous energy.

"No," she said. "Angela's not here yet."

"Forget her," he said. "It's time."

"Slow down, tiger."

"We don't have *time*."

"Get the snowmobile started. Give her a minute more." Juin shoved him toward the draped machine.

"Yes, June. Or should I call you *Juin*?"

"Shut up."

"What will you say when Angela arrives? Something in French, something *très glamoureuse*? You big phony."

Mr. Derrian was clearly feeling playful, but Juin wasn't having it. She stared down at her gloves. "I thought you said you found my tale-telling charming," she said.

"You can keep lying to me as much as you want. You'll always be my little girl from Iowa."

She smirked, but her voice came out sad. "You assume I was being honest about even that."

Mr. Derrian whisked the cover off the snowmobile. I realized with a shock that it would scarcely fit two people. *Maybe* three – but certainly not Carmen as well. Derrian adjusted settings on it, then was distracted by something in the distance. "Flashlights."

"Damn it, Angela," Juin said, staring out into the snow.

Holding my breath, I stepped out.

312

Chapter Forty-five

"Angela!" Juin said. "Get over here. And tell me you have the recordings!"

I didn't make a single step, just jammed my hands farther into my pockets. "You're not going to take me and Carmen with you, are you?" I asked.

Juin looked at Mr. Derrian and the snowmobile. "We probably have room for you," she said.

"*Probably*? Miss Iowa?"

"Oh. So I'm not French. Don't be so bourgeois. Come on."

"I'm not leaving without Carmen."

"Well, where the hell is she, then?"

"Right here." Carmen stepped out from the open hatch as the snowmobile whirred into life. She stood there awkwardly, clutching one arm. "I thought you had, like, a real *vehicle*. We have to go pick up Blank and Rebecca and Riley."

"And the rest of the purple thread," I added.

Mr. Derrian got on the snowmobile. "June, what did you promise them?"

"Look," Juin said. "There's no way a truck could get through this snow. And that fact is precisely what's going to save us, sweetheart. I'll take the snowmobile and go ahead with Derrian. None of the faculty will be able to follow. I'll get help, and then come get you guys."

"You said trucks can't come through," Carmen said. "So how are you going to get help back?"

"Stop sniveling," Juin snapped. "I'm going to call the TV networks and get the school shut down, that's how. Then we'll all leave."

"That'll take weeks," Carmen said glumly. "The rest of us'll be in solitary until then. Or worse. Like dead."

"June," Mr. Derrian said warningly, pointing at the flashlights approaching through the snowstorm.

"Come on," Juin said. "Angela, grab hold. We can take you, too."

As I watched Juin — or "June," I guess — get on the snowmobile behind Mr. Derrian, wrapping her arms around his skinny torso, I wondered where I'd wind up if I left with them. I wasn't about to let myself be the third wheel to some perverted couple. And I couldn't go to my parents, not back to Virginia. Not Houston, because my grandfather was dead and I doubted Trevor wanted to have anything to do with me. Maybe Carmen's parents would let me live with them, but the chances of them letting a girl stay with their daughter were pretty slim, what with them freaking out about her friendship with Ingrid. And Carmen would still be stuck at Hidden Oak, anyway.

If Juin dropped Derrian (which I imagined she probably would, as soon as possible), I could travel with her, making our way across the country, living on the lam, getting into all sorts of crazy adventures. But I also knew that teen runaways usually ended up involved in drugs or prostitution, and I didn't know what made me so special that I wouldn't wind up trapped in that, too. And the more I'd gotten to know Juin, the more the initial friend crush had faded; I'd realized she was impressive because she was so icy, not because she was so cool. She'd never shown any real sympathy toward any of us, never asked me a single question about my life, only set this cult up around her own personality. She was clearly sleeping with Derrian to get what she wanted. She threw Carmen off a roof to save her own neck. I looked at Carmen, then, standing there uncomfortably. Her greatest wish was just that her parents would be cool with her hanging out with whoever she wanted, so she could go back to being friends with Ingrid. She wanted company, compassion, support.

I was thinking all these things. But mostly, I wanted to get out of there.

Without fully realizing it, I'd allowed Juin to pull me onto the snowmobile behind her. We were backing out of the garage, reversing and turning at the same time, so we pitched hard to one side. I had to pin myself against Juin to hang on. Then we were off into the snow. I was too shocked to say anything, not that they would have heard me over the roar of the engine.

I clutched Juin, felt the sharp tips of her frozen hair whisk against my cheeks, felt her rib cage, so slender even under her heavy coat. I couldn't believe we were beginning our new lives with creepy Mr. Derrian along for the ride, and wondered how long it would really take Juin to find an excuse to shuck him off once we got to civilization. What did they have planned, an escape to a motel somewhere? Had Mr. Derrian even told Harrison he was leaving?

Harrison. I thought about Harrison.

Then I thought about that cock-and-bull story Juin had told the coven about living in France with Etienne. The stuff about writing checks was totally ripped from my own story. What was she really about? Regardless of her having made up all the Europe stuff, she'd clearly been through some heavy crap – you could tell when someone's grittiness was earned.

I am leaving Carmen and Harrison behind, I thought numbly. And yet I held on.

But it was more than Carmen and Harrison. I thought of Riley as I'd last seen her, doing whatever Juin told her to do, but with that crazy look in her eyes that meant she'd rather bash her head against the bleachers than tie up Vienna.

Or Blank, with her consciously erased history, or Rebecca, tough and self-aware. Or even Teresa, and the other girls who'd turned from Calista to me. All of them waiting to be rescued. For me to rescue them.

And I was leaving them for . . . what? Freedom? Breaking out with this cool girl who I'd always liked because she'd lived a life so much larger than mine? Juin – *June* – could really be anyone. I didn't know anything about her or what she was capable of doing. I wanted to be with her, but knew I shouldn't: All my therapy sessions with Zsilinska clicked in, and I knew that this time I should act on what I knew was better for me. The disconnect between what I knew Juin made me feel and what she actually *was* finally traveled to my arms.

For once in my life, I knew with some certainty what I had to do.

I took my hands off her body. I leaned back. I stopped myself from holding on. I let myself fall back into the snow.

When I trudged back to campus, it wouldn't be Juin's rebellion anymore.

It would be mine.

I hit the ground and buried myself in the freezing white. I was hidden within seconds, and felt oddly warm and protected, even as the chill cut me. This was the first time that being alone had ever felt really good. I heard the snowmobile slow, and then speed up again. When I finally pulled myself out of the snowdrift, there was no vehicle in sight.

Over the howl of the wind, I heard a thrashing so clumsy that it could only have been Carmen. I pulled myself out of the snow and joined her, hugging her to me.

The searchers came closer, their flashlights bobbing in the storm.

Chapter Forty-six

The lights were a narrowing circle. Our only hope was to stay hidden and pray they'd pass by us.

Carmen and I closed our eyes. We lay there, clutching each other, until eventually I heard snow crunch nearby, and my eyelids glowed red. I was caught in a flashlight.

"Up and at 'em, ladies," Harrison said.

My eyes sprang open. "How — ?" I sputtered.

He scanned about to see if anyone had seen him, then fell to the ground beside us. "I'm the one who actually knew where you were supposed to be. So I was bound to find you first. All I had to do was volunteer for the rescue party."

He reached an arm around me.

"Are you working for them?" I asked.

"Of course not, dumb-ass. Now, listen up. Zsilinska's got all the faculty out looking for you. She's called the cops, too, so they'll be here soon, as soon as they get through the storm."

I didn't want to tell him what I knew about his father, but I couldn't hold it back from him. "Harrison, your dad —"

He shook his head savagely. "Ugh. I think I know what you're going to say. Don't even talk about it."

"No, really —" I started to say.

"Not now. Let's go." He got to his feet.

I pulled him back down. "Wait."

"Yeah," Carmen said. "Where are we going?"

"We're not going back to the school," I told Harrison. "Ever. We're busting out." I'd thought about it. There couldn't be that many cops living in the area. The purple thread girls would still have a numerical advantage. They could hold out, at least for a while. And everyone would be too busy with them to go after a couple of escapees.

"Fine," Harrison said. "But two things: First, you guys aren't going alone. Second, you're not going on foot. Me and my dad have skis."

"Let's go get them," Carmen said.

"Wait," I said. "One of us has to go to stop by the gymnasium. If the standoff has ended, that changes everything. And if it's still going on, we have to make sure it continues."

"I'll go," Harrison said.

"No," Carmen said. "I'll go. You're the only one who knows where the skis are. I'll meet you outside the dorm, the door nearest your apartment, as soon as I can."

Carmen broke toward the far side of campus, while Harrison and I headed across the snow, keeping low to avoid any searchers that neared. At one point, Dr. Hundrick, the gym teacher, came near, but I crouched in the snow while Harrison blinked his flashlight and called to her that he hadn't seen anything yet.

The skis were in the back of the Derrian apartment, propped against a heating pipe. They'd been there in plain view the whole time, but I'd never seen them because of all the clutter.

Harrison waded through the room and yanked them from the wall, his coat riding halfway up his back as he did.

"There's only two sets," I said.

"Yeah, I guess it'll just be you and Carmen." I could tell he didn't mean it, though. He looked at me longingly.

"Maybe there's another one somewhere?"

He shook his head. "Not that I know of."

Harrison had to be one of the two to go, I realized. He'd grown up around here and had friends on the outside. And he was fit enough to survive the journey. "Maybe you and Carmen should go," I said. "I'll take care of your dog."

He dropped the skis and grabbed hold of me. The cold from our coats merged. Even as bits of snow fell between my pants and my ass, I could feel heat rise in my throat. "I don't think so," he said. "Carmen would be much better at taking care of the dog."

Right then, the door to the Derrian apartment banged open.

In strode Dr. Hundrick. Apparently, we hadn't played her as easily as we thought. "Of course," she said. "I should have figured you'd fall into the Harrison trap."

Harrison snatched a set of skis from the ground and held it in both hands, like a club. "Run," he said, "right toward her. We have to get past."

Before we could do anything, though, more of the faculty filed in. Alsanz. Churchill. And, finally, Spicer and Zsilinska. My vision wavered; the apartment suddenly looked impossibly full of people. There was nowhere to look without facing a hostile teacher.

I focused on Zsilinska. She'd changed out of her bed-clothes and gotten her look together, which in her case meant that she'd arranged her tackiness into her preferred order, the glasses high on her nose, the weird cone of hair standing tall. Next to her, Spicer looked like a corporate manager's assistant, hair pulled back tightly, hands folded over gray skirt. It was hard to tell whose expression was worse: Spicer's — unhinged, demonically angry — or Zsilinska's — mystified and wounded. "Angela," she said, "why do you insist on doing this?"

"Tell your little minions to back off," Spicer told me. "And to let Mrs. Vienna go."

Despite the shock of it all, despite seeing my chances for escape on the brink of vanishing, I smiled. Or I felt a smile inside. I couldn't quite get my face to move. "So they've still got her. You haven't broken through."

"Look, you slack-jawed little monster, we gave you our trust, and offered you every chance to get better. When we first met you, we had high hopes. Your little friend Carmen had distasteful tendencies but no urges that could really be called self-destructive. And while you'd devalued yourself into worthlessness, you showed a capacity for self-reflection and a latent determination to improve. You should have been a model success story. But we've never been proven more wrong. I hardly need catalog your misdeeds. Even before the Vienna incident, you set fire to a school building and broke into the headmistress's office, where you stole confidential school property. Which brings us to the matter of the discs."

Spicer pointed at my bulging waistline. "We did an inventory, and we know exactly which ones are missing. We can assume, from the fact that you stole them, that you were planning to humiliate your classmates publicly by airing all of their confidential experiences. Fortunately, Angela, you were unable to escape, and so we will be able to seize them from you. Your plot has failed in every way."

She turned her withering gaze on Harrison. "The question remains of how Angela got into the recording office in the first place. Given that you've previously been granted access to work on the computers, the answer is fairly obvious. So we'll add that to Angela's list of transgressions — using sexual fraternization to conspire to burglarize. Like father, like son, I suppose."

"That's enough," Zsilinska said, a crack in her voice. "We have a history of never expelling students once they've been admitted to the main school. We've never given up on anyone. When a girl acts up, we merely remove privileges. As you have put the school itself under assault, however, our remedies must evolve. You have placed the school's very existence in jeopardy. I can no longer entertain the idea of your staying. Solitary living clearly wasn't enough. I can't even move you back into the purple thread, given its current upheaval. We'll be sending you straight to the police, and then home, if they foolishly decide not to press charges. I'll call your parents immediately to inform them."

I couldn't believe it. Did Zsilinska really think I cared anymore about being *expelled*? Didn't she have any idea what was going on?

Harrison and I stared back at her. He still held the skis like a weapon, as if he thought we had a chance in hell of taking them all on.

"I'd expect you to be delighted," Zsilinska finished. "This was your goal all along, was it not?"

"Dr. Zsilinska," I started, "imagine a TV news story showing girls living in one large room like rats, educated for only a few hours a day, given free rein to jump one another in the hallways, dying from lack of medical attention, being the subjects of cruel mind games that pit one against another, all because some crackpot 'educational' theory claims that evil girls should be encouraged to get more evil, basically just to get more tuition money from their parents. That's how it works, doesn't it? If you cured us all, who'd pay the bills? Someone's got to pay — so you create a thread of girls who will never, ever get better. It's too bad Pilar died — you must really miss the checks her parents sent."

"Conversation's over, you little bitch," Spicer said. "We don't expect you to agree with how we run the school. But you're powerless to do anything. Whenever inspectors come, they are invariably pleased."

"But you don't take the inspectors into the steam tunnels, do you? You don't show them the purple thread."

"We are not getting anywhere by discussing this," Zsilinska said. "Our meeting is over."

And it was. I had nothing to hold against them. Our only hope was that Carmen would still escape with the discs she had. I had to cover for her the best I could, give her time to get away with them. I could only hope she would figure out what was going on and strike off on her own before they captured her.

I must have looked smug. Dr. Spicer slapped me hard across the face.

I put a hand to my cheek.

"You're going to tell your friends to release Mrs. Vienna, do you understand?" she said, leaning in close for dramatic effect.

I slapped her back, even harder. "Like hell I will," I replied.

"Vienna should have let you burn!" Spicer screamed. Hundrick could barely restrain her from jumping me.

"Veronica," Dr. Zsilinska said slowly, "what are you saying?"

"Please," Dr. Spicer said, whirling on her. "It's all in the service of your school."

"What? *What's* in the service of my school?" Her expression simultaneously broadened and narrowed as she realized the magnitude of what had been going on under her nose.

But Spicer couldn't care less. She was unrelenting as she stared at me; I shrank under her intensity.

When she finally lunged, I stumbled and panicked.

Harrison started to swing the skis toward her, but stopped.

Now it was Zsilinska who had wrapped her arms around Spicer, and gave little screeches of exertion as Spicer's pantyhosed legs kicked in the air. "Adrienne, hold her for me," she said. Hundrick was already there, pinning Spicer's arms. "I won't tolerate you harming a student," Zsilinska said.

"Are you kidding?" Spicer said. "Harming them is the only way to keep them in order."

"That is *not* our philosophy, and you know it," Zsilinska shot back.

"We're all bruised and battered, the purple thread girls," I said quietly. "It's a war zone. They let us do whatever we like to one another." I filled her in on what my experience in the purple thread had been like. Starvation, gangs, poor sanitation, blood and freezing and misery. And this time she listened.

She must have known something was going on. But she thought if she never stepped down there, it would make her innocent.

It didn't.

Dr. Zsilinska held her head high the whole time I spoke, but I could see the lights behind her eyes change color as it all sank in. I'd broken through; she felt defeated.

But I was the one who was truly defeated. I was the one who was always going to be stuck here.

"I'll take your words under consideration," Zsilinska finally said. "You may be surprised to learn that I've considered reforming Hidden Oak in the past, and have a few legal pads' worth of notes on how. Methodology for how to treat dangerous girls is by no means an exact science – schools are always changing their procedures, trying to strike a balance between respecting the student and providing sustainable boundaries. But that doesn't change the fact that you're acting immorally, coercing a school's administration under threat of blackmail. There will be no discussion, no terms to be offered or agreed to."

"Are you sure?" said a voice. The door to the apartment swung open, revealing Carmen in the hallway.

"Carmen!" I yelled. "Run!" We had to protect those discs.

"It's okay, Angela," she said.

And I understood. Because it wasn't just Carmen.

I saw Teresa, Isabella, and Shayla. Blank and Rebecca. Maybe five other girls from the purple thread. And, behind them all, staring feverishly into the apartment, Riley. They filled all we could see of the hallway. In my panicked and vulnerable state, they looked like an army.

"Our position is that you need to let Angela go," Carmen said. "And you might notice that numbers are on our side. We'd win if we were to vote on it, or anything like that." She sounded sweet and awkward, even when she was being threatening.

But I wasn't so sure that we were at an advantage at all. Hundrick was pretty built, and if Zsilinska let Spicer be released, I was terrified she might act out the crazy wildcat gleam she had in her eyes. All that changed, though, when Carmen pulled something out of her pocket.

A disc. It glinted blue-yellow.

Zsilinska put her hand over her mouth.

Spicer reached for it, but Carmen held it out of her reach.

"Don't expect that you'll be allowed to go anywhere with that," Zsilinska said.

"I don't imagine I will," Carmen said. "And that's why I've hidden three more."

A grin spread over my face.

"I had a while to wait while Angela was off in the snow," Carmen said clearly, as if answering a geography question. "So I hid my discs in some very creative places. You'd have to dismantle the school to find them all."

"You'll direct me to them immediately," Spicer said.

Carmen shook her head. "No, I don't think we will."

If there was one thing that had always been true about Zsilinska, it was that she was a damn good psychologist. She knew exactly what I was thinking, always. But I like to think that during our sessions I'd learned to read her just as well. I was able to interpret perfectly the look that passed between her and Spicer: *We'll lock them away forever,* Spicer's eyes said, but Zsilinska gave an almost imperceptible shake to her head. *I won't allow it.*

"Let Veronica down," Zsilinska said to Hundrick. She did, and Spicer stood there, waiting for her cue from Zsilinska, staring about menacingly and rubbing her arms.

"You're here," Zsilinska said quietly to Carmen. "So it would seem there's something you want from us."

Carmen deflected to me. She'd set it up; it was my turn. "We don't want to leak the discs, but we will if we need to," I said. "What we want is freedom."

"You'll die out there if I let you go," Zsilinska said.

"Did you hear Angela?" Blank said, stepping into the apartment. "It didn't sound to me like she was opening anything for discussion."

"I agree," Zsilinska said, nodding to Spicer and Hundrick. "I don't think talking is the best idea anymore." They formed a line with Alsanz and Churchill. Harrison and I on one side, the rest of the girls on the other. Divided.

"Let us go," I said.

"Those discs are still on campus," Spicer said. "So it seems your little blackmail threat doesn't have much firepower. No one will ever see them."

"We have enough to deal with right now," Zsilinska chastised Spicer, "without provoking them further. I need to get to the purple thread and see what's going on." She sighed. "I *hate* doing this. Any extreme discipline is supposed to be Mrs. Vienna's exclusive domain."

"Mrs. Vienna seems a little overwhelmed," Alsanz offered.

"How did you get out?" Zsilinska asked the purple thread girls, whirling suddenly. "Is the standoff finished?"

The purple thread girls stared back defiantly. Riley spat.

"Little bitches," Spicer said.

"Go to your gold thread rooms," Zsilinska said. "The purple thread girls can stay in the empty room, two-oh-eight. Dr. Spicer, I'd like you stationed in the hall."

"You'll be under constant watch until everything is sorted out. Is what Dr. Zsilinska just told you clear?" Spicer stared at each of us in turn, like she had that meeting when I first arrived at the school.

This time, not one of us said "It's clear" in return.

"I'm afraid Dr. Zsilinska is no longer in charge of this school," I said. "None of you are. Hidden Oak is ours now."

Like that, the balance of the room shifted. Before, the four adults had been the wall between us. Now we were two groups on either side of them. And we were closing in.

"What's it going to be?" I asked Zsilinksa. "Do you want to do this peacefully, or do you want us to start treating you the way you've been treating us?"

Dr. Zsilinska raised her hands.

"There's no need for violence," she said.

But Spicer wasn't having it. She lunged for me. I stepped back and Harrison lowered a ski between us. Then, before we could stop her, Riley leaped forward and clawed her across the face, then leaped back against the wall and stood there, giggling.

Spicer was terrified now, holding a hand against the three red lines slashed on her cheek. I could see the calculations running through her mind. We had the taste of her downfall on our tongues. She knew her chances were slim.

I didn't know what to do. I was the default leader of this

group, and despite all the hateful feelings I had for Spicer, I didn't want her hurt. But Riley was a loose cannon, and the other girls seemed invigorated by the chance for revenge.

"Dr. Spicer," Harrison said, standing at the front of the group. "I suggest you calm down." He'd had the same thought as I had. He was giving her a way out.

"Veronica," Dr. Zsilinska said. "It's over."

Shayla and Teresa had Dr. Spicer now, and Riley looked like she wanted a piece, too. Other girls grabbed Hundrick, Alsanz, Churchill, and Zsilinska.

"Wait a sec," Harrison said. He ducked into a closet, and came back with some rope. Only Spicer put up a fight when we tied up their hands. The rest submitted, like Zsilinska.

"You know you'll never get away with this," Spicer said to me. "The police will be here any minute."

She shouldn't have opened her mouth. Because the minute I heard her voice, I found what I'd wanted to hear:

Fear.

Chapter Forty-seven

I'd never skied before, so Harrison carried the pillowcase with all our supplies while I concentrated on just moving forward. Whenever my heart quaked and my determination waned, I focused on him gliding in front of me. Every painful stride I took, every movement that made my thighs ache and brought fresh lashings of falling ice against my cheeks, was easier when I thought of his smooth progress, the physics of his back and legs.

What happened once we arrived in town would be up to me, but the prospect of it was easier knowing I had capable company.

Carmen had packed the pillowcase for us, frantically stuffing it with whatever supplies she could get her hands on: toothbrushes (four, which I told her seemed like overkill), a box of minute rice, a hairbrush (which I tossed back out once we were outside), plastic bags, a water bottle. It was as random an assortment as the coven's bag of items.

Harrison had been unusually quiet while we prepared, lost in his thoughts. At first I figured he was thinking about his father and Juin. What went down with them was pretty heavy, after all. I imagined what would happen if we ran into them in town. Would they acknowledge us, and we them? In any case, it was totally unlikely that we'd ever see them, what with their head start and the fact that they'd taken, oh, a snowmobile, while we were on skis.

But while we were about to set off, Harrison had said, "It's probably not going to work, you know?"

"What do you mean?" I'd asked.

"The discs. Sure, we have footage. But Zsilinska will be able to spin whatever it shows. It's not like anyone's expecting bad girls to be treated that well. She's documented everything you guys have ever done wrong. Since they wouldn't be stupid enough to have cameras filming the purple thread, all you're going to have on record is what happens to the better girls. And that's not enough to get a school shut down."

I'd thought about it as I fastened Mr. Derrian's ski boots. "They threw me in a *freezer* while I was in the gold thread. And who knows what the faculty might have said while these were recording."

"Who says there's audio? And I'm not sure that the freezer episode would exactly make the nightly news. You'd be surprised by the low standards people have for girls like you."

"Hey, could you stop?" I said, cuffing him. I'd made sure I sounded playful, but I was pissed. It would be a hard journey no matter what, and I didn't want to feel like I was on a fool's mission.

He held up his hands in mock surrender. The move had an icky undercurrent, like the main point was to show that I was overreacting and he was just an innocent bystander. "No, maybe it'll all go well, and they'll shut the school down. I'm not saying it doesn't deserve to be shut down. And you're certainly going to get their undivided attention by locking up the headmistress and a large part of the staff."

"Let's not get into it right now, okay?"

"Yeah, okay."

As I skied, I concluded that he'd probably been upset about his dad and Juin the whole conversation, and that was why he was being so pissy and negative. I didn't know how to bring it up in a way that wouldn't make him defensive. Someday I'd figure it out. We'd figure it out.

As we kept on, leaving the cover of the trees and skiing across open spaces, the pain in my legs faded and I started to feel exhilarated. It's really rare that you can actually feel your life turning, that all the miniscule gear changes you've made in the last few years finally result in a turn of the big massive cog that's your existence as a whole. But something had changed. I'd gone from a girl sobbing in a Texas parking lot about a guy who'd never been worth it to a girl skiing through a blizzard, her survival at stake, the destiny of an entire institution in the possession of the guy confidently arrowing through the snowdrifts in front of her.

I'd been called dangerous before, and I'd never really believed it. I was often angry, bitchy, judgmental – sure. But they had it wrong about my being dangerous. I didn't belong at Hidden Oak. I never had. But now, tackling the faculty and racing away into the wilderness, I was doing the sort of thing that everyone expected a Hidden Oak girl to do. It was a school for dangerous girls, all right, but I'd always assumed that it *cured* the danger, that it made us polite and respectable. It had done the opposite for me. I'd become what they tried to starve out of me. There were all sorts of positive versions of "dangerous," used for people who were fighting for the right things. Assertive. Self-assured. Resourceful. Forceful.

We skied into town just as the moonlight gave way to the first seam of dawn appearing on the horizon. We found a phone outside a gas station whose awning sagged with snow. Harrison leaned against a propane tank a few feet away and stared at me: drawn, concerned, encouraging. I called collect.

"Mom," I said. "Listen up. And this time, I'm not giving you any option but to believe me."

Epilogue

When it finally came back into view, Hidden Oak seemed snug and almost cheery. Red brick chimneys sprang like candles from snow-frosted roofs. The yellow glow of desk lamps backlit the silhouettes of busy students. It could have been any prep school, anywhere; it was hard to think that these buildings contained any of my own history, that my previous world still existed somewhere within the gabled halls.

But it was definitely still Hidden Oak.

And it was definitely being shut down.

And I had definitely caused it.

Whoever designed Hidden Oak may have given it a tall fence, but what truly kept it secret from the rest of the world were the woods. Thick trees ringed the school, and in the winter the snow bowed their tips toward the ruins, as if nature had intensified her shield for those cramped months.

We didn't approach the school and the students lining up on the front lawn with what remained of their possessions. Instead we dodged the campus and headed into the trees. Once the school was out of sight, the forest opened up and became its own world, numb to the human drama occurring yards away. Chirping birds dotted the branches, their feathers fluffed against the cold. The occasional fox slunk between distant thickets, hunting the occasional rabbit.

The storms may have stopped, but the ground between the trees was covered in snow that had melted and resealed so often that its surface had hardened into glass. A raven passed overhead, its shadow reflecting a black triangle over the glittering ice.

The fallen tree house was piped in hardened snow. Voices murmured inside.

We paused outside the jagged entrance. "You were right," Harrison said. "They came."

I squeezed his hand. "Ready?"

We walked in.

Carmen broke off mid-sentence and stared at us.

It was my first time seeing her since I'd left. She looked worse for wear, but it almost suited her. She wasn't puffy and red-cheeked anymore; she was at home in her own body, no longer the blubbery fat girl I remembered from that first night in the mansion. Harrison's dog sat, tail swinging, in her lap.

Riley was seated next to Carmen, wearing a powder blue sweater with ripped-out elbows. I couldn't tell her mental state, but at least the smile she gave me was on the right side of normal.

Next to her were Blank and Rebecca. And Teresa.

"Angela," Blank said. "You're back."

"Hey, guys," I said, waving awkwardly.

They all stared at me. It was as if I had returned from more than the nearby town; I was back from the dead.

After a few awkward minutes, we were all chatting comfortably. The coven lit a fire in celebration, and I started to tell them about the month Harrison and I had spent on his friend's foldout couch, about the concerts we caught in Denver, about all the testimony I'd been called to give. In return, the coven told me and Harrison the basics of what had been going on at the school. The police had arrived soon after we'd left and released the faculty. A reporter showed up at the gate a couple of days later, and Spicer barred her from coming inside. Four more showed up the next day, followed by a government investigator. It had been a downhill slide since then, the campus a riot of flashbulbs, camera crews, and officials in beige suits with government badges pinned to the lapels. During the swift investigation, all the faculty had been on their best behavior. "Which still," Rebecca noted, "was pretty crappy."

"They're scared," Carmen said, "that they'll never be employed again."

"Carmen," I said, "they *shouldn't* ever be employed again."

"Hey, wait a second," Blank said twinklingly, "what's a *boy* doing in the coven?"

They teased Harrison for a while, and he took it good-naturedly enough, laughing and staring at the ground, then returning with a jibe about the zit right on the tip of Blank's nose.

Then Teresa asked for more about how it all went down on our end.

Harrison explained that we'd watched the discs at his friend's, how they looked bad for the school, but weren't slam-dunk damning. The footage was grainy, and silent. There was no recordings of the purple thread, or anything that couldn't be explained away by a scheming administration. Which Hidden Oak certainly had.

I told them how I'd e-mailed a few clips to my mom, that she saw how everything wasn't on the up-and-up, and that we were in touch now. "She wired me money to come home," I said, "but I don't want to. So I spent it. On stuff. You'll see in a minute. I'll pay her back later or something."

"Wait, wait," Rebecca said, refusing the bait. "You guys are saying you didn't have anything that could shut down the school?"

"Not at that point," I said.

Because we hadn't seen the footage of Juin and Vienna yet.

The clip had shown Juin sitting in solitary, then Vienna coming in. It all passed in silence, but we saw Juin stand up and start yelling, until Vienna brought something from behind her back, a little glass globe, and smashed it into Juin's face. Juin had fallen into a crouch, and Vienna had left.

I'd remembered the first time Juin rejoined the coven after she'd entered the purple thread, how she'd had those bruises over her eyes.

"So we sent a copy in to the local paper. And they must have told their contacts. I don't know what you guys know about how big this story's blown, but it's national," I said.

We all stared at one another. Teresa rubbed her mittened fingers. I wasn't sure if the coven was despairing or jazzed.

"You look great," Blank said, to break the moment.

I laughed. But she was right — I looked a hell of a lot better. When we'd first arrived at Harrison's friend's place, I'd ducked into the bathroom and checked myself out in the mirror. I'd nearly cried. My hair had grown out over the months, and my braids had gone halfway to dreadlocks, the colors faded and interwoven like the back of old embroidery. My fingernails were cracked and rimmed in black from all my time in tunnels and dirty solitary rooms and snowfields. But a daylong trip to the mall with the money my mom had wired had fixed all of that. I slid my backpack off my shoulder. "I brought supplies."

They gasped in delight, even Riley. Shampoo, conditioner, hairbrushes, volumizer, exfoliant, blush, mascara, lipstick, perfume. I'd even picked the right color foundation for everyone. Except for Teresa, but she said she didn't wear foundation, anyway. Riley busted open a highlighting kit and handed everyone bits of foil. As Teresa and Blank started mixing chemicals, Rebecca went to fill a pail with water from the stream. If anyone was crazy enough to dye her hair in the forest and rinse her head in ice water, it was Riley.

Carmen skipped the divvying of supplies and hung back, sitting in the corner with me and Harrison.

"When does everyone head home?" I asked her.

"Rebecca's cab is in a couple of hours. Mine's a while later," she responded. "Say, any word from Juin?"

"Nothing," I said. I put my hand on Harrison's knee. "No word from her or Harrison's dad."

"We're all surviving, you know?" Carmen said. "It's not like, now that we're getting out of here, we won't still have to concentrate on surviving. It might be even *harder*." She picked at a shoelace. "For me personally, at least, I'm glad that I'll be surviving with you back in my life. Do you want to come to Connecticut with me? My parents wouldn't let you stay in my house, I'm sure, but Ingrid's parents might."

I laughed. "Wow. Saturday nights with me, you, and Ingrid. Can Harrison stay with us, too?"

Carmen had been serious, and I was treating it like a joke. But for the moment I was just too manic from the constant realization that I'd closed down an entire school. "The craziest thing? It actually feels good to be back on campus. I'm almost sorry that it's all over." I cupped my hands, as if holding all of Hidden Oak in my grasp.

"Yeah, *almost*," Carmen said. "Hey, what do you think's going to happen to the school, like the actual buildings?"

I shrugged. As I watched Blank, Rebecca, and Teresa surround a giggling Riley and start dyeing random chunks of hair, I felt Carmen take one hand, and Harrison the other. In a way, I did still have the school in my grasp.

We all did.

You could never undo a dangerous girl.

You could only ask her to be dangerous for the right reasons.

Acknowledgments

I'm indebted to my agent, Richard Pine, and especially to my editor, David Levithan, who showed up to lunch one day with a great idea for a book.

To Do List:
Read all the Point books!

Airhead
Being Nikki
By Meg Cabot

Suite Scarlett
By Maureen Johnson

Sea Change
The Year My Sister Got Lucky
South Beach
French Kiss
Hollywood Hills
By Aimee Friedman

And Then Everything
Unraveled
By Jennifer Sturman

The Heartbreakers
The Crushes
By Pamela Wells

This Book Isn't Fat,
It's Fabulous
By Nina Beck

Wherever Nina Lies
By Lynn Weingarten

Summer Girls
Summer Boys
Next Summer
After Summer
Last Summer
By Hailey Abbott

In or Out
By Claudia Gabel
In or Out
Loves Me, Loves Me Not
Sweet and Vicious
Friends Close,
Enemies Closer

Point

www.thisispoint.com